Mystery Gre
Gregson, J. M.

Too much of water

TOO MUCH OF WATER

Recent Titles by J M Gregson from Severn House

Lambert and Hook Mysteries

AN ACADEMIC DEATH
DEATH ON THE ELEVENTH HOLE
GIRL GONE MISSING
JUST DESSERTS
MORTAL TASTE
TOO MUCH OF WATER
AN UNSUITABLE DEATH

Detective Inspector Peach Mysteries

DUSTY DEATH
TO KILL A WIFE
THE LANCASHIRE LEOPARD
A LITTLE LEARNING
MISSING, PRESUMED DEAD
MURDER AT THE LODGE
A TURBULENT PRIEST
THE WAGES OF SIN
WHO SAW HIM DIE?

TOO MUCH
OF WATER

J. M. Gregson

This first world edition published in Great Britain 2005 by
SEVERN HOUSE PUBLISHERS LTD of
9–15 High Street, Sutton, Surrey SM1 1DF.
This first world edition published in the USA 2005 by
SEVERN HOUSE PUBLISHERS INC of
595 Madison Avenue, New York, N.Y. 10022.

British Library Cataloguing in Publication Data

Gregson, J. M.
    Too much of water
    1. Lambert, John (Fictitious character) - Fiction
    2. Hook, Bert (Fictitious character) - Fiction
    3. Murder - Investigation - England - Gloucestershire - Fiction
    4. Detective and mystery stories
    I. Title
    823.9'14 [F]

    ISBN-10 : 0-7278-6262-6

Typeset by Palimpsest Book Production Ltd.,
Polmont, Stirlingshire, Scotland.
Printed and bound in Great Britain by
MPG Books Ltd., Bodmin, Cornwall.

To Ray and Margaret Smart,
who represent all that is best in New Zealand

Autism is touched on here, briefly and superficially, within the confines of a detective novel. For anyone anxious for further reading on the subject, an excellent lay person's introduction is *George and Sam* by Charlotte Moore, published by Viking Press.

'Too much of water hast thou, poor Ophelia,
And therefore I forbid my tears.'

Hamlet, Act 4, scene 7

One

Heat. An intolerably heavy, humid heat, hanging every-where, like a tangible malign presence. The kind of heat which makes people do silly things, bad things, criminal things. Evil things.

A damp, oppressive, English heat, hanging in every cleft and hollow of the ancient English city of Gloucester. A heat oozing softly into every ancient crevice of the old stone build-ings around the cathedral and every modern hollow of the pedestrianized city centre. A brooding, overwhelming heat, which will be rent by thunder before the night is out.

Mischief is abroad in the city. As midnight approaches on this, the longest and hottest day of the year, the binge drinkers tumble from the pubs and seek out devilment, a danger to themselves and others. The sweltering night is rent by cries of cruel laughter, cries of excitement, cries of alarm, cries of fear and cries of pain. And then rent anew by the crash of broken glass, the yells of drunken laughter, and the sudden, horrifying screams of agony.

And so the still, stifling night is suddenly full of noises. Police sirens, all too familiar to the citizens of the town at this hour on a Saturday night. The sober, experienced voices of authority, making arrests, curtailing a revel gone wrong. And then the suddenly subdued voices of those arrested, protesting their innocence as they are pushed into the police vans, whining in sudden sobriety as their deeds collect un-expected retribution.

A little below the centre of the ancient city lie the docks, where ships sailed up the tidal reaches of the Severn and brought treasures to the city from Roman times, long before the cathedral was built. There is trouble for a few minutes only. Then the police arrive here also, amidst a harshness of blaring sirens, and contrive to disperse the hordes with no more than a couple of arrests.

Yet despite all this noisy activity, the worst thing of all goes undetected. It does not happen in the city. It takes place a mile away. But through the stillness of this sweltering night, it is within earshot of the turbulence and violence which spills from the taverns.

But this evil is silent, purposeful, undetected. It is conducted under cover of a darkness which seems thicker amidst the all-pervading heat, in a silence which seems more profound against the sudden outbreak of noise from the city.

No one sees it, but any observer would see only the stealthy movement of shadows beneath the low cloud of a moonless, starless sky. He might be able to discern that the thing which was carried was heavy, from the laboured movements of its bearer. But he would not be able to see enough beneath the darkness of the beech trees to decide that the burden had once been a human, living thing.

The corpse slides softly into the tepid waters of the river, which are oily to the touch after three weeks of this intense heat. It moves sluggishly away from the bank, then catches the quicker current of the central stream and is gone.

The dark shape which has deposited it there stands motion-less for several minutes beneath the trees, then moves softly away.

The silence and the crushing heat hang over the city and the river for two hours longer. Then the first white blaze of lightning forks the black sky, and heavy drops of rain spatter river and stone.

Two

Superintendent John Lambert was not having a good Wednesday.

He had begun his day in court, standing erect in his best suit and tie and striving to remain both patient and alert as a sharp young counsel for the defence tried hard first to trip him and then to rile him. The loan shark had gone down for three years, in the end, but it had been a more closely run thing than it should have been, and if one of the villains he had employed to terrorize and beat up his customers had not slipped up when giving his evidence, the man might even have walked free. It all made for a tense opening to the day, and Lambert told himself, not for the first time, that he was getting too old for this sort of contest.

That was a thought which returned to him now, in the stifling confines of the small, square, windowless interview room. He did not trouble to disguise his distaste as he looked at the massive forearms which were folded and resting on the square table in front of him. The tattoos of Union Jacks on the right arm and the naked woman with the big bust on the left seemed at this moment to have been designed as a deliberate challenge to him.

Lambert forced himself into a calmness he did not feel as he said, 'You were there, all right. We have witnesses to that.'

'Never said I wasn't, did I? Going about my legitimate business, when I became a victim of police brutality.'

'The brutality was on your side. The officers applied no more force than was necessary to make an arrest.'

A grin from the coarse-featured face with the plaster above the left eye. 'Police brutality. I'll be discussing the matter with my brief. You'd better get ready to apologize, if you don't wish us to press charges. Superintendent.' He rolled out the

3

rank with a sneer of relish, as if it was the greatest epithet of contempt imaginable.

Lambert wished he had his dependable detective sergeant, Bert Hook, at his side instead of the inexperienced, fearful young woman DC who was sitting just behind him to learn the CID ropes. As if she read her chief's thoughts, the girl said feistily, 'You're the one who'll be facing charges, Benson. You and your friends were causing an affray.'

The thug looked her up and down. His wandering eyes came to rest appreciatively on the rounded chest beneath the uniform shirt; an insulting leer spread slowly over the coarse features. 'I don't know where you get that idea from, love. I don't see how anyone as pretty as you could be deliberately telling such lies. I'm going to give you the benefit of the doubt and say that it's mistaken identity.'

'There was no mistaken identity, Mr Benson. You were kicking a defenceless man on the ground when we arrested you.'

'Oh, I don't think so, love. You'll have to prove it, and you won't be able to do that.' He looked from the earnest young face to the older and graver one beside it and shrugged his contempt. Then he looked round the narrow confines of the square box of a room and said, 'This is no place for a pretty young piece like you, girl. You should be out living life with us. I could do you a bit of good if—'

'Racially motivated, was it, the violence you offered last night?' Lambert's cool voice cut through the bluster. His contempt was colder and more edged than that in his opponent's blundering lechery.

'Man insulted the country's flag, didn't he?' The burly man in the torn and bloodstained shirt ignored the cautionary raised hand of the thin-faced lawyer at his side. 'Refused to bow before the Union Jack, didn't he? Black bastard deserved all he got, if you ask me.'

'They aren't asking you, Wayne,' said the lawyer, glancing nervously at the cassette turning silently on the table beside them. He resumed the neutral tone he had used in their previous exchanges. 'My client has nothing to say about the incident at this stage.'

'Except that the black bastard deserved all he got,' his client repeated, truculently and unwisely.

4

'We shall certainly be charging you with grievous bodily harm,' said Lambert, forcing confidence into his voice. It was a decision he had only just taken, and it broke all the unwritten rules he had set down for himself over the years. You didn't let scum like this get under your skin; you didn't make decisions in a fit of animosity or personal pique; you didn't charge people until you were sure that the evidence was there to convict them, however sure you were of their guilt.

'Load of bollocks!' said the bully-boy on the other side of the table. But he spoke automatically and there was apprehension rather than conviction in his voice as he went on, 'I was provoked. It wasn't me who struck the first blow, and you'll never be able to prove it was.' He glanced automatically at the lean figure beside him, hoping for approbation from his brief.

He got none. The young man was a member of the National Front, but he was regretting offering his legal expertise to them. They were all brawn and no brain, the ones who got themselves into trouble. And they blundered on like this young tough, spewing forth hate and insults when they should button their lips and leave the talking to their lawyer. He said as confidently as he could, 'Mr Benson has nothing to say at this stage. However, he will certainly deny any charges of the sort you have indicated. As far as I can see, there is little or no evidence to support them.'

'Oh, I think there is plenty of evidence,' said Lambert grimly. 'When we put what Mr Benson has volunteered alongside the statements which have already been made by his companions, I think you will find that there is a very strong case against him. That is the reason we are contemplating such a serious charge. The court will decide the matter, of course, but I have little doubt that a custodial sentence will be the outcome. Quite a long custodial sentence, I expect.' He nodded his satisfaction on that point, secretly elated by the fear which crept over the big face opposite him as he enunciated the familiar phrases.

'You'll have to prove it first, pig. And you've bugger all evidence.' But conviction was draining from the voice even as he tried to show his scorn.

'We've the man in hospital, for a start. Four fractured ribs, a broken nose and internal injuries which are yet to be fully investigated. I shouldn't like to be in your shoes, Benson. Or rather your boots. Especially when forensic get busy on the photographs of the injuries. They're quite hopeful of a match with the boots you wore to kick him so hard when he was down.'

'He won't give evidence. The silly black sod will keep shtum when . . .'

The guttural voice faltered and died. His eyes dropped too late to the slim hand his lawyer had raised in ineffective warning.

It was Lambert's turn to allow a smile to steal slowly onto his long, lined face. 'When your friends have finished intimidating him? I'm glad we've got this on tape, and that you've been so helpful to us with your brief sitting beside you. Because your lawyer only wants to see justice done, of course.' He let his world-weary contempt for lawyers who chose to defend actions such as this flood into his voice.

The thin-faced young man roused himself in the face of the superintendent's contempt. 'I would remind you that my client has done no more than give his opinion that this man in hospital will not give evidence against him. That is no doubt because Mr Benson is not the man responsible for these dreadful injuries. Any comments he has made here should not be construed as more than a routine "no comment". The tape to which you refer will not be admitted as evidence, as Mr Benson has not yet been charged.'

Lambert looked hard into the narrow, crafty face, hating it at that moment far more than that of the coarse-featured brute beside him. This man was educated, qualified to practise the law which was the basis of a civilized society. And yet he was sitting here defending the indefensible, the random racially motivated violence where might was right and was all that mattered. Lambert looked in vain for a mistaken fanaticism, for an attitude driven by a conviction, however mistaken. He saw none: despite his membership of the National Front, this slim figure with the sly, knowing features was motivated purely by mischief, by a desire to make trouble and enjoy it.

The superintendent told himself that this was a game which had to be played, a game where policeman and brief knew exactly where they stood. But another, more insistent voice told him that there should be no game, that the stakes were too high for that. And this second voice told him that he was too old for this grim charade, that he was demeaning himself to be going through the motions of a game when there was no game.

He reached across and slammed his hand down on the stop button of the recorder, shouted, 'Why the hell do you—'

He was saved by the sudden opening of the door. He caught the startled look on the face of his young female colleague as he whirled at the interruption, knew in that moment that he had been saved from an indiscretion which might have cost him dear.

DI Rushton was apologetic but insistent. He glanced at the thug and his lawyer, then took Lambert outside the door and out of earshot. 'Very sorry to interrupt, sir, but I thought you'd want to know immediately. There's a body been fished out of the Severn down at Lydney. Looks like a suspicious death.'

Relief flooded over Lambert, followed immediately by an access of guilt. Some poor soul was dead, probably murdered, and here was he exulting in the fact. There must be something seriously wrong with his personality to find relief in an event like this.

It was a fleeting guilt. His self-reproach lasted no longer than a moment. It was overtaken by that eagerness to begin the chase which was a familiar feeling after a quarter of a century of detection. Every CID man is a hunter, and the most efficient ones are the men and women who have the exultation of the hunt coursing most strongly through their veins. A murder: the most serious crime of all. Evil clearly defined, after the untidy edges of the violence he had just left behind him in the interview room.

Superintendent Lambert almost raced out to his car, in his eagerness to begin his pursuit of this unknown, welcome killer.

Three

The tutor was harassed. He had to see the dean of the faculty later that morning, and he had been told that the students had made complaints about his teaching. He did not know whether it was really so – you could never be sure when that young fool who taught psychology was serious – but it was worrying. When he had begun working at the university, no one had ventured to comment on your efficiency.

And now here was this grave and serious young woman, taking his time up when he wanted to be alone to compose himself. He said, 'This is not something I should get involved in, you know.'

The girl frowned. 'But you are Clare's personal tutor, as well as mine. I thought I should come to you first.'

Harry Shadwell pondered the implications of that word 'first'. Could he be accused of dereliction of duty, if she went to someone else after he had done nothing? Life was all very confusing, nowadays. This was another complication in it: one he could have well done without. As often when confronted with some human dilemma, he was confused. Shadwell knew a lot about the sociology of groups, could give a whole series of lectures about it, but he was not very good with people.

He said desperately, 'How old is Clare?'

'Twenty-five, I think. She's definitely older than me. Classified as a mature student, for grant purposes.'

'Then she's definitely an adult, you see. Students are classed as adults at eighteen, as you know. Clare's much older than that, and definitely in charge of her own life. We shouldn't interfere with the actions and decisions of students. It's not part of our remit as tutors to do so.' Harry smiled weakly as he repeated this useful mantra, and tried not to sound too satisfied with it. He failed dismally.

8

'You think we should do nothing?'

Shadwell pursed his lips and steepled his fingers on the untidy desk in front of him, seeing the opportunity to pass the buck back whence it had come. 'As her friend and flatmate, you must make your own decisions, Anne. I really think it's not our province as tutors to interfere.'

'Even when she's missed three days of lectures and a personal tutorial?'

'Students do miss classes. It may be regrettable, but we have to allow them a certain degree of latitude.'

'Clare hasn't missed them before. She's very conscious of the opportunity that's been offered to her. Most mature students are.' Anne Jackson was surprised at her boldness. It wasn't characteristic of her, but she was annoyed by the inertia of this balding figure with the thick-rimmed glasses and the hunted air.

And Shadwell in turn was irritated by her persistence. It irked him all the more because she seemed to have a valid point. 'Clare may have gone home to see her parents for the weekend, as you suggest. She may have found sickness or some other crisis there which needed her attention. If she has, I don't think she would welcome our interference. She is, as you have pointed out, a mature young woman of twenty-five, with her own concerns and her own decisions to make.'

It was as dismissive as he could get. He stirred the papers vaguely on his desk to indicate his multitudinous other concerns. Anne Jackson wanted to go on arguing with him, but she saw that she was going to achieve nothing. She stood up and said, 'I thought you would feel that the disruption of Clare's studies warranted your attention. My own feeling is that something is wrong.'

Shadwell stood up also, glad to indicate that this tiresome interlude was at an end. He sought for some compromise on which to end the exchange, sensing that he ought to give the girl something if she was not to go away and grumble to her peers. 'It does seem that Clare is a conscientious student, and that this is a disruption of the normal pattern of her life. If she has not returned to her work and her residence by the end of this week, I suggest that you should report her absence to the relevant authorities.'

9

Anne thought that she had just done that. It seemed not. The problem was back with her. She wondered when she had left the tutor's office just who these mysterious 'relevant authorities' might be. The police, perhaps.

Like most law-abiding people, Anne Jackson shrank from the thought of informing the police. There was surely some rational explanation for her flatmate's absence. She decided that she had better leave matters as they were for a little longer.

Hadn't her personal tutor just told her that this was the right thing to do?

Detective Sergeant Bert Hook wondered why he had volunteered himself for the post-mortem examination. It might be more than usually harrowing. No one knew how long the corpse had been in the water when the walkers discovered it in the Severn.

He smiled to himself as he went into the laboratory and caught the familiar scent of the formaldehyde. This was the one area where he was better than John Lambert, whose stomach had remained sensitive through a quarter of a century of CID work and experiences like this. Bert knew he wouldn't throw up, would remain professionally inquisitive and alert throughout the pathologist's dismemberment of the corpse. He was too old a hand now to be shocked by the innards of a human body and whatever they might reveal about the life that was gone.

He began his notes on the information which the Home Office pathologist spoke tersely into the microphone at his lips as he proceeded. Oldford CID would have the full report in due course, but Hook could save time by noting anything of interest now. The doctor had the microphone attached to his neck by an adjustable collar, so that he had both hands free for his work. Those hands now moved with swift efficiency into actions which laymen found gruesome but the pathologist had long since learned to regard as purely scientific.

Bert Hook, watching unobtrusively as the police representative beside the table where the scientist worked, tried hard to see the thing beneath those expert hands as merely material for intelligent work and scientific conclusions. But

10

despite considerable and various experience in such situations, he remained a policeman, not a medic. What lay on the bench might now be meat and bone which could be dismembered for its revelations, but Bert Hook's reactions were dictated not by what this material was but by what it had so recently been.

The corpse which had brought him here today remained to Hook a young woman, a life which had been abruptly arrested for ever in its prime.

For that much already had been made evident. The pathologist had told his recorder before he made the first cut on the body that this was a young woman, probably between the ages of twenty and thirty, who had no external evidence of serious disease. Now, in less than a minute, he removed the breastplate to look at the heart and lungs. The quiet, unemotional voice told its microphone that the heart had been healthy; that it was still in its pericardial sack and not enlarged; that it had no apparent abnormalities. It weighed three hundred and forty-seven grams. The pathologist drew a sample of blood from the heart to send for toxicology. You could be much more certain of your conclusions with a corpse than with a living being.

The lungs contained only a little river water and had been darkened by the sucking in of blood, the pathologist announced in calm, deliberately matter-of-fact tones. DS Hook knew well enough what this meant. This woman hadn't died by drowning. She had been dead when she was put into the river. The 'suspicious death' of the police jargon had in this moment been translated into a coroner's court verdict of 'murder, by person or persons unknown'.

And now, without any alteration in tone, the pathologist announced calmly, 'The cause of death is almost certainly strangulation. There is severe bruising about the throat and the carotid artery has been crushed.' It was what Hook expected. There was other, more superficial damage to the young skin, cuts and abrasions which could have occurred during the body's journey down the river, but the blackness around the throat had always suggested a strangling.

Body odours are what any attendant at a post-mortem examination remembers most vividly. Bert Hook was not going to retch and run for the lavatory bowl, as many novices in these

11

things did. But he had to steel himself and his nostrils all the same as they reached the fourth part of the examination, the stomach and its contents, when the scents of the investigation prevailed over even the smell of the formaldehyde, which had originally seemed all-pervading.

The average stomach stretches to accommodate two to four pints after a meal. This one was no exception. Within two to three hours of eating, food moves out of the stomach and into the small intestine. Because the process stops at death, this is one of the most valuable areas for detectives investigating foul play, often enabling them to assess the time of a particular death. This woman had eaten a meal of fish and chips some three hours before she died, in the pathologist's opinion. He set the stomach contents carefully on one side in a sealed container for further investigation. Hook wondered if this anonymous woman had ever had such detailed attention paid to her diet when she was alive.

Meanwhile, the pathologist was preparing to examine the tissues of the brain, that most intricate and subtle of computers, which had now been stilled for ever. It was the noisiest part of the autopsy, as he followed the incision he had made from ear to ear at the back of the skull with the electric saw to remove the skullcap. Hook flinched a little despite his experience: the clinical brutality of this assault to reveal the most complex part of human existence, the brain, which elevates man above the other living things on the planet, still took him a little by surprise.

He was glad when he was out in the dazzling light of a high summer noon, blinking with the shock of the sunlight after the white, artificial illumination of the Chepstow pathology lab.

They had a murder victim all right. A young woman, as yet anonymous, stone dead before she was ever thrust into the wide, concealing waters of the Severn. Now they had to decide where to begin the investigation.

Four

This crime was not going to be easy.

A Scenes of Crime team had examined the reach of the Severn and the bank beside it where the corpse had been discovered. The civilian head of the team was apologetic about the paucity of their findings. They had discovered a little detritus to bag and take away for examination. A battered comb, a ballpoint pen, a few fibres of some man-made fabric, a couple of hairs which were almost certainly human rather than canine. But these probably derived from walkers along the riverside path rather than from the corpse or anyone who had been in contact with it.

Superintendent Lambert nodded resignedly and told himself he had expected nothing. You had to conduct these examinations, in case something helpful turned up unexpectedly. But the Severn was tidal here: its twice-daily rise and fall and its fast-running waters would quickly remove anything not securely attached to the corpse. More importantly, this was not the spot where the murder had been committed. This woman had been dead when she was consigned to the river, might have been killed many miles from the water. They did not even know the spot where she had been dumped into the river, which would have been much more significant than the location where the body was eventually found.

Indeed, it was the absence of a real Scenes of Crime investigation which was one of the greatest problems of the case. In cases of serious assault and murder, the crime team comb the scene of the incident for any tiny detail of the 'exchange' which takes place between a criminal and his victim. Even experienced criminals usually leave behind some scrap of themselves: a fibre from clothing, a hair, a trace of saliva, sweat or semen. A SOCO investigation is normally the starting point for any investigation. Because of increasingly sophisticated DNA and other forensic techniques, it is also in effect the finishing point in a surprising number of cases, since the material gathered at the scene is more often than not the key evidence in securing a court conviction.

Lambert's team did not know the scene of this crime, and they might never know it. As yet, they did not even know the identity of the victim. The pathologist's view was that the body had probably been in the water for between two and four days before being discovered. As the riverside walkers had come upon the corpse at Lydney on Wednesday morning, that indicated that it had probably been consigned to the Severn at some time during the preceding weekend.

DI Rushton's trawl of the Missing Persons register had so far produced no obvious candidate as the victim.

House-to-house enquiries were being instituted in villages and towns within five miles of the Severn, but unless and until the CID had a clearer idea where the victim had been deposited in its waters, it was far too wide an area for Lambert to be confident of success. It was a way of using the manpower resources immediately afforded to a murder enquiry, but not, the chief superintendent feared, a very productive way.

The team's first break came in unlikely clothing. The diffident and unprepossessing man who presented himself at the reception desk of Oldford police station was embarrassed to be there at all. He had never been in a police station before, and his fragile confidence drained away as he spoke to the duty sergeant. His assertion that 'It's probably nothing really!' meant that he was left waiting on a bench for twenty minutes whilst a shoplifter was processed and the details of a missing dog were entered in the register.

It was only when he went up to the desk again and said that he thought he might be able to throw some light upon the identity of the Lydney corpse that he was ushered briskly through to the CID section. There Chris Rushton listened to his first halting sentences and decided that John Lambert would want to hear what this uncertain figure with the clean but frayed shirt collar had to say.

Once he was invited to speak, the words tumbled from him like a fall of scree. 'My name is Harry Shadwell. I'm a tutor at the university. I thought you should hear what one of my personal students told me yesterday morning. We each take a personal responsibility for three or four students in each year, you see. They can come to us with personal as well as academic problems. I thought at first that it was probably nothing, but on reflection—'

'On reflection, you thought we ought to know about it. Your second reaction is the right one, Mr Shadwell. It's a pity that it took twenty-four hours for you to decide to come here, but better late than never.'

Curiously, the rebuke emboldened Harry Shadwell rather than checked him. He was not the most efficient of teachers, and he was used to being chivvied in his academic work. He plucked the cuffs of his shabby leather jacket straight, fastened onto the idea that his information was to be welcomed rather than derided, and became more precise. 'This concerns one of my personal students. A young woman called Clare Mills. She seems to have gone missing.'

Lambert made a note of the name. 'Missing since when, Mr Shadwell?'

'Only since the weekend. And there's probably a perfectly good explanation for it. It's just that I thought—'

'Thought that you should act as a good citizen and give us the information. Quite right, Mr Shadwell. If she proves to be alive and well and merely embarrassed, so much the better!'

Yet Lambert knew that a part of him was hoping that she wouldn't be alive, that this was the body which had been cut up to reveal its secrets on the previous afternoon. He tried to conceal his growing excitement as he asked, 'How normal would it be for a student to disappear from her studies for a few days like this?'

'For many students, quite normal, I'm afraid. But not for Clare Mills.'

'And why is she an exception?'

'Clare's a mature student. Twenty-five years old, and determined to make the most of the opportunity she's been given to read for a degree. They're often the best, you know, the students who come to higher education a little later. Better sense of perspective, better attitude to work, better—'

'They also often have other responsibilities. You don't think that it might be some other concern, some family matter for instance, which has required this student's attention?'

Harry Shadwell smiled in spite of himself: this was so near to his own initial reaction that it gave him confidence. He looked over the top of his glasses at his questioner and spoke as if outlining a difficult idea to a student. 'That was exactly my initial reaction when her flatmate came to me yesterday, Mr Lambert. I thought the girl was probably busy with some other concern. But another twenty-four hours have gone past and there is still no news of her. Moreover, I have given some thought to the matter, as I indicated earlier. For Clare Mills, this is atypical behaviour. She does not miss lectures and tutorials: she is a most conscientious student. If she had needed to miss them – if she were ill or she had some family concern which needed her immediate attention – Clare would have been sure to let her tutors know that she was going to be absent.'

Lambert reflected that all this had been so twenty-four hours earlier, when Shadwell had first been made aware of the situation. The tutor had wasted a full day, when days were precious; it was a statistic of CID life that the further away you got from the date of the murder, the less likely you were to solve it. But that was history: at least the man was here now, pinning down a possible victim for them. 'Was this lady married?'

'No. Well, I don't think so.' Harry Shadwell felt a familiar panic at his own inefficiency. He should know the backgrounds of his personal students, but he could remember little about Clare except that she had been an able and diligent student, and thus no trouble to him. 'She was sharing a flat with another girl.'

Lambert smiled at the man's naivety. 'She could be separated from a spouse. She could be divorced. These things are highly relevant, if she's disappeared. As is the whole of her family background, and any friends and enemies she may have made whilst on her course at university.'

'Yes, I see that. Well, I can check her file and—'

'We'll need to have that file, Mr Shadwell. And if she does prove to be a murder victim, we'll need to talk to her friends and her tutors at the university. Does anyone else know that you have come here today?'

16

'No. It was my own initiative.' Harry Shadwell seemed suddenly rather proud of himself.

'Then please tell no one of it. The fewer people who know about this, the better. If the girl is alive and well, there is no need to stir up a hornets' nest. If she isn't, people will know soon enough what we are about.'

One of the host of people who had surrounded Clare Mills in the teeming buildings of a modern university might have strangled her. There was no reason to let him or her know that the hunt had begun.

They called him Denis.

It had seemed a strange name to him at first, and people had laughed as they said it, but he had got used to it now. In the early days, he had failed to react to it a couple of times, and there had been much laughter. Denis had grinned sheepishly at his error, but he hadn't been laughing inside.

He knew that not responding to his new name could be dangerous for him. So he didn't make that mistake any longer.

He had been here for six weeks now, picking the strawberry crop under ten-foot-high polythene tunnels in Herefordshire. It was stifling work, toiling for long hours in oppressive conditions in the hottest part of the year. You could see why the British did not want to do it, when they could get other work. You could see why the farmer had to assemble a polyglot workforce, the desperate and the defeated from all parts of Europe.

Denis was a Croatian, living in the wrong part of Kosovo at the wrong time. He had been training to be a doctor once. He had completed four years of his course, before war and all the things that went with it had intervened. Now he had lived so long by his wits that those student days seemed to belong to another person altogether, living a very different life: someone impossibly young and carefree, without the experience of horror, without the ruthlessness that came with it to enable you to survive.

Someone from the days before the medical student had turned into someone who killed people.

It had cost him money to get here, far more than he could afford. Everything he had owned in Kosovo had gone. And

17

the passport he had been promised had never materialized. He could do nothing about that: he had as much chance of pinning down the man who had taken his money as he had of flying to the moon. He had learned to live life day by day, to survive and to save every penny he could from his earnings.

Denis was a natural linguist, and he had quickly picked up enough of the language to get by with. He trusted nobody, and he tried to anticipate trouble and keep away from it. You kept yourself to yourself, you saw trouble developing, and you kept away from it. 'Keeping your nose clean', the English called it. Denis worked very hard to keep his nose clean. At first, he had counted off the days he had been in this strange new country. Then he had begun to measure his success in weeks, even occasionally to feel quite relaxed.

He was an excellent worker. The man who had hired him and a lot of other foreign labour to pick his strawberries was pleased with him. He even told him that, which was unusual for a farmer, Denis thought. He asked him to stay on to pick raspberries when the strawberries were finished. And after that, if all went well, he said, there might be work in the apple orchard, well into the autumn.

It wouldn't get him a passport. Denis didn't see how he was ever going to do that. But in the caravans the farmer had crowded onto the smallest of his fields to house his motley army of fruit-pickers, Denis listened and noted. He heard people say that if you could stay in this country for a long time, you had a better chance of being accepted here permanently. He had no idea whether this information was reliable, but it was an idea he clung to as he sweated out his days beneath the polythene tunnels. He didn't discuss it with anyone. He stored the notion away and kept his own counsel.

People learned to leave him alone. He got a reputation as a loner who didn't want to make friends. People thought he knew nothing of the language and couldn't converse. That suited him well. He listened and learned. Many of the people around him would never have been so open in their conversations if they had realized how much was understood by the wiry man with the very black hair and the deep scratches on his forearms.

When he had been in Herefordshire for three weeks, the

police visited the site where the three hundred temporary workers were housed. Twenty of them were taken away for deportation.

The ones without EU documents or passports.

Denis spent a tense and uncomfortable time in a ditch by a wood, half a mile away from the fields where they worked. His face was altogether too close to the vestigial socks and odorous feet of a huge Lithuanian who had fled there with him, but neither of them dared to move for three long hours, until the sun had set over Wales and the police had driven away with their cargo of human misery.

Denis put this disturbing visit out of mind in the days which followed. Another crisis endured and survived. He had trained himself now to think in the present and the future, not the past. The one thing he had to do was to learn from things like this. He knew that he should not stay for too long on this temporary site, that it was too dangerous a place for people like him to live. The police would return in due course, and he might not be so lucky on the second occasion. But where else could he find work, where else would he be accepted without questioning?

The farmer was anxious not to lose a good worker, a man who kept his head down and caused no trouble. When he told Denis he wanted him to stay on through the summer, he gave him the address of a man who rented out rooms in Gloucester. He also allowed him to purchase, for a mere three-pound stoppage from his wages, a rusting bicycle which had remained untouched for ten years in a disused barn. Denis cleaned it and oiled it and repaired its punctures and shone up the ancient Raleigh crest on the front of its frame.

The man who rented out the rooms asked for the first month's rent up front, but otherwise made no conditions and asked no questions. Denis found himself in the rabbit warren of a high Victorian house whose rooms had been subdivided to maximize the letting income. The other residents came and went as shiftily as he did, but they asked no questions and expected no answers from the lean young man, who said little and was not curious about them.

It took Denis nearly an hour to ride to work, but he set off at five thirty in the morning and was there before the rush-hour drivers were peering blearily at the queue of vehicles in front of them. When Denis hinted that there might be work for him on a building site nearer to his new base in Gloucester, the farmer gave him an extra ten pounds a week, which helped to pay for his room.

He was still cheap labour, with no card to be stamped and no records to be kept. And Denis had picked up enough now to know that the farmer was acting illegally in this law-conscious country. His employer wouldn't talk to the police, wouldn't even acknowledge the presence among his work-force of this quiet, industrious man from Eastern Europe.

Things were going well for Denis. As well as they could go for one in his desperate situation. And then, on the longest day of the year, when things had seemed to be at their bright-est, came the setback.

In the days which followed, he tried to keep to his maxim of putting things behind him, of looking forward rather than back, of preparing himself to cope with the next challenge. But this was bigger than any other thing which had happened to him. This could blow his whole world apart, if the police ever got to the bottom of it. And they would. He listened to people talking in the house, at work, around the streets of this old city where he had begun to feel safe. They all said that the police in England got their man, when it was murder.

He tried desperately to put the events of that fateful Saturday out of his mind, to tell himself that there was no way anyone could connect him with what had happened in the darkness on the banks of the Severn.

But even now, five days later, he could not get it out of his mind.

Five

Thursday evening. The weather still warm, but unsettled, as it had been ever since the thunderstorms of the weekend. A brisk shower fell as the police Rover moved through the Gloucestershire countryside, darkening the sky above the high treetops of the Forest of Dean.

Bert Hook sensed the unease in the young uniformed woman constable next to him. He knew it stemmed from the mission they had, but he chose to divert it to the more general theme of their surroundings. 'Race apart, the Foresters. That's what they used to say when I started to work round here, afore you were born, girl.'

She was reassured by his soft Herefordshire burr, felt comforted rather than patronized. 'So I've heard. Keep themselves to themselves, they say. Close ranks when people like us come among them.'

DS Hook smiled as he swung the car round a wide bend through the woods, keeping his eye on the sheep which roamed unfenced in this part of the Forest. 'It's less so than it used to be. But you still get it, in the villages especially. I don't object to it, myself. Part of that community spirit which we're asked to foster, if you ask me.'

He was content to make small talk, to try to relax the girl. It was the first time she had been to break the news of the sudden death of a daughter to unsuspecting parents. And this one was much trickier than most.

For a start, they weren't certain that the corpse from the Severn really was their daughter. People didn't thank you when it turned out to be a false alarm. After their first overwhelming flood of relief, their next reaction was usually a fierce resentment against the police bunglers for putting them through such an ordeal.

21

And it was much worse when the child was a murder victim. Parents always found this much more upsetting than a random tragedy like a road accident. But it was much more difficult also for the police who brought the awful news. You had to be conscious that it might not be news to them at all. Beneath your compassion for them as parents suffering the worst loss of all, the death of a child, you had to be coolly observant of their reactions.

There has been a huge rise in gangland killings in the last twenty years. Yet even now, over seventy per cent of killings are committed by members of the victim's families. Even parents may be murderers. But it is much more likely that they will have some shrewd ideas about who within the family might be responsible.

The address they had picked up from the university files was in a quiet village, four miles from the bustling little town of Cinderford, which was one of the hubs of life in the Forest of Dean. A quiet place, closed in upon itself among the high oaks which had been planted in the nineteenth century, to replace the trees felled to construct the fleets with which Nelson had fought off the bogeyman Napoleon.

Though the cottages and the sporadic outbreaks of modern housing now all sprouted television aerials, not much else seemed to have changed here since those trees were planted. Yet Bert Hook knew as he drove up the narrowing lanes that this was an illusion: life in the Forest had changed radically in the last half-century. Most people who lived here now worked outside the Forest and brought a different perspective home with them at nights. Nor were the families as in-bred as they had been, even in the days only a generation ago, when he had first ventured into the Forest as a fresh-faced young constable.

About the same age then as the uncertain young woman at his side was now, he thought as he followed her up the path to the house: the thought made him feel at once protective and far too old.

It was a high stone house, three hundred yards away from the next residence. There were extensive and well-planted gardens around it, but what had once been a cottage garden beside the oldest part of the house was now largely gravel, providing a wide turning circle for vehicles. The broad oak door was opened before he could ring the bell beside it. Bert Hook took the initiative.

'I'm Detective Sergeant Hook and this is Police Constable Lipton. I rang you earlier.'

The woman nodded, scarcely bothering to listen. 'You'd better come in.' She was a well-preserved ash-blonde, probably in her late forties, with alert brown eyes and a sophisticated hairstyling that had nothing rural about it. Only a certain rigidity about the lower part of her face hinted that she might be feeling a certain strain. She led them into a surprisingly light sitting room, with windows on two sides. She said, 'You said you might be coming here with bad news.'

Hook hadn't said that, but he had been evasive when she pressed him on the phone. 'It may be, I'm afraid. I hope it isn't.' He meant it, even though a blank here would put them back to the beginning of a baffling investigation, without even an identification of the victim. He hastened to cloak his compassion with the routine formalities. 'Are you the mother of Clare Mills?'

'I am. My present name is Hudson, but I was Mills when Clare was born.'

'And is Clare's father still alive?'

'He is. Something's happened to her, hasn't it? Something's wrong.'

'I'm afraid there may be, yes. When did you last hear from your daughter?'

'I don't know. Not in over a week now. Tell me what it is that's wrong.'

'Would that be usual, Mrs Mills? Or would you expect her to have been in contact with you over the last few days?' It was a technique he had learned from Lambert. You fed in as many questions as you could, whilst they were nervous and uncertain. An emotionally uncertain witness was more likely to say revealing things than one who was certain of the facts. It was cruel, but this wasn't a routine death; they knew now that this was the first stage of a murder investigation.

'I've been expecting her to ring for the last few days. Since the weekend. She usually rings at the weekend.' The banal repetition trailed away into the corners of the quiet room. 'Something's happened, hasn't it? Something bad.'

Hook nodded to the young woman beside him, who went tremulously into the sentences she had prepared for this moment. 'You may have read that a female corpse was discovered on Wednesday in the Severn at Lydney. There has been no formal identification made yet, but we have reason to think—'

'It's Clare, isn't it? That's what you think! That's why you're here.' Her hand flew involuntarily to her mouth. White teeth gnawed at her well-manicured fingers, as if like a child she had to stop herself from screaming. Yet Hook had the curious feeling that she was acting out the symptoms of grief, rather than genuinely affected.

'We have reason to think that it might be your daughter. She has been absent from her flat since the weekend, and if she hasn't been here—'

'I knew it! I knew something was wrong when she didn't ring me. She always rang me, at least once a week.'

'The body is a female of about your daughter's age. There was a university library card in the pocket of her jeans. The library computer tells us that this belonged to your daughter. We shall need a formal identification before we can be certain, but—'

'I'll do it. I'll come with you now, if you want me to!'

There was a febrile excitement about the woman, almost an eagerness to have her worst fears confirmed. Hook deduced nothing from that: grief affected people in a host of different ways. 'The corpse is somewhat damaged, Mrs Hudson. Seeing it will be an ordeal. Perhaps Clare's father, or your present husband, could do the—'

'Clare's father is in New Zealand. And I don't want my present husband doing this. I'll come with you myself. I'll come with you now.'

They waited a few minutes, listening to her movements upstairs. She came down in a dark dress, as if already in mourning for her daughter. The body was still at Chepstow, and Hook phoned the morgue there to warn them of their impending visit.

24

He wondered why this brittle woman had been so determined that her present husband would not do the identification.

Clare Mills's flatmate was nervous.

Anne Jackson raced around the rooms in something like a panic when the phone call came through to say that the police were coming. They wouldn't say why they wanted to see the flat, but it sounded bad to her. The students at the university were all talking about the body that had been fished out of the Severn and speculating that it might be Clare. Harry Shadwell hadn't told her that he was going to the police. It was just like him, that, dithering so uncertainly about what action to take when she had been to see him and then rushing off to inform the authorities himself the next day, without telling her what he was doing. Other people seemed to have been allotted personal tutors who were much more on the ball than Shadwell.

Anne moved the things she had been looking for, then hastened to tidy the place. She gave the bathroom and the kitchen a quick clean, wiping the surfaces and removing the clutter of make-up in the bathroom and the beakers in the kitchen which seemed part and parcel of student life. She realized with a little start of guilt that it had usually been Clare who did the minimal cleaning they allowed themselves in the place. She put her notebook and the books she had got from the library on the table under the window: might as well play the virtuous student.

She was surprised when they arrived, exactly at noon as she had suggested. Anne had expected a couple of uniformed people, probably about her own age, who would go through a standard list of enquiries. Instead, she got a superintendent and an inspector: top brass, as her father would have said. They were both in plain clothes. The tall, lean one with the beginning of a stoop was Superintendent John Lambert, the man who Severn Radio had just told her was taking charge of the case. He had a lined, intelligent face beneath his iron-grey hair. He also had a habit of studying her as she replied to his questions, which she found disconcerting.

The younger man was introduced as Detective Inspector Rushton. He was probably in his early thirties, she thought, with well-cut brown hair and clean-cut features. He was what her mum would have called dishy and what she and her contemporaries called fit. But his manner was rather stiff and Anne, who had a weakness for romantic fiction, thought that there was a sadness in his large brown eyes which suggested a failed relationship. Anne hoped that he would be the one who put the questions to her about Clare. Instead, he seemed content to take notes whilst the superintendent did most of the talking.

He asked how long Clare Mills had been missing, and when Anne had begun to grow anxious about her friend's absence, and what action she had taken. All routine stuff, no doubt. But Lambert's attention never strayed from her face and his eyes never seemed to blink. It was as though he felt that she had something to hide from him. Yet he certainly couldn't have any real knowledge about that, she told herself firmly.

Then he said, 'What kind of a girl was Clare?'

She felt suddenly very defensive. 'Ordinary, I suppose. She was a good friend and a good student. Is this really important?'

'It is if Clare Mills is identified as a murder victim, which it now seems probable she will be. We have to build up a picture of a girl we've never met, to find out what sort of enemies she had, to see what circles she moved in, if we're to determine who it was that killed her. I'd have thought you'd be anxious to help us.'

It was like an accusation, when she had done nothing. Anne was still trying to cope with the idea that the girl who had laughed with her so often in this room might be dead. She said, 'Of course I want to help you. It's just that Clare Mills was – well, kind of ordinary, I suppose. I'm not saying she wasn't pretty enough, when she wanted to be, but she didn't wear outlandish clothes or anything like that. She wouldn't stand out in a crowd.' She realized with a little spurt of cold fear that they were now talking about her in the past tense.

'No one is really ordinary, you know. For a start, Clare was older than the average undergraduate student, wasn't she?'

'Yes. She was twenty-five.'

'And was she a good student?'

'Yes. She was very conscientious. And bright, too, though

26

she said she wasn't. She'd got excellent grades in all her assignments. We're only halfway through our course, but we all thought Clare was in line for a first.'

Lambert gave her his first smile. 'There you are, then. She wasn't ordinary at all! Where do you think she went on Saturday?'

The sudden switch, the abrupt question, disconcerted her. She should be grieving for her friend, if what they feared was true, and yet she felt as though she had to watch what she was saying all the time. 'I've no idea. Really I haven't!' She wondered if she was blushing; it felt as if she was. 'I didn't think anything about it at the time. I suppose I thought she'd gone to visit her family – I've never met them, but they live not far away from here, in the Forest of Dean. It was only when she didn't come back that I began to worry. When she wasn't back by Wednesday and I hadn't heard anything from her, I went to see our personal tutor, Mr Shadwell, about it.'

Lambert took his gaze from her face for the first time in several minutes to gaze round the room. 'If she's dead, as we now believe her to be, we'll need to send a team in here to conduct a systematic search.'

Anne forced a smile, tried to thrust confidence into her voice. 'That won't be a problem. The landlord will let you in, if I'm not here. He lives on the premises.'

'Miss Mills had her own bedroom?'

'Yes. We shared this room, and the kitchen and bathroom, but we each had our own small bedroom.'

Lambert nodded thoughtfully, studying her again in that disconcerting manner which seemed to imply that she was holding things back from him. Then he stood up and walked into each of the rooms in turn, as if he wanted to commit the layout of the place to his mind. He did not touch anything, did not open any of the drawers, as she had feared he might. Inspector Rushton gave her a small, sympathetic smile, as if in apology for his chief's brusqueness. He had a nice smile. She wouldn't mind getting to know Inspector Rushton properly, but she didn't suppose she ever would.

Lambert stood for a long moment looking into Clare's bedroom, as if the neat, narrow bed could tell him something about the woman who had spent her nights there. He said, 'Have you tidied the room? Did she leave it like this?'

'No, I haven't touched it. Clare always made her bed before she went out in the morning, even when she had an early lecture.' This time Anne was sure she was blushing. She looked not at Lambert but at the window and the white clouds in the blue sky beyond it. She told herself that she would burst into tears for her friend when he had gone. In the meantime, she would be careful about what she said.

'Rather a good flat this, for students.'

'We had our loans. And my mother gives me a little, when she can. She says she'd rather I lived in a decent place than a slum.'

'And Clare?'

'We didn't discuss money. She may have had some savings before she began her course. I told you, she was a mature student.' She wondered if it rang true, if she was talking too much. Her explanation sounded odd in her own ears.

'Was Clare Mills meeting a man on Saturday?'

'No! Well, I don't know, do I? I don't know where she went. I don't know what her plans were.' She was suddenly annoyed by his persistence. She was sure it showed, and there was a reaction from Rushton, but her discomfort didn't seem to have the slightest effect on the older man.

'If this proves to be a murder investigation, as I'm sure it will, we'll need to know about all her acquaintances over the last few months. Please give the matter detailed thought. As Clare's flatmate, you may have key information.'

'I didn't know her all that well, you know. She was four years older than me and she kept herself to herself a lot of the time.' It sounded defensive, as if she had something to hide, but it suddenly seemed important to convince them that she wasn't going to be of any great help to them.

'Nevertheless, you may know things which seem to you insignificant, but which may supplement what we learn elsewhere and prove to be vital. We have to begin somewhere, and the sooner the better. If Clare Mills is dead, I'm taking it for granted that you will want to see the person who has harmed your friend brought to justice.'

'Of course. That goes without saying.' Yet she'd given him

the chance to say it, hadn't she? She'd been sounding deliberately unhelpful. He'd nettled her, and made her reveal things about herself that she hadn't wished to show them. She turned deliberately to Inspector Rushton. 'I'll certainly give proper thought to the matter, and I hope that I come up with something which might be useful to you.'

He smiled at her as he shut his notebook, as if apologizing for Lambert's attitude. 'I'm sure you will, Miss Jackson. And you really can be quite helpful to us, you know. Trivial things may turn out to be quite important, as we begin to put all our findings together.'

DI Rushton had driven a mile before Lambert said to him, 'I think you made a hit there, Chris. Could be a promising liaison there for you. Once all this is over, of course.'

Rushton had been divorced for two years now, but hadn't found new relationships easy. He did not respond to the suggestion. He found it difficult to be certain when the super was teasing him about these things; it was even worse when the man got together with Bert Hook, the officer who had been his CID sergeant for ten years and more: the two older men were always twitting him about his sexual attractiveness and his exotic – and unfortunately imaginary – love life.

Chris Rushton gazed resolutely at the road ahead and said stiffly, 'She seemed a typical student to me, sir. I'm sure she thought me much too old for her. And she seemed anxious to help us find her friend's killer. I hope the search of the girl's room turns up something useful.'

He thought he had managed to turn the conversation away from the pretty Miss Jackson. Until Lambert said after another half a mile, 'I wonder what it was that the girl was trying to conceal from us.'

The young woman constable tried her best to put Judith Hudson at her ease as she sat beside her in the police Mondeo on their journey to the mortuary at Chepstow. But she was not herself comfortable in the situation, and the woman beside her spoke more to Hook, who was driving, than to her. Perhaps it was the experience of the older man which gave him the empathy for a situation like this.

The staff at the morgue tried to warn Mrs Hudson about

the condition of the body, but she nodded curtly and seemed anxious to have this over with. At her request, Hook accompanied her into the identification room to view the corpse which he had lately seen mutilated at the post-mortem.

He was always pleasantly surprised by how much of their work the pathologist and his assistants managed to conceal from the relatives. The girl's plentiful hair covered what had been done to the skull. The sheet would mercifully conceal the stitching at the front of the body. He stood at the back of the room behind Mrs Hudson and watched her steeling herself for the moment of truth. Then she nodded to the assistant.

Hook listened for the familiar gasp of emotion from the parent as the still, lineless young face was revealed. This time he did not hear it. Two long seconds passed before Judith Hudson said in a low voice, 'That's her. That's my daughter. That's Clare Mills.'

They gave her a cup of tea before they took her out to the car for the journey back to that high, isolated house in the Forest. She seemed very composed, but Hook, accustomed to seeing grief in many forms, deduced nothing from that. He didn't attempt to make conversation. That would have been banal, even tasteless.

He was trying to think what it was that had been unusual about this particular identification. Something small, but something definite. They were driving through Cinderford, turning onto the road which led to Mrs Hudson's village, before he realized what had struck him as different. It was the manner of the identification. Normally parents, however affected, gave just the forename of their child: 'That's James' or 'That's Debbie'.

This one had given the child's full name. 'That's Clare Mills,' she had said. He'd never heard a parent do it like that before.

Six

Ian Walker was a sheep-badger in the Forest of Dean.
It is a local term, a definition of those people who have
no farm of their own but make a living by grazing sheep
through 'commoners' rights' in the Forest of Dean. It is one
of the ancient rights of people who live in the Forest that they
are allowed to graze sheep without charge on certain tracts of
it. Most people think the privilege derives from a medieval
ruling by the monarch, although few are certain of the origin
or the detail of the statute.

Others claim that what are now usually called the commoners' rights were originally given to a group of gypsies with
the splendidly inappropriate name of DuBunny, and were
granted by the then Prince Edward to make this group self-
sufficient. Modern sheep-badgers claim descent from this
group, though most of them could not trace the lineage to save
their lives.

The rights of free grazing related to the woods of the Forest
of Dean, with no mention of roads, for the simple reason that
the tracery of modern roads which runs through the Forest did
not exist, except as ancient tracks and bridle paths. According
to opinion, the modern sheep-badgers, 'hefting' their sheep
amidst the woods and open spaces, are either practitioners of
an ancient custom, who should be treasured as part of
England's heritage, or unscrupulous opportunists, taking
advantage of loopholes in the nation's law to live rent-free
and make a quick buck at the expense of more conventional
citizens. Both opinions are fiercely expressed by those who
live in the Forest, and sometimes, less pardonably, by those
who live outside its boundaries.

Ian Walker would not have denied the charge that he lived
by his wits. He would probably even have been prepared to

31

boast that he did so, when he was in the right company. He was swarthy and dark-haired, with a scar on his temple which might have been a symbol of the way he had lived. Whereas aristocratic Germans used to carry duelling scars as a badge of honour, Walker's injury denoted a life of casual violence, an inclination to solve every dispute with his fists, a succession of brawls in the pubs and back streets of Gloucestershire towns.

He had convictions for burglary in his teens, cautions for his part in an affray and for assault, a ban for driving without tax or insurance. He had never received a custodial sentence, though it had taken a good brief and a lenient court to give him the benefit of the doubt and save him on a couple of occasions.

It didn't look on paper like the background of a murderer.

But John Lambert was studying the man from a hundred yards away with the dispassionate gaze of a man who took nothing for granted. And Bert Hook was telling himself that murder was the one crime where you could not rely on criminal records. That anyone who had shown a predilection for casual violence could easily let that impulse spill over into something more serious.

The sheep-badger had his back to them. He cursed his flock roundly as he herded them away from the road with a stick hewn from the nearby trees. It is always difficult to tell with people who live life in the open air, but he seemed unconscious of the presence of the two big men behind him as they left the unmarked car and moved closer to him.

They were within three yards of him before Lambert said evenly, 'Are you Ian Walker?'

'What's it to you?' He whirled on them, answering question with question, his voice almost a snarl, his immediate reaction aggression.

Lambert moved even closer, almost a foot taller than this stocky, powerful man. He flashed his police card briefly beneath the dark eyes. 'It's a matter of considerable interest to us, as a matter of fact. Important enough for us to take you in to the station to question you, if you are not cooperative.'

Walker glanced past the two men in shirtsleeves to the houses visible beneath the canopy of foliage five hundred yards away. 'That Johnson bugger been fuckin' complainin' again, 'as 'e? Needs to mind 'is own fuckin' business and keep out of my way. I've every right to 'ave my sheep 'ere and 'e knows it. Needs to fence 'is garden off properly if 'e wants to protect 'is bloody plants, don't 'e?'

'This isn't about what you let your sheep get up to, Mr Walker. If there are complaints, uniformed officers will deal with that.'

Ian Walker looked at them with undiminished hostility. He'd known they wouldn't send a superintendent after him, not for a few harsh words and the threats he had offered over his sheep. He dropped into the sudden, automatic denial he had practised for ten years with policemen. 'I ain't pinched nothing. You're wasting your time coming after me. You got the wrong man.'

'Are you the husband of a woman we know as Clare Mills?'

'No. I fucking was though, once. She divorced me. Stuck-up bitch. And if she wants maintenance, tell 'er I can't fucking afford it!'

Both of them studied him unhurriedly, watching him breathing hard, savouring his frustration as his language failed to make any impression. Then Bert Hook said, 'She's dead, Ian.'

'Dead?' It was a low-key reaction. Neither of them could be sure whether or not this was news to him.

'Dead. And we're here to find out what you know about it.'

He looked from one to the other of the two faces, from Bert Hook's weather-beaten countryman's visage to John Lambert's longer and more lined features. Both were equally serious, equally observant. He dropped his eyes in the face of their unrelenting scrutiny. 'I know nothing about it. It's news to me that she's dead.'

He had dropped his obscenities; perhaps it was the nearest he could come to recognizing the solemnity of death. But he didn't remove the stained baseball cap, which let his dark hair escape untidily at its edges. Nor did he ask how the woman who had once been his wife had died. Bert Hook, trying hard to put himself inside the mind of this alien maverick, thought that Walker should have done that. Unless, of course, he already knew how Clare Mills had perished.

'Were you still in touch with her, Ian?'

'No. Hadn't seen her for ages.' The denial came perhaps too promptly, too automatically. But this man's urge would no doubt be to dissociate himself from death, whether or not he had any connection with it. He looked full into Hook's face and said, 'I hadn't seen Clare for a long time.' Walker produced the name clumsily, as if he was belatedly conscious of the need to show some sort of respect.

Bert studied the swarthy face. There was defiance in the set of the chin, but apprehension in the dark eyes. Bert said, 'You may wish to think about that statement, Ian. You haven't asked us yet how she died.'

He had made a mistake, then, and they were letting him know it. Ian said sullenly, 'Well, how was it, then?' And then, with desperate invention, he added, 'Car accident, was it?'

He stood breathing heavily, clutching his long stick as if he planned to use it if things did not go his way, waiting for Hook to reply. Instead, it was Lambert who said quietly, 'She was murdered, Mr Walker.'

'Murdered?' His jaw fell stupidly. It seemed that the word carried its normal overtones of awe and fear, even for this man.

'Murdered, Mr Walker. We are investigating a serious crime. The most serious one of all.'

So that's why he had plain-clothes men here plaguing him. That's why he had a superintendent and a DS, more rank than he had ever been accorded before. He said with automatic denial, 'Well, I didn't kill her, did I?'

'That's one of the things we're here to find out. The nearest relative is always a suspect, Mr Walker. But I expect you know that.' Lambert checked himself: he mustn't allow himself too much enjoyment in the spectacle of this boorish creature squirming.

'Course I know it. But I didn't kill Clare, did I?' Almost as an afterthought, he repeated his earlier statement. 'I 'adn't seen her for months, 'ad I?'

'I don't know, Mr Walker. I have to accept what you tell me. Of course, it will be checked against what other people have to tell me, in due course.'

'You threatening me?'

34

'I'm providing you with information about how a murder investigation operates, Mr Walker. You should be aware that any untruths, any information you withhold from us, will come out eventually. Deceiving us now would be regarded very seriously.'

Ian Walker told himself that he had heard this sort of thing before, that this was the way the police always behaved, throwing their weight about, trying to make people like him lose their nerve. Well, they wouldn't succeed. 'I don't know nothing about this. You can't pin this on me, copper.'

Bert Hook said, 'No one wants to pin anything on you, Ian. Nothing you didn't do, anyway. We need your help, if we're to find who killed Clare. Surely you want us to find out who killed her?'

He wasn't going to be caught out by this softer approach. The cop with the weather-beaten face spoke in an accent like his. Perhaps he was trying to make out they had something in common. Well, it wouldn't work. 'I haven't seen Clare for months. Didn't want to see 'er. I know bugger all about this.'

He smiled, not at them but towards his sheep, pretending with the return of his accustomed swearing that confidence was back with him. Lambert said, 'How long is it since you were divorced from Clare, Mr Walker?'

Walker looked at him as if he thought it was a trick question. He thought for long seconds before he decided it was something he had to answer. 'Nigh on two year. We'd been separated well before that, mind.'

'On good terms, were you?'

'I told you, we was divorced.'

Lambert allowed himself a sour smile. 'Some people manage to be divorced and remain friends, Mr Walker.'

He looked as if he was considering a strange idea. 'She were a stuck-up bitch, were Clare. She seemed to think—'

'Why were you divorced?'

'In-com-pat-i-ble. That's what the papers said.' He pronounced each syllable as if it were a separate word. 'That's how the snobby cow wanted it. Said that was the easiest way.'

'Knock her about, did you?'

'Who told you—?' He stopped quickly, though not before he had incriminated himself. Then he glared suspiciously at his questioner and said, 'Course I didn't. We should never have got wed, that's what it was.'

'Hit women a lot, do you, Mr Walker?'

'You've no reason to bloody say that.' He glanced from side to side, like a cornered animal looking for a path of escape. Then he fell back on a phrase from his youth. 'This is victimization, this is.'

'This is the police pursuing enquiries, Mr Walker. I doubt if you'd recognize victimization if it rode in here on a bicycle with a label round its neck.' Lambert let his contempt flow over the man for a moment. 'So we know you hit Clare Mills during the brief period when she was Mrs Walker. What we have to decide is whether you killed her last Saturday.'

'I didn't. Didn't go near the snobby cow.' But he wasn't looking at them. He kicked a tussock of grass viciously in his frustration, and the sheep started away from him, gathering fifteen yards away, keeping a nervous eye upon him as they resumed their nibbling of the sparse grass around the base of a tree.

Lambert nodded to Hook, who resumed the questioning. 'When did you last see Clare, Ian?'

'Dunno. Months ago, must be.' He dragged his toe across the dust of the bare patch of earth where he stood, as if seeking to draw some sort of line on the conversation.

'But you've seen her since you were divorced.'

'Dunno. Might have.' His face set like that of a sulking child.

Hook controlled his anger, made himself pause before he said quietly, 'It's a murder enquiry, Ian. Be best if you co-operate, won't it?'

'All right, I've seen her since we were divorced. Can't be expected to remember when, can I? Not just like that.'

'You'll need to work on that, then, force your memory into action. Why did you see her, Ian?'

'Can't recall, can I? Not just like that.'

But he immediately looked even more shifty, and they knew it hadn't been a chance meeting. 'Trying to get money out of her, were you, Ian?'

Walker looked across to his sheep, then down the valley towards the distant houses. 'It's not all profit, this game, you

36

know. People think it's easy money, sheep-badgering, but there's expenses.'

Hook was almost drawn into asking him what they were. Instead, he said, 'Did you get money from Clare, Ian?'

'Did I bloody 'eckers like! She said she'd given up her job and become a student now. Another bloody parasite!' He thrust his resentment into the insult he had heard in the pub, though he'd no real idea what a parasite was.

'And when did this meeting take place?'

'Dunno. Months ago. Six months, mebbe.'

He stood breathing heavily, watching the toes of his trainers, refusing still to look at the CID men, even through the pause which they let stretch beneath the warm sun. Lambert said, 'Do you have a vehicle, Mr Walker?'

'No.' He turned his back upon them for a moment to look at his sheep, straggling away in groups beneath the trees of the Forest of Dean. 'I don't need wheels to heft sheep, do I? I borrows a van from a mate, when I needs one.'

They left him then, walking stiffly away like the townies he took them for. Their car was a hundred yards away. They sat watching him for a couple of minutes, whilst he shouted some guttural commands to his unheeding sheep and tried to look purposeful. Then they drove slowly away, with the burly sergeant watching him until they passed out of sight.

You kept the fuzz in the dark on principle, lied whenever you could. They surely couldn't know which were the important lies.

Seven

Sara Green watched the police team working its way around the Social Studies department at the university and tried hard to keep calm.

They had said they planned to be unobtrusive, to disturb the work of the faculty as little as possible. But the dark uniforms stood out against the jeans and T-shirts of the student community at exam-time: they had as much chance of being unnoticed as Martians. Sara was surprised how many officers there were: half a dozen at least, she thought, maybe even more. And you were always being told that the police were overstretched, that there weren't enough of them to go round. It certainly seemed like that, when you had a burglary at your house or someone went joy-riding in your car. They hadn't done more than go through the motions when her mother's house had been broken into last year, just told her that she could tell her insurance people that the police had been informed.

But this was a murder investigation, and that seemed to pull in the resources. A team of fifty altogether, the reporter had said on television last night. They seemed to be talking to as many of the students as they could get hold of, as well as the academic staff. Sara wondered if they were asking everyone the same questions. It was routine, she told herself. There was nothing to get worried about.

She was wearing her usual dark blue trousers and flat shoes. She had thought last night that she might wear jeans and trainers; she could still pass for a student when she wanted to. After all, Clare Mills had been a student, and Sara was only eight years older than her. But in the end, she had chosen to look her age, to blend as easily as she could into the role of tutor which sometimes felt so alien to her. She had put on her best green silk blouse, which she knew made the most of her small but definite breasts.

With its delicate tracery of embroidery around the neck, it made her look very feminine. She had already had a few compliments on her appearance, so that she wondered if she was attracting attention rather than the anonymity she craved. But it was the male staff who had been most fulsome about her attractiveness today, and men were suggestible creatures at the best of times.

Sara wondered if it would be a male police officer who came to question her, when they finally got round to her. Whoever it was would surely put the same set of queries to her which were being put to everyone else. She would give them an equally dull set of replies and send them on their way. There was no reason why they should be more interested in her than anyone else. She was just someone who lectured in psychology. Just one of the many lecturers whom Clare Mills had come across in the course of her studies. Neither more nor less important than a dozen other people.

Sara Green wondered if she would have to sign a statement. It would be important not to let them see that she was nervous.

They were ushered straight through by the PA in the outer office. It was a luxuriously carpeted room, with expensive prints of the Brecon Beacons and the Black Mountains on the walls and two deep armchairs in front of the big desk, but a room which was curiously without a distinctive character or atmosphere.

The first words of the man after the introductions had been made were equally inscrutable. 'She was a lovely girl. I can't think of anyone who could possibly have wished her any harm.'

It was a conventional enough thought, one they had heard voiced many times before in murder cases. And Lambert's practised reply was equally conventional. 'We're sorry to have to intrude at a time like this, Mr Hudson, but I'm sure you'll appreciate that we need to gather as much information as we can about a murder victim, as quickly as we can.'

'I still can't believe that Clare was murdered. Why would anyone want to do a thing like that?'

Another platitude. It was impossible to tell how genuine people were, when they spoke in grief or in shock. It was not even possible to tell which of these two emotions predominated. 'We have to begin with those who were closest to the victim. We need to know as much as possible about her friends and her habits.'

'I was her stepfather, not her father, of course. But you'll have deduced that from the name.'

'Indeed. Were you close to Clare?'

'Yes, of course I was.'

'There's no "of course" about it, Mr Hudson. Stepdaughters often find a new man in their mother's bed hard to accept.'

Roy Hudson looked for a moment as if he would bridle at the directness of this. He was a little older than his wife, probably around fifty, with deep-set, watchful brown eyes in a tanned face. He was a handsome man, greying at the temples but still with a good crop of dark hair. He had the slightly florid complexion which often comes from a comfortable lifestyle and a surfeit of good food and wine, but there was no sign of the corpulence which might have accompanied such indulgence. He controlled himself and asserted tersely, 'Clare and I had a good relationship.'

'But she chose to keep the name of her real father.'

'That was her prerogative. I believe it is not unusual in these circumstances.' They were fencing with each other already, two naturally combative men who had dropped into a contest. Lambert wondered how it had happened, why it was that this successful man was behaving as if he had territory to protect.

'How old was Clare when you came upon the scene, Mr Hudson?'

'Sixteen. She was eighteen when I married Judith. Is this relevant?'

'It may or it may not be. We shall only know when we have a much fuller picture of the life led by a girl who cannot speak for herself.'

Lambert wasn't averse to ruffling a man who struck him as a smooth operator; people who were angry usually revealed more of themselves than they intended. He was wondering why Hudson had chosen to see them here in his luxuriously appointed office rather than at his home. Did he for some reason not want his wife, the girl's mother, to overhear these exchanges? Lambert said, 'Clare must have lived under the same roof as you for a number of years.'

'She came with her mother when I married her.' He made her sound like a family pet which had to be accommodated as part of a deal. 'There was plenty of room in the house for her. She wasn't with us for very long. She chose to get married herself.' The words tripped out without any hesitations, almost like part of a statement he had prepared in advance. But there might be nothing sinister in that: there was no reason why he should not anticipate their questions and prepare his answers.

But the nature of their work turns CID men into suspicious creatures; prepared statements suggest to them that the speaker may have something to hide. 'So how long did you live in the same house as your stepdaughter?'

'Six months or so. She made a hasty marriage, against our advice. Marry in haste and repent at leisure, they say. It was certainly so in Clare's case.' Perhaps Roy Hudson thought he sounded too satisfied that it had turned out so, for he added lamely, 'It was a great pity for her, a great sorrow for us.'

Lambert wondered if Roy Hudson was anxious to turn the talk away from his own relationship with the dead girl to that of Ian Walker's. 'Would you say that Clare Mills and you had a happy relationship during those six months when you lived in the same house?'

'Yes. Excellent.'

'Forgive me for saying so, but that would be unusual, in our experience. There are usually problems of the kind I have suggested when teenagers have to accept a new head of the family. We need you to be quite frank with us.'

Hudson pursed his rather thin lips. 'I wouldn't say there were major problems. As a matter of fact, Judith had more trouble with her daughter than I had. I think Clare blamed her for the break-up of her first marriage. I never met Clare's father. He was off the scene before I even met Judith. He's in New Zealand now.'

Hook looked up at this point from the notes he had been making. 'So how would you summarize your own relationship with Clare Mills, Mr Hudson?'

41

'Close and friendly.' Again there was the sense that this was an emollient phrase he had prepared for this very question.

Hook nodded. 'We were given access this morning to Clare's bank and building society accounts. That is quite normal in the case of a murder victim.'

'Yes?' The man behind the big desk could not see where this was going.

'She had quite a large student loan. No larger perhaps than that of many students at her stage of a degree, but quite substantial.'

'So?'

'Nothing, really. But it's surprising how often a murder victim's financial situation tells us significant things about their life. I just thought that in view of the fact that you enjoyed a close and friendly relationship with her, you might have chosen to supplement her income whilst she was at university.' He put the thought apologetically, where Lambert might have made it confrontational. Then he looked round the conventional affluence of the office rather than at the man at the centre of it. Bert Hook did rather a good line in innocent speculation.

Roy Hudson controlled himself with difficulty and said icily, 'Clare was an independent young woman. She wouldn't have accepted charity from me.'

'I see. Did you offer to help her?'

Hudson paused to consider his reply. These men and their team were going to talk to many other people, to unearth much more about Clare than they knew at present, a lot more than he was going to offer them. 'I knew her well enough to know that financial support from me would not have been welcome. I told you, we had an excellent relationship.' His manner rather than his words told them that this was a man not used to being challenged, a man who ran a highly successful small business, whose word was law during his working day.

'When did you last see Clare Mills?'

He took his time, suspecting now that they might be happy to irritate him, accepting the rules of the game and playing to win. 'Three months ago, approximately. I couldn't be precise. I didn't expect to be quizzed about it by policemen.' He allowed himself a small, mirthless smile on that thought.

Lambert answered this thought he had heard hundreds of times before with a wry smile of his own. 'But we believe that Clare went home regularly to visit her mother. Does this mean that you did not see her on those visits?'

'If she visited the house during those last three months, I didn't see her. I assure you there is nothing sinister in that fact. Hudson Plastics is a prosperous business, but it doesn't run itself.'

'Did Clare communicate any sort of anxiety to you or to her mother?'

'None whatsoever. Though as I say, it is some time since I saw her. But I'm sure Judith would have mentioned anything which was worrying her daughter to me, if she thought it serious.'

'Was Clare in any sort of trouble?'

'No. As far as I know, her studies were going well.'

'Yes. The university confirms that she was an excellent student. Both her tutors and her fellow-students were expecting her to get a good degree. And yet someone chose to kill her.'

'Couldn't this have been something quite random, quite unconnected with her normal life?'

People, even totally innocent people, always wanted this. They found some unpredictable violence easier to take than a planned murder, involving someone who had been close to the victim. Lambert said, 'It's possible, of course. But even in today's world, such deaths are rarer than the public thinks. We normally find that someone has secured some advantage from a death. For what it's worth, the post-mortem did not reveal any sign of a sexual attack upon your stepdaughter.'

He would have expected the man to have asked about that at the beginning of the interview: people close to the victim usually wanted to be reassured that there had not been a rape before a strangling.

As if he recognized the omission, Roy Hudson said hastily, 'That's something at any rate, I suppose. I hope Clare suffered as little as possible.'

Lambert was irked by his urbanity, by his lack of any obvious emotion about a girl he claimed he had been close to. He said abruptly, 'So who do you think killed Clare Mills, Mr Hudson?'

'I haven't the faintest idea. If I did, I'd be offering you my thoughts, obviously.'

Not so obviously, thought Lambert. You're concealing something, but until I know more about you and this strange murder victim, I can't begin to conjecture what it might be. He said as he stood up, 'If you think of anything at all which might be helpful, please contact me or Detective Inspector Rushton at Oldford CID immediately. We shall no doubt wish to speak to you again in due course.'

He made that sound as much like a threat as he could.

Bert Hook hoped to complete an Open University degree within the next year. But, having been a doughty Minor Counties seam bowler with Herefordshire for fifteen years, he still tended to think in cricketing metaphors. To his mind, Roy Hudson had played a straight bat to fairly standard bowling. Bert looked forward to making him hop about a bit on the back foot, when they got him on a stickier wicket.

The insurance broker gave him a price which was cheaper than anything else he'd had. It was probably from a dodgy company, but it would make him legal, which was all that mattered.

Ian Walker said, 'I only want third party, fire and theft, mind. You sure that's the lowest you can do?'

'You won't beat that price. And you're sure the vehicle is garaged every night?'

'Oh, yes. Locked and barred, with the keys removed.' He remembered the lies you had to tell. Probably the man on the other end of the line didn't even believe him, but that wouldn't matter.

'Once we've cleared your cheque, we'll send you the certificate by the next post, Mr . . . ?' The broker was anxious to get on to more important things; there wasn't much commission in third-party insurance on an old van.

'I'm paying cash. I'll be there in an hour. Have the certificate ready and I'll pick it up.'

In the circles in which Ian Walker moved, cash was still king. You trusted that and very little else. He pulled the tin out from its hiding place under the stained sink and extracted the grubby notes he needed. He took a blank cheque too from the scarcely used book and put it and the money carefully into the pocket of his jeans. Then he reversed the old white van out from the grass beneath the trees and drove into Gloucester, more carefully than usual. He parked in his usual place near the cattle market and went to collect the insurance certificate. There was still a month left on the van's MOT, so that was all right.

The broker looked at the unshaven man suspiciously as he entered the narrow office. The soiled baseball cap, with the greasy black hair protruding untidily from its edges, and the scar on the temple didn't inspire confidence. Walker, who was used to working outdoors, looked round uneasily within the confines of this cramped little room, as if he feared someone might spring out on him from behind the filing cabinet. But he presented exactly the right money, in a variety of dog-eared notes. The broker counted it carefully and handed over the certificate. Any claims would be a matter for direct negotiation between the client and the insurance company, he explained. He wasn't going to be a middle-man for this very dubious customer.

Ian Walker accepted that information with scarcely a nod of acknowledgement. He was busy checking the certificate: he didn't have to do a lot of reading nowadays. But he was literate enough, when it was needed. He filled in the form in the post office, explaining that he had only just acquired the vehicle which he had actually been driving for the last four months. Then he posted it off, with his cheque for six months' tax and the MOT and the new insurance certificate, to the DVLC at Swansea.

He scrawled a 'Tax in Post' message on a scrap of paper and put it over the out-of-date tax disc. If the police were coming calling, you'd better be legal. There was nothing the pigs liked better than catching you out like that.

Perhaps he shouldn't have told that snotty superintendent that he didn't have a vehicle; it had been his natural instinct to deny it when he knew it wasn't taxed or insured. When he was back in the Forest of Dean, he'd throw a couple of the sheep in the back for an hour or two, let them piss on the bit of old carpet, if they wanted to.

No one would be able to tell that he'd scrubbed the van out on Sunday, once they'd been there.

45

Eight

M artin Carter thought he was in the clear.

It had all seemed to go quite well when the uniformed constables had taken his statement about Clare Mills. They had been a man and a woman, both younger than him, and he had moved from being stiff and nervous to being quite relaxed. He had made a few jokes with them about how the university was detached from real life, about how these people in uniform were working away at the crime face whilst he did research, studying crime from the outside and making portentous pronouncements about trends and possible solutions.

He confided to them that he had even considered entering the police through the graduate-recruitment scheme at one time, but had then recognized that he could neither take the discipline nor join in the team work that was required of people in the modern police force. 'So I became a postgraduate student instead,' he had concluded wryly. 'Put off entering the real world for a little longer, as you might say!'

He had explained to his visitors that he was researching 'Recidivism in the Modern Criminal'. He had planned further self-deprecatory remarks about the advantages of studying crime from the elevation of an ivory tower, but they hadn't shown much interest. You couldn't expect PC Plods to show much imagination or sense of humour, he supposed.

They'd made notes on what he had to say about Clare Mills, without asking him anything very searching about it. They had seemed to accept his story, but they must have been suspicious of something in it. Because now these two older blokes in plain clothes were here to see him. So that was one up to the PC Plods.

Lambert and Hook saw a diffident young man with dark red hair and a thin, watchful face. Unusually in this university setting, he wore a conventional shirt and a tie on a sweltering day at the end of June. He had also assumed small-lensed glasses, which sat rather ridiculously halfway down his nose, as if he wished to accentuate the impression of the egghead postgraduate student. The suspicion that the spectacles were not strictly necessary for him was reinforced by the way he took them off and studied them thoughtfully as he made his replies to their questions.

'We won't be disturbed in here on Friday afternoon,' he assured the two big men. He shut the door carefully behind them as they entered the room. It was the book-lined study of one of the tutors in the department, the kind of accommodation Martin hoped to attain for himself if he ever got a permanent appointment in this or another university. He decided against opening the north-facing window, despite the heat, feeling an instinctive need to close this meeting off from the ears of the world.

Martin sat down behind the tutor's desk, trying to look at home there, resisting the temptation to send up his own aspirations, which was his reaction to nervousness. 'I'm happy to give any assistance I can with your investigation into poor Clare Mills's death, though I can't think I can possibly offer anything more than you already know. I saw very little of Clare.'

'Really?' Lambert managed to inject a scepticism into his delivery of the single word which was quite remarkable. He paused for a moment as if gathering his thoughts, though he knew quite well where he was going. Silences always made edgy men more edgy, and he had noted already that Martin Carter was apprehensive. 'We are here to follow up one or two queries which have arisen as a result of statements taken here yesterday by junior members of our team. And to check whether you have recalled anything which you did not tell them yesterday.'

Experience counted for something: Lambert managed to make the routine introduction sound heavy with menace.

Martin had that too-revealing complexion which often goes with red hair. The light skin of his face coloured now as he said, 'Really, I scarcely knew the girl. I was devastated to hear of her death, of course, as we all were, but—'

47

'You seem to have conducted rather more meetings with Clare than you recalled to our officers, Mr Carter.'

Martin didn't like that word 'conducted'. It made it sound as if he had been controlling things. He said, 'I'm sure I told your uniformed officers everything I could.' He could feel his face hot from the blood beneath the skin. 'Perhaps you're not aware of the set-up here. I'm a postgraduate student, doing my own research, using the libraries of this and other universities. Clare was a second-year undergraduate. In the ordinary course of events, we might never have met at all.'

'Nevertheless, in this case you did. And for Clare Mills, life did not follow "the ordinary course of events" or she would not have ended up murdered and thrown into the Severn.'

'No. But I didn't put her there.' He regretted that ridiculous thought as soon as he had voiced it: it seemed to put him closer to the death.

'I'm glad to hear it. Let me explain why we are here.' Lambert stretched his long legs out in front of him as he sat on the upright chair, perfectly at ease as the tension grew in the young man behind the desk. 'Let me explain what happens in a murder investigation of this sort, Mr Carter. We take initial statements from as many people as possible who were in contact with the victim. Where it appears that there are discrepancies or omissions in the statements of individuals, more senior officers return to follow up these interesting anomalies.'

He made it sound as though he were outlining the procedures from a lectern to an audience of interested students, and Martin nodded, as if playing his part in the exchange. Lambert said weightily, 'Sometimes people quite innocently fail to mention certain things, either because they have forgotten them or because they do not consider them relevant.'

Martin Carter waited for him to go on, to add the logical conclusion to his argument, that sometimes people withheld information from more sinister motives, that sometimes people wished to deceive the police. But Lambert said nothing, merely continuing to examine his man's face with that steady, unrelenting stare which Martin was already finding disturbing. He said unwillingly, 'And you're saying that I forgot to tell you something.'

Lambert gave him a small smile. 'I'm saying that there are

48

discrepancies between what you have told our officers and the information we have collected from other people who knew Clare here.'

He had carefully failed to say that these were innocent discrepancies, and Martin was aware of it. 'If I have forgotten anything, I apologize. I can't at this moment think what it might be.'

In his concentration on the long, watchful face of the superintendent, he had almost forgotten the more easy-going presence at his side. DS Bert Hook now opened his notebook, looked at a page of notes he had there, and said, 'You say there was no reason why you and Clare Mills should have come across each other at all in the ordinary course of events. So how did you come to meet?'

Martin forced himself to be calm. They couldn't really know anything, not anything that mattered. 'It is part of the post-graduate ethos in this university to be available to help more junior students.' He was aware that this sounded pompous, and he heard himself give a small involuntary giggle as he added, 'Clare came to ask me about a subject she was considering for her dissertation next year. I believe her tutor suggested that she consult me.'

Hook nodded. 'This was on the fourth of March, I believe. Was that your first meeting with Ms Mills?'

Martin was shaken by the precision of this. That was part of the police method, he supposed. You'd expect them to be good on detail; they'd have to be, with court cases and the like to consider. 'Yes. I couldn't have given you the date, but I'm sure you're right.' Again that incongruous giggle came trilling in on the end of his words, when he least expected it and least wanted it.

'She came to see you about her work.'

'Yes. Not that I was able to help her much. I just told her to narrow the scale down, for a dissertation. You don't want anything too wide, or you can't handle it, when you only have twenty thousand words. People begin by wondering how they're ever going to write so much, and end up by having far too much material to deal with in the space available.' He knew he was going on too much, wanting to enlarge upon this safe area where there could be no traps for him.

49

'But Clare appreciated that?'

'Immediately.' He nodded his head several times in emphasis, as if praising a good pupil to her parents. 'She was a bright girl, who saw the point immediately.'

'So why did she need to see you so often subsequently?'

They'd trapped him, after all. He'd thought this slightly overweight man with the weather-beaten countryman's face would be easy after the gaunt, intense one, but he'd led him straight into this. Martin told himself to be careful, to say as little as possible. 'She didn't. See me very often, I mean.' He felt as though his brain was coming apart with his syntax.

Hook looked down at his notes. 'That's not what other people tell us, Mr Carter. Are you saying they're wrong?' He ran a finger down the page in front of him, and for an awful moment, Martin thought he was going to reel off a series of dates, giving chapter and verse to the lies he had told.

'I – I may have forgotten one or two meetings, I suppose. I wasn't counting, at the time!' Again that awful giggle came in on the end of his words.

'And not all the meetings were in the university, were they?' This was Lambert, back in again, giving him the impression that he was being attacked from all sides, that nothing he said would now be trusted.

'No.' He wondered if he could get away with telling them that they'd met informally to talk about her work, that these meetings had just been a continuation and extension of the first one. But he'd already told them that he'd offered all the advice she needed at that first meeting. And he'd shot himself in the foot when he tried to enlarge on what had seemed the safe area of work. He took the plunge and said, 'Look, you might as well know, I fancied her. Clare was a pretty girl. And she was the same age as I am, because she was a mature student, you see. Twenty-five.'

He wondered if he had the air of a man eagerly enlarging upon an idea which had just occurred to him. That fear was reinforced when Lambert said acidly, 'So why conceal this from us? Why pretend you'd hardly seen a girl with whom you were trying to establish some sort of relationship?'

'The authorities wouldn't approve. They couldn't do anything about it, we're neither of us married. But it would be frowned upon for a postgraduate student to be dating a second-year undergraduate. The older men who control the appointments in the university would think I was taking advantage of my academic status to start a thing with a young student.'

It was thin, desperately thin, and it sounded so even in his own ears as he said it. Lambert said quietly, like a man being as kind as he could to a dumb animal, 'But you were the same age. You just told us that.'

'Yes. I doubt if the men I'm talking about would see that, though. And they're important to me, you see, those people. I'm hoping to get a permanent appointment in the university, after I've completed my Ph.D.' He wondered if professors in the faculty would refute the idea that an appointment to work alongside them was such a prize. Probably not: academics always had exaggerated ideas of the standing of their own university.

But Lambert said inexorably, 'But why conceal it from us? Why lie to police officers who were conducting a murder enquiry?'

The giggle came out this time before he had said anything. 'I wouldn't say I lied, exactly. I might have been a little economical with the truth!'

He managed a weak smile, but it drew no answering smile from the men sitting on the upright chairs on the other side of the desk. He wished suddenly, inconsequentially, that he had not chosen to come into this room here for this meeting, had not attempted to play the academic in his book-lined study.

Lambert said, 'Oh no, Mr Carter, you lied to our officers. You said specifically that you had seen Clare Mills "only once or twice" and not at all in the recent past. It's never a wise thing to start with a string of lies when talking to police officers, and when they're pursuing a murder enquiry, it's positively stupid.'

'Yes. I see that now. I suppose—'

'It immediately makes us wonder not only what the actual facts are, but why someone is lying to us. The reason for lying is usually even more interesting to us than the lies themselves. It often puts people behind bars.' It was time to turn the screw on this strange young man, to get what they could from him whilst he was on the defensive.

'I was a fool. I can see that now.'

'Can you, Mr Carter? I hope so.' Lambert found himself playing the heavy schoolmaster to this penitent young man, who looked suddenly younger and more vulnerable.

Martin turned the steel-rimmed spectacles between his fingers, then folded them and put them down on the desk, as if recognizing with that gesture the course of action he should have taken originally. 'I'm sorry for wasting police time. The truth is that I fancied her, as I say. But it turned out Clare Mills didn't fancy me. We had a couple of meetings – you couldn't even call them dates, I suppose. She let me take her for a drink in a pub during the evening.'

'You had meetings during the day in the university and the town, too.' It was a statement, not a question.

Martin forced a laugh, hoping that it came out better than that wretched giggle. 'Yes. Clare and I met seven or eight times altogether. At first I pretended I could give her more help with her work than I could, and got two or three meetings that way. But she was too bright to need much help from me with her second-year studies, and both of us realized that pretty quickly. We stayed friends and had the odd coffee together. I suppose that when it came to the questioning, I was too vain to want to document the story of my failure to your officers.'

Martin felt himself blushing again, but it was surely natural enough for him to be embarrassed over this confession. Then the giggle came, falling into a silence which seemed suddenly profound in that small room, with its books from floor to ceiling and its isolation from the real world outside.

Neither Lambert nor Hook afforded him the smile which might have eased his embarrassment, which might have signified that the account of his foolishness in concealing the real facts of his relationship with Clare Mills had now been accepted. Instead, Hook made a new entry into his notebook with a sceptical air, while Lambert regarded the face of the man opposite him with an unblinking gravity. Then the superintendent said quietly, 'When did you last see Clare Mills, Mr Carter?'

52

'Thursday of last week.' Martin stared at the desk in front of him, hoping that the precision of this would convince them that he was hiding nothing from them now.

'Two days before she died.' Lambert answered with a matching precision, watching his man as if he expected a false move at any moment. 'And where did this meeting take place?'

'In the Lamb and Flag hotel.' Martin found that his brain seemed to be working again. He told himself that for all their experience, there was nothing these men could do, if he kept it simple.

Lambert watched a group of students, newly released from an exam, comparing notes and talking in excited relief on the lawn outside. They were no more than forty yards away, but through the double-glazed windows they could not be heard, and the mime show reinforced the impression that they were cut off here, playing out a drama which was quite divorced from and altogether more serious than the action on the sunlit grass outside. He made his question heavy with import as he said, 'And exactly what took place at this last meeting between the two of you?'

'Nothing of moment.' Martin froze his features into a mask, but he was thinking furiously.

Hook looked up from his notes. 'That won't do, Mr Carter. This is a murder investigation. And you met the victim two days before she died.'

'Yes. Sorry. I suppose I was just trying to preserve my self-esteem. Silly, really, when the poor girl's been killed. Well, she turned me down at that last meeting. Finally turned me down, I mean. We'd never been more than friends, even though I'd wanted it to go further. We agreed that evening that there was nothing in it for either of us, that we wouldn't meet again. I – I'm sorry I've wasted your time like this.'

The last of his involuntary giggles rang out like a bizarre epitaph on the interview.

Nine

'Denis' was acquiring an identity. An official identity, he hoped.

But he was more worldly-wise now than when he had come into the country from Croatia. He had money, but it had come from grinding toil in the fruit-fields of Herefordshire. He wasn't going to give up the money he had worked so hard to earn without having something in his hands to show for it. You didn't buy things in pubs: that was one of the first things he had learned from the people he had spoken to in this strange, exciting land.

So he had refused to give the man with the hooded anorak even a first payment on the document. Rather to Denis's surprise, the man had accepted that. But he said that without an advance deposit, the passport would cost four hundred rather than three hundred pounds: take it or leave it.

Denis had taken it.

It meant that everything he had saved so far would be gone. But he would have something to show for it. The man pulled the hood even closer about his head and agreed that he should have the passport on Friday night. Indistinguishable from the real thing, he said. Good enough to get you a work permit anywhere in the EU, he said. Denis found it difficult to take a man seriously who slid a hood over his face in that melodramatic manner, when there was so little danger around: no flying bullets, no machetes which could take off a limb with a single descending blow. Seeing the things Denis had seen gave you a real perception of danger.

Denis wanted to tell the man to stop playing games, to point out that the way he was behaving was more likely to attract attention than to help him to pass unnoticed. But he couldn't afford to insult him, not if the man could really provide the services he claimed to offer. They agreed a price. The man looked from side to side suspiciously along the wall of the small, deserted room at the back of the pub and said, 'What name do you want on the passport?'

'Pimbury,' said the man from Croatia impulsively. 'Denis Pimbury.' The name had sprung to his lips without a conscious thought about it. He remembered that he had seen it somewhere in the newspaper, one day during the week; he read *The Times* in the evenings, to improve his English. He couldn't remember the context, but the name must have appealed to him, to come straight into his mouth like that. Just occasionally, the instinctive things were the best.

The man made him spell out the name on paper, then nodded and put it into a hidden pocket. He insisted that he would only meet Denis again after darkness had fallen: he was a creature of the night, he implied, who could not operate outside his natural environment.

That meant that three days later, Denis was now sitting with his half of lager in a corner of the pub as the noise grew and the people around him got rowdier and rowdier on Friday night. The English with the weekend ahead of them were a revelation to Denis. There was something frantic about their enjoyment. It was as if they would be breaking some sort of rule if the laughter did not get louder and louder as the evening proceeded and their world passed into a warm summer darkness.

After the storms at the beginning of the week, the weather had settled again and the temperatures had climbed. Denis glanced from time to time through the narrow window behind him, watching the approach of the darkness, trying to catch the first sight of the evening star which had shone upon him in those savage days of fighting in Kosovo. Eventually he could stand the waiting no longer, and went out into the yard behind the pub. He stood among the empty steel kegs, watching the sky turn from rich blue to navy, willing it towards blackness. The English darkness fell slowly, especially when you were anxious to have it drop protectively around your shoulders.

It was warm out here, with not a breath of wind within the old brick walls which enclosed the yard. With the high elevation of the pub behind him, he could see only a tiny section of the sky, and as yet very few stars. Without any warning, the thought sprang into his mind that this was not unlike the stifling darkness of six nights earlier, when Clare's life had been so abruptly ended.

He went back into the small room where they had agreed to meet at the back of the pub. He had lost his seat with his absence. He stood awkwardly in the corner, but after a couple of minutes, the group which had taken over his spot made a noisy exit, and he was able to slip again behind the small round table, where he could watch the door.

The landlord called for last orders, and people rushed to the bar in that other strange English ritual. It looked as if the man was not coming. Well, you won't be any worse off if he doesn't, Denis told himself. You haven't handed over any money, this time. All the same, he felt a desolation, as if he had been made more alone and vulnerable in the world by this attempt which had failed. Then he began to wonder if he had been betrayed. He had grown used to a world of secret police, where the knock at the door at night was the most feared sound of all. Would the British police come here tonight, nodding to each other when they saw him, taking him without a word to a cell? Would this strange and exciting odyssey, which had taken him across Europe and into the lotus-land of Herefordshire orchards, end as quietly as that?

Then he saw the man, just inside the door of the pub, with the hood still up on his anorak on this stifling night. He was so relieved that he wanted to shout a welcome. As he had done when he had arranged this transaction, he found himself wanting to tell this ridiculous figure that he was attracting attention, not escaping it, by his strange garb on a hot night at the end of June.

Instead, Denis said nothing. Instinctively vigilant from years of experience of danger, he signalled that he had noticed the man only by the faintest nod. The man stood still for a moment, looking back behind him into the noisy pub. Then he stepped into the small room and sidled over to Denis, lowering the hood and sneaking glances around the room, like a pantomime villain. 'You got the money?' he asked hoarsely.

'I've got it.' Denis could scarcely believe that this comic-opera figure was going to produce what he needed. He told himself that this was just a go-between, that the real work, the real deception was performed by a skilful forger with a powerful lamp at his shoulder, in some quiet workshop miles from here. Denis fingered the money in the pocket of his jeans. At least this man seemed to be on his own. One of his fears had been that he would come up against three or four anonymous heavies, who would beat him up and take his money without even pretending to offer him the goods. He said, 'I want to see it, before I pay.' Then, as the man moved automatically towards the door into the yard, he said, 'Here, not out there. Where I can examine it. See how genuine it looks.'

This creature of the night glanced longingly at the door and the darkness, then looked him fully in the face for the first time. 'All right!' he said. 'I suppose that's fair enough.'

In that moment, it flashed in upon Denis that this man had not done much of this trafficking before, that he was almost as inexperienced in these transactions as Denis was himself.

The knowledge gave him confidence. 'Listen to me,' he said with soft menace. 'I'm going to inspect the goods before I pay. On this table. There's no one watching us: I've been here for an hour. If the work's as good as you promised, you'll get your money.' He noticed how his accent came out more strongly with his excitement, how his sibilants hissed with the tension of the moment.

The man looked round the crowded pub, took in the various groups of noisy, unheeding drinkers. He was younger than Denis had thought at their first meeting, with delicate, almost girlish hands. Denis noted them with surprise as the man produced the document like a conjurer from the recesses of his clothing. 'You'll find it's good,' he said. 'Let's have the money!'

He kept his hand on top of the envelope, and there was a slapstick moment when it seemed that neither of them trusted the other enough to make the first concession. Then Denis waved his bundle of notes briefly in front of him and the man reluctantly slid the envelope towards him across the table.

Denis extracted the slim, dark-red booklet from the envelope and looked at it. His first reaction was that it didn't look much for four hundred pounds. Gold capital letters spelt out 'EUROPEAN UNION. UNITED KINGDOM OF GREAT BRITAIN AND NORTHERN IRELAND.' Then there was a coat of arms, with Latin he did not understand, and beneath it the magic word, 'PASSPORT.'

Denis looked inside. There were pages of writing he did not understand. Then he turned over the page and saw the photograph he had taken of himself in the booth in Gloucester staring out at him. He should have allowed himself to smile a little in the darkness, he thought: this man looked more foreign because he was glaring so tensely at the lens. But beside the photograph it said that this man was Denis Pimbury, born in Bristol on the twentieth of December 1978. And then the magic description in capitals: 'BRITISH CITIZEN'.

'Get you anything you want, that will,' said the man. Denis had no idea whether he was right, but by now he was looking round so nervously and theatrically that Denis feared again for their safety. The sooner this was over, the better. He slid his four hundred pounds swiftly across the small metal table and slipped the envelope carefully into the front pocket of his jeans.

There were drunks upon the streets. He skirted a couple of groups carefully, wanting no trouble, feeling the slim package against his thigh with every step, hoping it was not as noticeable as his raging senses told him it was.

Back in his room, he studied his costly trophy for a long time, working out the meaning of the officialese of its opening pages with a strange combination of difficulty and relish. Belatedly, he realized that he had no real idea of what a passport should look like. And now that Clare was gone, there was no one he could turn to for advice or reassurance.

But he spent a long time staring at the page with his photograph on it, as if by doing so he could make his new identity part of his very bones. He was Denis Pimbury now, British citizen, born twenty-six and a half years ago in Bristol. He signed that name in the space beside the photograph, as the man who brought this treasure to him had told him to do.

He would tell the farmer on Monday, make himself a proper employee. He would 'get his feet under the table'. He hadn't been able to comprehend that expression when someone had first used it to him, but he thought he understood it better now. It meant you were one of the tribe. One who could pass unnoticed. So long as you thought yourself properly into the role. So long as you became the person in your passport.

Denis Pimbury, British Citizen.

Ten

Judith Hudson stood looking down from the doorway of the high stone house as Hook parked the car in the turning circle in front of it.

She took them into the comfortable sitting room where Hook had come with the young woman constable to bring the first news of her daughter's death. It had wide sash windows on two sides and a Degas reproduction on the longest wall. A tray with a coffee pot and what looked like home-made biscuits had been placed on the low coffee table in the middle of the floor.

When Hook had introduced his chief, Mrs Hudson said, 'I thought you'd appreciate coffee, as you're having to work on a Saturday morning.' She was almost like she was trying to sell them the house, thought Lambert. And she was wearing what looked to him a very expensive grey dress, as though she was trying to make the best possible impression on her visitors. Perhaps she was trying to sell herself. But he had never known a woman who had lost her daughter try to do anything like that, in the days following the death.

He said, 'I'm sorry to intrude at a time like this. But I'm sure you will understand that if we're to track down the person who killed your daughter, we have to move as quickly as possible. And that means getting to know as much as we can about a girl who cannot speak for herself from those who were closest to her.'

'I understand. And it goes without saying that I want to see you put the man who killed Clare behind bars as quickly as possible.'

She was curiously controlled: unnaturally so, it seemed to Lambert, who was well used to the various manifestations of grief. And she had immediately spoken of their murderer as a man, when he had carefully left the gender of the killer open in his conventional introduction. He said, 'There is no objection to your husband being present for this meeting, if you prefer it. Perhaps, indeed—'

'He isn't here today. Pressure of work, you know. Sometimes you have to go in on a Saturday morning, when you run your own business.'

Yet Hook had stated when he arranged this meeting that they would need to talk to both husband and wife, that it would be quite in order for Roy Hudson to be present when they spoke with his wife. Lambert wondered which of them had taken the decision to ignore that suggestion. Was it that man who had so carefully kept them at arm's length on the previous day, or this well-groomed woman who was now composedly pouring coffee, with no outward sign of grief for the daughter whose body she had identified on Thursday? Or had they agreed together, for some reason that he could not begin to work out, that they should be seen separately?

He said, 'The last time Clare was seen was apparently by her flatmate last Saturday afternoon. We are presuming that she was killed some time on the Saturday evening. We haven't yet got the full written post-mortem report – it may be waiting for us at Oldford CID this morning – but we know that the findings support that timing. I presume you have no reason to think that she was alive after that.'

'No. I hadn't heard from her for some days before that.'

'Did she seem in any way distressed or fearful when she spoke to you?'

'No. I can't even remember the details of our conversation. It was just a conventional mother–daughter exchange, I expect.'

Many people would have broken down on that thought, with a searing regret that the last exchange had not been more meaningful, that they could not even remember the details of what had been said. Instead of that, Judith Hudson touched her well-coiffured ash-blonde hair with the back of her hand and said, like the most conventional middle-class hostess, 'Do help yourself to the biscuits, Sergeant Hook. They'll be wasted if you don't eat them, you know.'

Lambert thought of his own daughters, who were about the

same age as this girl who had died so mysteriously, and how he would feel if either of them was killed. Irritation cut through his carapace of politeness as he said, 'We need your help. You must know things about your daughter which are going to be vital in this investigation.'

She looked at him with intelligent brown eyes and said, 'I'm not even sure how Clare died. Was she drowned?'

It was wrong again, unnatural. If she really didn't know, she should have asked the question much earlier, when Hook had seen her with the woman constable to inform her about the death, or at the latest when Hook had taken her to identify the body on Thursday. 'No, Mrs Hudson, she wasn't drowned. She was strangled. And then someone, presumably the murderer, took her body and dumped it into the Severn.'

He had made it as abrupt and brutal as possible, certain now that there was no real grief here. But she merely nodded quietly and said, 'Where was that?'

'We don't know, as yet. We may never know. The corpse had been in the water for about three days when it was found at Lydney on Wednesday morning.'

'Yes. Sergeant Hook here warned me that there was some damage from the water when I went to identify the body. It wasn't as bad as I expected, not on the face, anyway.' She sounded as if she were reporting on some minor scientific experiment.

'She had not been sexually assaulted, as far as we can tell.' He volunteered the information most parents would have demanded in the first shocking minutes of their knowledge of the death.

'That is good, I suppose.' She spoke not spontaneously, but like one picking her words with care.

'Mrs Hudson, please do not take this the wrong way, but I have to say that you seem to me unnaturally calm about this.' Almost like one who was expecting it, Lambert thought. But of course he could not say that, not yet. Not until they had a lot more evidence against this strange woman. He was striving not to dislike her, because the code said that personal feelings should never be allowed into an interview, since they would obviously affect your objectivity. Yet in the thirty years since he had been a fresh-faced young constable he had never

61

met a mother who seemed less affected by her daughter's death; perhaps this was one you couldn't play by the book.

Judith Hudson sipped her coffee and looked at him coolly. 'I think "unnaturally calm" is probably a fair summary. I find myself calmer than I could ever have imagined myself in the face of this week's news. Superintendent, I think you should know that Clare and I were not as close as other mothers and daughters.'

He wanted to say that he had seen that already, that it seemed to him patently an understatement. Instead, he said, 'And why was that?'

She smiled. 'Perhaps a psychiatrist could tell you. No doubt it reflects some serious defect in my character.'

Lambert let out a little of his irritation with this infuriatingly calm woman as he said sharply, 'We're trying to find who killed Clare. The least you can do is give us the fullest possible picture of her relationship with you.'

She smiled, accepting the logic of his argument. He wondered for a disconcerting moment if this woman ever lost her control, whether she shouted her passion between the sheets with that other enigmatic figure, Roy Hudson. As he hastily banished that image, Judith Hudson said, 'It was better when she was a child. Even then, I never seemed as close to Clare as other mothers were to their children. When I met her out of school, for instance, she never seemed to need me the way other children needed their parents.'

Lambert, feeling like a psychiatrist listening to a patient, looked rather desperately at Hook, who said, 'And how did Clare get on with her father?'

'She was always closer to him than she was to me.' Judith Hudson seized on that idea eagerly. 'I used to tell myself that girls always liked their fathers best, that I shouldn't be jealous of Ken. Adolescent girls are always half in love with their dads, aren't they?'

Hook smiled at her sudden animation. 'I only have sons, myself, Mrs Hudson. But I'm told that's true. Perhaps I'm missing out. So how did Clare receive the news that you were getting divorced?'

She looked as if she had been slapped across the face. Bert Hook got people off their guard quite effortlessly, with his genuine, avuncular interest, and then threw the difficult question at them when they were least expecting it. 'She didn't take it well. She was very upset, if you must know.'

'We must, I'm afraid. But it's not unusual, you know, for adolescent girls to be disturbed and difficult, in circumstances like that.' It was stating the obvious, but this woman seemed emotionally ignorant, to be lacking any knowledge of those instinctive responses which were the essence of being human. 'Did Clare keep in touch with her father?'

'Yes. She wouldn't hear of taking my new name of Hudson when I remarried. Her father was working in Oxford for a year or so, and she visited him a lot. It was a real blow to her when Ken found himself a new wife and emigrated to New Zealand.' A small smile crept onto Judith Hudson's face, as if she were relishing the memory of her daughter's distress.

Hook said, prompting her towards further revelation of herself, 'You must have had some trying times, in those years.'

'It wasn't easy. She made life as difficult as she could for me and for Roy. And then she made the most unsuitable marriage. I sometimes thought that it was part of her defiance, that she took up with Ian Walker just to annoy me.'

'So tell us about him, please.'

Judith shrugged. 'There isn't much to tell. He's a rogue, pure and simple. He's been in and out of trouble since he was a boy. But he's more intelligent than he pretends to be: don't let him fool you about that. Clare had known him a little at school. She flounced in one night and told us she was going to marry him. I thought it was just a bad joke at first, something she'd engineered just to annoy me.'

There was another explanation, thought Bert Hook. A girl, desperately unhappy at home, snatching at the first opportunity to get out of it, however unsuitable the means. He felt the familiar frustration that a murder victim, unlike the victim of any other crime, could never balance the scales with her own version of events. He said, 'We know about Ian Walker's record. We spoke to him ourselves, yesterday morning.'

'Then you'll know what a thoroughly unsavoury character he is.'

'You must have been glad when the marriage ended without any children.'

'Yes. But he'd ruined her education, among other things. She'd left school when she should have been going on to university. In effect, she gave up her education to get a job and support that waster.' There was a sudden hiss of hatred on the last phrase. It was what you would have expected, in the circumstances she described, but coming from this emotionless woman, any display of feeling was almost a relief.

'Are you still in touch with Ian Walker?'

'No. I haven't seen him for years.'

'He seems to have been in contact with Clare, not long before she died.'

'He'd be after money, then, I expect. He's a sponger, as well as everything else. I could cheerfully murder Ian Walker myself.' But she said it without passion, as if she were studying herself objectively and being surprised by the thought.

'Were you aware that he was still in touch with Clare?'

'No. It doesn't surprise me. But any contact from him would be bad news, I'm sure.'

'Do you think he killed Clare, Mrs Hudson?'

She examined the notion for a moment, as dispassionately as if she were considering the murder of some girl she had never known. 'He might have done. He hasn't the guts or the intelligence to plan a murder, but he might have strangled her in the heat of the moment, if they had a row. He'd certainly have known some quiet spot to dump her body in the Severn.'

It was so exactly what Lambert had thought about the man that it made the hairs rise on the back of his neck, coming from this source. He said hastily, 'We have as yet no reason to suspect Mr Walker of this crime. And it would be best if you kept your own thoughts on the matter to yourself.'

'Of course. Detection is your business, not mine.'

Lambert nodded and took up the questioning again. 'Do you know anything about a man named Martin Carter?'

'No. I don't think Clare ever mentioned him. Who is he?'

'He's a postgraduate student, doing research for a degree at the university. He helped Clare a little with her studies. He was pretty well the same age as Clare. I thought she might have mentioned him when she was at home.'

'No. Not that I can recall. Look, Superintendent, there's something you should know. Clare didn't come home during these last few months. My contacts were by phone. She made regular calls, to keep in touch.'

But you didn't report any disquiet to the police or the university when the regular phone call never came last week, he thought. As an ordinary mother might have done. But they'd already had ample proof that this was no ordinary mother. He said, 'Why did Clare stop coming home?'

She looked as if she was considering the question for the first time. 'A variety of reasons, I should think. Excitement over her new studies at university: she was a bright girl, who should have been reading for a degree five years earlier. When you start late, you want to make the most of it, people tell me. New friends: she hadn't had many of those, during her years with Walker. Perhaps a new boyfriend, for all I know. What about this man you mentioned a moment ago.'

'Martin Carter? He says not. It seems he would have been willing, but Clare wasn't.'

'Someone else, then. I know from the phone calls that she was enjoying being at the university.'

'Yes. It must have been quite a decision for her, embarking on a degree course as a mature student. Did you offer her any financial assistance?'

'No. She wouldn't have accepted it.'

The same reply as her husband had given them. Lambert would have given a lot to hear the exchanges in this strange household when Clare Mills had announced that she was going back into full-time study. He said, 'Do you think one of the reasons why Clare no longer came here was the presence of your husband in the house?'

For a moment, it looked as if she would react angrily. A flash of temper would have been a relief from this disturbingly composed woman. But then she collected the coffee cups and put them back on the tray, like a stage actress using props during a pregnant pause. 'I shouldn't think so. Roy and Clare had their problems, during the early years, but they now have – had – an excellent relationship.'

The same phrase her husband had used. Lambert wondered how much collusion there had been over what they would tell him. 'Did they see much of each other?'

'Very little, over the last year or two.' She smiled at him.

'I won't deny that that probably contributed to the improvement in the way they got on with each other.'

Lambert wondered just how well she herself got on with the absent Roy Hudson. Each of them had so far seemed determined that they would not meet him together. He said rather desperately, 'Is there anything you wish to ask us?'

He would have expected her to ask when she could have the body for burial. That was one of the things which always upset parents, when he had to explain that the body had to be retained indefinitely, that when someone was eventually charged with this killing he would have the right to a second, independent post-mortem examination, if his defence requested it. Instead, Judith Hudson said after a moment, 'Are you close to an arrest?'

He smiled. 'You probably realize that I would hardly be likely to tell you if we were. Until we actually have someone under lock and key, most of our findings have to remain confidential. But I will tell you that we are at present still in the early stages of the enquiry. That is why we need all the help we can get, from the relatives and friends of Clare Mills.'

He had used the girl's full name like a rebuke, and Judith Hudson said immediately, 'Yes. I'm sorry I haven't been able to be more helpful to you. But you will appreciate that owing to the circumstances surrounding her, I haven't seen much of Clare in the last few years. First of all, she was involved in a marriage of which Roy and I both thoroughly disapproved, and then she was studying at the university.'

She made both of these circumstances sound like deliberate attacks upon her by the dead girl. He said, almost accusingly, 'But you must have been happy to see Clare justifying her educational potential at last. You said you had been upset when she gave up the chance of university in order to get married.'

'Yes, of course. And it's good to hear that she was doing well.'

But apparently you didn't know that until I told you today, thought Lambert. And shouldn't you now be desperate to get into her flat in Gloucester, to retrieve whatever souvenirs you can of the daughter who has gone?

Lambert stood up and said, 'Please get in touch immediately

66

if anything occurs to you which might have a bearing on this death.' He paused in the doorway as she nodded dutifully. 'I'm afraid we can't release anything from Clare's flat at the moment. We've had to bag up a lot of her belongings and take them away. We don't know yet what may prove to be evidence later in the case.'

'What belongings?'

'I couldn't be precise. Our Scenes of Crime team will have taken away whatever they think might eventually be significant.'

'What sort of things?' She was showing more interest than at any time since they had arrived in that high, comfortable room.

'Photographs. Letters, if there are any. A diary, if we're exceptionally lucky. But I understand there was no diary or list of engagements, in this case.'

He had thrown that fragment he would normally have concealed at her to see what reaction it would bring. It was difficult to be certain of anything with this unnaturally composed woman.

But he thought he caught a fleeting glimpse of relief in her face.

Eleven

Detective Inspector Christopher Rushton enjoyed being in CID on a Saturday morning.

There were people around, of course, but nothing like the same buzz of activity as on weekday mornings. Crime does not shut down for the weekend, but policemen, like other workers, only work on Saturdays and Sundays if the rotas demand it. Chris Rushton appreciated the time to check through his computer files, to make sure that everything had been recorded as it should be, and, most importantly, to do the cross-referencing that sometimes threw up significant connections and led eventually to arrests.

You could only make these complex connections and use the modern technology to its full potential if you had time to yourself, in Chris's view. That old reactionary Lambert and his faithful dog Hook were out seeing Clare Mills's mother this morning. That would allow the inspector, who was co-ordinating the documentation of the case at Oldford police station, the opportunity to concentrate and do his own thinking. He was relishing the time at his computer when the duty sergeant made a call from the reception desk to say that there was a young woman who wanted to see him, who had indeed asked for him by name.

The sergeant plainly thought this a matter for levity, but Chris ordered him brusquely to send the lady through to see him.

She was a pretty, dark-haired girl of around twenty, he thought. She announced herself as Anne Jackson, and it took him a moment to remember that she was the student who had been the flatmate of the dead woman, Clare Mills. That she was in fact the girl they had talked to when he had visited that flat with Superintendent Lambert only two days earlier.

He was annoyed with himself for not recognizing her immediately: it should be part of a CID man's mental equipment to remember faces and pin names upon them immediately, in his view. But she had jettisoned the ubiquitous student's dress of jeans and T-shirt and put on a very pleasant green cotton dress and make-up. And Chris, who was no expert in these things, thought that she had acquired a new hair-style in the last forty-eight hours.

These things couldn't possibly be for his benefit. It was probably that like many people she was nervous about venturing into a police station, and had responded by putting on her best clothes and her best appearance. He tried not to read anything flattering into the fact that she had asked for Inspector Rushton by name. She must simply have remembered it from their meeting on Thursday.

He tried not to sound like the older generation as he said, 'And what can I do for you, Miss Jackson?'

'It's a bit embarrassing, really.' She blushed. It went very prettily with the green dress. 'There's something I should have told you, when you came with your superintendent to see me at the flat the other day.'

Rushton, who was normally both very stern about such omissions and completely devoid of small-talk, heard himself saying, 'I'm sure it can't be anything very serious, in your case.' He followed that unwarranted assumption with an encouraging smile.

Anne smiled back at him. He was really rather attractive to look at, and he seemed quite nice, when you got through his grave manner. 'Anyway, I'm glad I've been able to get you and not Superintendent Lambert. He frightened me to death!'

'John Lambert?' He enjoyed using the superintendent's Christian name. Normally, with his exaggerated consciousness of rank, he found that difficult, but this morning he was happy to show his familiarity with the great man to this pretty girl. 'Oh, John's bark's much worse than his bite. He comes from the old school, you know. His methods may be a little antiquated, but he gets results.' He wondered what the chief would think if he heard his inspector being so patronizingly magnanimous about him.

'Yes. Well, I've never been involved in anything like this

69

before, and I got a bit confused, I think. I was thrown by the way he kept looking at me all the time. He never seemed to blink, and he seemed to be weighing up everything I said and wondering whether it was really the truth.'

Chris smiled encouragingly. 'Well, fortunately, I've never been on the wrong end of John Lambert's interrogations. I think I see what you mean, but I can assure you he can be much fiercer than that, when he feels that anyone is really trying to conceal things from him.'

But he was thinking back to Thursday and Lambert's remark as they drove away from her flat: 'I wonder what it was that the girl was trying to conceal from us.' He hadn't noticed anything himself, had thought at the time that the chief was just being fanciful, trying to give himself mystique. But it seemed the old bugger had been right.

Chris Rushton said, 'I think you'd better put things right, then. Let's hear all about this terrible thing you were confused into concealing.' He couldn't really believe he was playing this so lightly, when he would normally have been as stern as a Victorian parent. It surely couldn't be anything to do with Anne Jackson's large, attentive eyes. They were a very dark, very intriguing blue, he thought.

Anne smiled at him again, to show him how grateful she was for his sympathy. You'd never have thought he was a policeman, really, not in his powder-blue sweater and his neatly creased navy trousers. He didn't seem to have a single grey hair. He must surely be very bright, to have become an inspector when he was still so young. She fumbled in the big leather shoulder bag she had brought with her, finding it surprisingly difficult to take her eyes from Inspector Rushton's face and concentrate upon the contents of the bag.

Anne said, 'It's this, you see.' And she held up a mobile phone in her small hand, as dramatically as if she had produced a knife dripping with blood.

'Yours?' said Rushton.

'No. It belonged to Clare Mills.' The name of the dead woman dropped between them like a barrier, and she wondered if he was going to rebuke her, to tell her that she had been concealing evidence, or something of that sort. Then she rushed on with an explanation, feeling herself blushing furiously as she changed tack during it. 'I forgot all about it at the time. Well, no, that's not strictly true. I knew that Clare had just put some money on it, and I thought I might as well use the calls up and save myself a bit of cash.' It came out all in a rush; she felt she should be standing like a naughty school-girl and pleading for mercy, not sitting comfortably opposite this attractive man.

Chris said as harshly as he could, 'We really should have had this at the time we saw you, you know. It might give us some leads.'

'I know. I realize that now. I'm sorry.' She wanted to say again how glad she was that she'd got him and not that horrid Lambert, but she'd done that one already.

'You should have given it to the Scenes of Crime team when they examined the flat and took away some of Clare's belongings.'

'Yes. But I wasn't there when they searched the place, you see. I was at the uni. The landlord let them in.'

'Well, at least you've brought it here now. And I suppose it's less than two days since we saw you.'

'Yes. And I haven't used it at all. I've scarcely touched it. Everything that was on there when Clare left should still be there now.'

He was suddenly torn by conflicting emotions. The CID man in him was desperate to conclude the formalities and see her gone, to examine the phone and find what it could tell him about the contacts the dead woman had made in the last days, perhaps the last hours, of her life. But another part of him, asserting itself surprisingly and startlingly, wanted to prolong his exchanges with this girl, who grew more attractive with each minute of her embarrassment, who seemed so grateful for the understanding he was according her.

Chris Rushton said, 'As I told you just now, you've done the right thing in bringing this to us. I think I can assure you that there won't be any recriminations from John Lambert for your forgetting to mention it on Thursday.'

He'd said 'forgetting' when both of them knew that she hadn't forgotten it at all on Thursday. She was grateful to him for that, was still thinking how human and understanding Inspector Rushton had been when she was back in the bright sun outside the police station. She had a feeling that she might see him again.

Inside the CID section Chris Rushton was so affected that he sat looking at the wide blue sky beyond his window for a moment. You couldn't get too friendly with people who might be involved, however peripherally, as witnesses in a murder case, he told himself. Anne wouldn't even know that he found her attractive, he thought bleakly. And he hadn't even managed to give her his first name.

Roy Hudson was waiting for the call. The phone hardly rang before he had the receiver in his hand.

'They've gone.' His wife's voice was quite calm; he felt the contrast in his own racing pulses.

'Only just gone? I've been expecting you to phone for the last half-hour. They must have given you quite a grilling, then.'

'They've been gone ten minutes now. I wanted to make sure they weren't coming back before I rang you. You said we had to be careful.' She looked at the clock in her kitchen, noted that it was two minutes slow. Perhaps the battery was running down. She felt almost unnaturally calm.

He should have been grateful for that calm; he had counselled her towards it, after all. Instead, he found it infuriating. 'What did they talk to you about?'

'Nothing much, really. I gave them coffee and biscuits to lower the tension, as you suggested. They raised the things we'd thought they'd raise. How I'd felt about Clare. How close we were to her.'

'So what did you say?'

'What we'd agreed. That I hadn't seen a lot of her recently. That we'd kept in touch by phone.'

'And they believed you?' He tried to keep the anxiety out of his voice.

'I think so.' Like many people who are detached and self-contained, she was not good at estimating other people's reactions to her.

'Why do you think so?' His impatience leapt into the question.

'Well, they didn't question me too much about it. I made it a sort of concession, you see, to tell them that she'd only been phoning me. They'd thought Clare was still coming home regularly, and I said, no, she wasn't, that we were only in touch by phone. And they didn't have to trip me up to make me say it. I volunteered the information. That's what we agreed, isn't it?'

'Yes, that's what we agreed. We thought they'd be bound to find out from someone else that she hadn't been coming home. From her flatmate, or someone else at the university.' It was almost like recalling it to a stranger.

'Yes. They didn't seem to have found that out, though. They seemed to think she had been coming home. So I'm sure they thought I was being completely honest with them when I disabused them of that notion.'

She was so perfectly cool. He envied her that. And yet he knew that it was a dangerous coolness; her disconnection from ordinary feelings helped her to play out situations cleverly, but made her insensitive to what others were feeling about her. 'Did they ask about me?'

'Yes. I told them you had an excellent relationship with Clare. That was what we agreed, wasn't it?' It was her first touch of uncertainty. She was pathetically anxious to please him.

'Yes. Insofar as I had a relationship with her at all. I'd not been in touch with her in the months before her death, don't forget.'

'No. I told them that.'

'Did they talk about Walker?'

'Yes. I said neither of us liked him. Said he'd been a disaster for Clare. They said he'd been in some sort of contact with her, quite recently. I got the impression they think he might have killed her.'

He was suddenly impatient with her. 'Of course they do. A husband is always a suspect. And a husband like him even more so.'

'Perhaps he did kill her.'

'It's my bet he did, Judith.' He tried to put all his old affection into the name. 'Let's hope they soon arrest him.'

He looked at the phone thoughtfully for a moment when he had rung off. It was terrible when a husband and wife couldn't trust each other.

Twelve

Sara Green strode around the cottage for the third time since she had received the phone call. She knew by now that there was nothing they could find suspicious, but she could not sit still. Movement was release of a kind; even feverish and repetitive movement like this.

They came precisely at one fifteen, just as she had suggested. She had the one-day cricket on when they arrived, flannelled fools flitting to and fro in a green scene which seemed a world away from the one into which she had put herself. She hastened to switch it off, but they appeared in no hurry, seemed for a moment to be almost like normal visitors.

'Sergeant Hook was a doughty practitioner at that game,' said Superintendent Lambert with a smile. 'Seam bowler, who's made a few good batsmen hop about a bit, in his time.'

'I know. One of the linch-pins of Herefordshire cricket for fifteen years and more.' She found that she was absurdly pleased to be able to produce this snippet of information, which one of her male colleagues at the university had retailed to her.

'Other times, other places,' said Hook with a dismissive smile. But he was obviously male enough to be pleased to have his prowess recognized. Sara wondered whether to tell them that she had once been quite good at the great game herself, that she had played women's cricket to county level. But something told her that there was a limit to how matey you could get with such people, that this was a business visit for them and she should give her full attention to that.

And sure enough, Lambert said at that moment, 'Let me explain why we wanted to see you, Miss Green. At the beginning of a murder investigation, our team gathers in a huge amount of information, from all sorts of different sources.

When this has been digested and cross-referenced, we follow up any small contradictions which present themselves. It's as simple as that.'

'And that's why you've come to see me on a Saturday afternoon.'

He smiled again. 'Yes. How well did you know Clare Mills?'

After the polite preliminaries, the question fell like an accusation into the comfortable room, with its low, beamed ceiling and its cottage suite. Sara swallowed, her throat suddenly very dry. 'I knew her as a good student. As an able woman, who was going to get a good degree and sort out her life.'

Lambert studied the serious, unlined face beneath the neat black hair for a moment before he said slowly, 'That is what you told our officers when they made the original enquiries.'

'Yes.'

'But other people have indicated to us that your relationship with Clare was rather closer than that.'

The gossips. Malignant as usual, doing all the harm they could to you, as they had when Clare had been alive. The people with trivial, boring lives, who lived out their small, petty excitements through studying the behaviour of other, more daring and original spirits.

Sara forced an acerbic smile, then said, 'Some people like to speculate about such things. I said Clare was a good student. We had interests in common. I suppose you could say we became friends. I wasn't going to claim that. Some people claim friendship very easily. I like to think it goes a little deeper than the number of times we spoke, when I assert that someone is a friend.'

'Commendable, I'm sure. But that's a different matter from claiming that you hardly knew a girl who is now dead. Especially when she is a murder victim. I should have thought you would want to be as frank as possible, to assist in the hunt for her killer. Unless, of course, you had something to hide from us.'

He was staring at her steadily, unnervingly. She was not used to it, and it upset her. She felt she should show that his insinuation infuriated her. But all she did was to say limply, 'I don't know why you should think that.'

His grey eyes seemed to look into her very soul in the pause which followed. Then he said quietly, 'I think it is time you told us the truth, Miss Green.'

She wanted to do just that, wanted to have the relief of confession, like a child bursting into tears and revealing all. But she was not a child; she was a responsible adult in her thirties, with all the restrictions that put upon your conduct. When you had embarked upon deception, you could not let it drop away from you like a child shedding a coat. She knew the situation was hopeless now, but she struggled on, as if having her pretences stripped away was part of some elaborate ritual. 'I'm surprised you listen to gossip and mischief-making like this, Superintendent. Perhaps you are not aware that academics can be as petty as anyone else. Perhaps more so, in some circumstances.'

'And what about the other evidence? Are you prepared to deny what we found in Clare Mills's flat?'

'What did you find there?' The question was out before she was aware of framing it, as if it came from someone else.

Lambert nodded to Hook, who bent over his briefcase and began to search methodically within it. Everything seemed now to be in slow motion; Sara wanted to scream at this stolid man to speed up his movements. Detective Sergeant Hook produced a small folder, said with irritating deliberation, 'These are some of the items removed from Clare Mills's bedroom by the Scenes of Crime team. They are copies, of course, not the originals.'

He handed her three photographs.

Sara's pulses seemed to stop for a moment as she held the pictures in her hand. There was one of herself in profile, looking towards the ceiling in that silly Hollywood film-star pose which they had laughed at together. There was one of her in shorts, on the balcony of the Shakespeare Memorial Theatre at Stratford, overlooking the river. And there was the one the passer-by had taken for them outside the cathedral in Worcester, with their arms shyly around each other's waists, smiling boldly and defiantly at the camera together.

That was the one she had kept on her own dressing table in the bedroom, the one she had swept away into the drawer of the sideboard when she had known these men would be coming. She looked automatically now at that tightly closed drawer, and the gaze of that hateful man Lambert followed the movement of her head. For an awful moment, she thought he would rise and walk over to the sideboard. That he would pull open the drawer and reveal the dozen small intimacies she had stowed so hastily away from their view.

Instead, he said quietly, almost sympathetically, 'It's time you told us everything you have to tell, don't you think?'

She said defensively, as if she were defending herself to her professor, 'Clare was twenty-five. And she wasn't a student of mine. There was nothing improper in our association. Certainly nothing illegal.'

Lambert gave her his first smile. They all knew she was going to talk now: he was interested only in encouraging her. 'Of course not. But I urge you now to be completely open about this.'

'Well, I liked Clare from the first. And I think she liked me. We became firm friends quite quickly.' She nodded a little to herself, as if she was checking her recollection, and finding it a true and acceptable one.

'And as time passed, you became a little more than friends.' John Lambert's grey eyes were as observant of her as ever, but his tone was patient, understanding.

Sara Green glanced at him sharply. She had been expecting the condemnation she felt among her peers, the so-called enlightened intelligentsia of the university, the people who sniggered behind hands and shook their heads in judgement. She had almost been wishing to meet that condemnation of her actions, she now realized: you could feed off opposition, use your resentment to fight. Now she must guard against being too relaxed, too accommodating to this man who had transformed himself so easily from interrogator to sympathetic listener. She said with an attempt at defiance, 'We became lovers, Superintendent. Does that shock you?'

His smile was genuine. She lived in a narrow world, this one, despite the supposed freedoms of university life. 'If I were shocked by things like that, I would long since have ceased to be a CID officer.' He looked for a moment at the photographs she still held in her hand and his tone hardened. 'What shocks me is that people lie to us during a murder investigation. You have done that, Miss Green. If you want us to believe the answers you are now going to give us, you must take pains to be wholly honest with us.'

'I understand that. Fire away!' She felt suddenly buoyant. It would be a relief to be open, to talk about Clare as she had not done to anyone before.

'Was Clare Mills bisexual?'

She was shocked despite herself by the abruptness of that question. They didn't mess about, these men. Didn't bother with the tactful lead-ins of normal conversations. 'No. I don't believe she was. But she's dead now. Is her sexual orientation of interest any more?'

'Of extreme interest. We are trying to build up the fullest possible picture of someone who cannot speak for herself. Of her likes and dislikes. Of her passions, indeed. They may be even more relevant.'

'It seems prurient, you see. As one who loved her, I am upset to see her private life being turned over like this.'

That seemed obtuse, when you were a CID man. But it was a normal enough reaction, Lambert knew. His mind flew back as it usually did in this situation to Hardy's *Mayor of Casterbridge*, in which a peasant woman lamented that a dead woman's small private secrets were exposed, her drawers turned out and all her tiny, private intimacies brought out for strangers. It was a normal enough reaction, in those who had loved a dead one: Hardy had got that right.

But any detective had to remind himself that it was also the reaction of someone who feared that such trawling would reveal something about not just the dead one but herself. And perhaps about her own part in that death. He said quietly. 'We don't know who killed Clare Mills. We haven't even got what we usually call a prime suspect yet. It's by following up the secrets of her private life that we shall arrive at that prime suspect.'

'All right. The answer to your question is that I don't think that Clare was bisexual. I know she'd had heterosexual relationships – she'd been married, for God's sake! – but I believe she found herself sexually with me. She was only going to be interested in same-sex relationships for the rest of her life.'

Her voice caught on the last phrase. Lambert waited for a

moment for her to compose herself before he said, 'Are you saying that you think the two of you would have lived together?'

'We were planning to do that. Who knows what would have happened, when she died so young? I believe that we might have spent the rest of our lives together.' She felt a tear, let it run unchecked down her left cheek. It was a moment of pride, as well as grief; she had never been able to make this assertion whilst Clare was alive.

It was only when the burly man beside Lambert spoke that she realized he had been making notes of her replies. Hook said simply, 'And do you think that Clare Mills believed that too?'

'I don't know. Life is a long time, and Clare was still young. Eight years younger than me.' She spoke as if it was a gap she had considered many times. 'We hadn't discussed plans for the rest of our lives. There didn't seem to be any need for that. All I know is that she was serious about us. She kept the photographs in a position of honour in her room, didn't she?' That sounded to her like a rather childish assertion of her importance to Clare, but she had needed to make it. Sara pulled out a handkerchief and wiped away her tears.

'And when did you last see her?' Hook was so quiet and understanding that he gave the impression it was no more than a dull routine enquiry, rather than a key question in a murder investigation.

'Thursday night. Three days before she died.' There was a defiant pride in the precision.

'And you parted on friendly terms.'

She coloured, and for a moment Hook thought she was going to show her anger at the suggestion it might not have been so. But she controlled herself and gave him a tight-lipped, 'Of course.'

Lambert took up the questioning again. 'Did Clare seem to be upset about anything when you last saw her?'

'Not really. I've thought about it a lot since she died, as you'd expect, but I couldn't say she was seriously upset about anything. Certainly not in fear for her life. She wasn't happy about her parents, but that was nothing new.'

'Yes. Tell us about her relationship with her parents.'

She looked at them sharply, as if she had not considered the extra horror of one of the Hudsons being involved in the killing until now. 'Her mother was an odd fish, by all accounts. I haven't met her, but she never seems to have been very close to her daughter. I know they fell out over Clare's marriage. That was understandable enough, from what Clare told me about Ian Walker. I met him once, about a month ago, at Clare's place. He was a nasty piece of work.'

'Do you think he was capable of killing Clare?'

She pursed her lips. 'I'm trying to be fair, because I don't like the man. I think he's a rogue, but probably a small-time rogue. I can't imagine him planning a murder, but I can see him losing his temper and killing someone during an argument. But if he had, I should think you'd have him under lock and key by now.'

It was a fair summary of what Lambert himself thought about Walker. She was a shrewd woman this. And a likeable, no-nonsense one. He had to remind himself that she'd lied to them at first, that she was still a suspect in this baffling case. 'What about Roy Hudson?'

She took her time, frowning a little with concentration. 'He was only Clare's stepfather, of course, and she was very close to her natural father: she was planning to visit him in New Zealand next year. To tell you the truth, I couldn't quite work out what she felt about her stepfather. They seemed quite friendly when she began her studies, but over the last eighteen months she'd got cooler towards him, I think. She wouldn't really talk to me about it, but I don't think she wanted to meet him any more. I think it was Mr Hudson who arranged all their meetings in the last few months before she died.'

Lambert kept a perfectly straight face, nodded as if she was merely confirming previous findings for them. He said casually, 'But she was still in touch with Roy Hudson?'

'Oh, yes. Fairly regularly, I think. As I say, Clare didn't seem to want to talk about it, but I gathered she saw her stepfather quite often.'

This was a direct contradiction of what Roy and Judith Hudson had told them: it would need following up, in due course. As would the meetings Clare had had with Ian Walker. Lambert wasn't surprised that Walker had been in touch with his ex-wife and had denied it. He thought the sheep-badger found lies came more naturally to him than the truth, when he was speaking to the police.

But Roy Hudson was an altogether more interesting case. John Lambert felt the familiar quickening of the pulses, the sharp interest of new suspicion. He mustn't show that to this alert woman. 'Is there any working acquaintance of Clare's who you think might have killed her? We speak in confidence, of course.'

'No.'

Had the blunt negative come a little too promptly? He studied the sharp, unlined features beneath the dark, short-cut hair. With her small, neat features and wiry frame, Sara Green looked like an alert kitten, who might spring unpredictably into movement at any moment. 'What about Martin Carter?'

Sara knew now that she should have mentioned him herself. But she didn't know how much they had already discovered about the research assistant. She said as casually as she could, 'Martin? He was an embarrassment to Clare, nothing more.'

Lambert had been watching that well-formed face for any sign of jealousy. He saw none. So he said, 'I understand he was something of a suitor to Miss Mills himself over the last few months.'

Sara smiled, perfectly relaxed, it seemed. 'He wasn't in with a chance. Clare was too kind-hearted to choke him off as she should have done. I suppose the fact that he was a postgraduate student gave him a certain standing with her, at first. But I told you a few minutes ago that Clare had discovered the nature of her own sexuality. That is rather a cliché, but it was appropriate in her case. She should really have told him about me and got rid of him. But we were very discreet, for a long time. She was probably trying to protect me when she didn't send him on his way.'

As always, he would have liked to hear what Clare Mills had to say about this, whether she was in complete agreement with it. Sara Green certainly didn't seem to have felt sexually threatened by that attractive but rather gauche young man. He said on impulse, 'What do you think would have happened to you and Clare, if she hadn't been killed?'

'She would have come and lived with me here, as soon as she had completed her degree.'

'That was agreed between you?'

She paused. 'Tacitly agreed. We hadn't even discussed it, in those detailed terms. But I am confident that that is what would have happened. You asked me to be completely frank with you, and I am trying to be just that.'

He thought she might have broken down again with the domestic picture she had just given them, but she seemed to have done with tears, though she still clenched her handkerchief in her hands.

Lambert found himself admiring her composure and the way she bore her loss as he and Hook went back to the car. Then he reminded himself that sexual jealousy was the passion which above all others drove people to murder.

Thirteen

The full post-mortem report was waiting at Oldford police station when Lambert and Hook arrived there late on Saturday afternoon.

Rushton had copies ready for them, and the three men pored over the details without speaking for a few minutes. Then Lambert said, 'We knew she wasn't drowned. She was strangled, probably manually, possibly by someone wearing gloves, though the days in the water make it difficult to be certain. This report suggests that in all probability she wasn't killed near the river. She'd been lifted, they think, to judge by the slight bruising on her legs and beneath her arms. And there was some small evidence of hypostasis, even after three and a half days in the water.'

Rushton nodded eagerly. He had read the report three times whilst waiting for his superintendent to come in. 'Yes. The blood seems to have settled in the buttocks and the backs of the thighs, implying that the corpse was left lying on its back. The pathologist says that she probably lay somewhere for an hour or two after death before she was consigned to the river. He doesn't commit himself to how long and he says it can only be his informed opinion. That's pathologist-speak for saying he wouldn't swear to it as a fact in court.'

'We'll need to run a check on transport, whenever we can,' said Lambert. 'But we may need the owners to volunteer their vehicles for forensic examination, as things stand.' He shook his head in frustration. Examining vehicles was a difficult area; like search warrants for houses, permission to examine vehicles was difficult to obtain until the CID team had collected more definite evidence against particular individuals. Yet how did you assemble that evidence when you were hamstrung by restrictions?

Hook was looking at the last paragraph of the report. 'It says here that certain fibres found on the dead girl's clothing have been sent for analysis. And something which looks like hair.'

'Can't see either of them being of much use to us, not after three days in the water,' said Lambert gloomily.

Which goes to show that even the Great Detective can sometimes be wrong.

'Denis Pimbury' was growing used to his new identity.

There had been an awful moment on the first day when the farmer had called his name out and he had failed to respond, for fully two or three seconds. In some of the battle situations in which he had found himself back in Kosovo, such a delay would have been fatal. In the more relaxed context of a Herefordshire fruit farm, he had got away with it. Many of the fruit-pickers were much worse at the language than he was, and those who were British had shaken their heads and smiled superior smiles at the obtuseness of foreigners. Denis had put his hand up sheepishly and claimed his pay. He didn't mind if people thought him a little stupid; he had found by now that it could sometimes be quite useful if people underestimated you.

But the main principle, the one you had to remember above all others, was to keep out of things.

When he heard the two men who had driven up in the shiny new car using his name, his first instinct was to flee and hide. There weren't as many people as usual working on a Sunday; there were only about half the normal workforce, people like him who needed the extra money. He felt more exposed. He wanted to seek the sanctuary of the ditch at the edge of the farm as he had done on that previous occasion when men came looking for illegal immigrants. But he controlled the urge. You couldn't run for ever, and wasn't it for this very reason that he had acquired his expensive new identity?

He bent again over the row of strawberries, picking slowly and methodically, watching the shallow basket fill with the fruit even whilst he listened to the sounds behind him. He was apparently totally engrossed in his task when he heard the farmer's voice say behind him, 'This be Denis Pimbury.'

He straightened slowly, stilling the trepidation he felt in his breast, and turned unhurriedly to greet the men who stood beside his employer. They were wearing clothes which were far too neat for this place. He brushed the sweat from his face with the sleeve of his forearm, in that gesture he had seen the local men use. He was adopting the habits of the men of Herefordshire and Gloucestershire whenever he could now. Trying to be inconspicuous had become a habit with him.

He couldn't conceal his accent, of course. His English was becoming better every day, but he had the careful enunciation of the foreigner rather than the cheerfully slurred tones of the locals. He used the right phrases, spoke them a little too slowly. 'I'm Denis Pimbury, yes. What can I do for you?'

They were big men, both of them. It was the shorter and more solid of the two who said, 'Not a common name, that. And you're not from round here, are you? Not from England at all, I should think.'

'I have passport.' He resisted the impulse to reach into the pocket he had sewn onto the inside of his shirt and produce the precious document. He had never yet been asked to produce it, but he never went anywhere without carrying it upon his person. He gave them the words he had rehearsed so often at nights, trying to make them sound as though he had not gone over them a hundred times, 'My father was English, but he died when I was a boy. My mother was Croatian. I have been abroad for some years, but I kept my English passport.'

The tall, thin man had not spoken since they arrived, but he seemed to be weighing every word Denis said and every move he made with his cool grey eyes. Now he said, 'Where do you live, Mr Pimbury?'

He pronounced the name politely but carefully, as if he did not quite believe it. Denis gave him the name of the street in Gloucester. People who knew the city often said that it was very near the place where the infamous multiple murderers Fred and Rosemary West had lived. Denis was ready to nod sagely and produce a comment if these men had done that. He had learned a little about the awful Wests; it was part of the business of being a local to be able to comment upon them.

85

He had been past the place where they had lived and killed so many young girls: it was now a quiet garden of remembrance for the victims.

But this man didn't mention the Wests. He chilled Denis Pimbury's blood with the mention of another and altogether more familiar death. 'We're investigating the murder of a Clare Mills, who lived very near to you in Gloucester. We'd like to ask you some questions.'

'I do not know anything about this death.'

He articulated the words carefully, but his denial was surprisingly prompt. Too prompt. Lambert made it a statement rather than a question as he said, 'But you knew Clare Mills.'

Denis found that he was surprisingly calm, now that the moment had come. He must be careful what he said, especially in this strange language where you could so easily give things away. But these English policemen were not like those sinister figures he had known in the last days in Croatia. Those men came in plain clothes like these two, but they came during the night and they knew what they were going to do before they ever saw you; it was no use being careful about what you said to those men, because whatever you said had no effect. He said, 'I don't know if I knew this Clare Mills. I have not seen picture of her.'

He thought they might now produce a photograph. That would give him the chance to study it and the time to gather his thoughts, before he eventually admitted that he had known this woman. Instead, Lambert said confidently, 'You knew her all right, Mr Pimbury.'

Again he spoke the surname as if it were in inverted commas, as if this were merely a title he was giving to the man to humour him. But that nuance was wasted on the man from Croatia, whose mind was on very different things. Denis said carefully, 'I knew girl called Clare. She was kind to me.'

'Yes. That was Clare Mills. We need to know when and how often you saw her.'

Denis nodded seriously, his swarthy face the model of a man dutifully trying to help. 'I saw her near the docks at Gloucester the first time. I asked her the way to my street. The one where I had been told I could stay. Six weeks ago. Maybe seven.' He frowned hard, as if anxious to give them the most accurate information he could. It was surely a good idea to dwell on this perfectly safe area.

'But you saw her again, in the weeks which followed.'

Again it was a statement, not a question, and Denis noticed that. These men had talked to a lot of people, seemed perfectly confident. He wouldn't deny them then: not here, where the truth did not matter. 'She was kind lady, Clare. She said she lived near my street herself, and she took me there, showed me the way. I said could we meet again, and she said yes.' He wouldn't tell them about her hesitations, about how he had needed to assure her in his halting English that he was not a danger to her, how he had explained that he had not a single friend in this new land. There was no need for them to know any of that.

Lambert watched him carefully as he picked out his words. That scrutiny did not upset Denis as it upset most people; he was used to police who studied your every movement, waiting for you to make a mistake. And he was not surprised when the superintendent said, 'Our information is that you met her again, several times. What was the purpose of these meetings?'

'I told you, Clare was kind lady. She said she would do what she could to help me to establish myself here.' He was proud of that last phrase; he had got it from Clare and used it many times since: now it seemed the right one for this moment.

'Establish yourself?'

Denis thought there was the ghost of a smile about the tall man's lips as he repeated the phrase. The Croatian lifted his hand to stroke the stubble on his chin, wishing he had shaved before he came out so early on this Sunday morning. It hadn't mattered at work, of course: the men who worked here shaved after they had finished their work, if they shaved at all. But he felt at a disadvantage with these strangers in their clean long-sleeved shirts and their well-creased trousers. It was an unexpected reminder of those days he thought he had discarded for ever, when he had been training to be a doctor, when he had been used to dressing as a professional man.

He picked his words carefully as he said, 'I was new here. I did not know the language of the country or the customs of this nation. Clare helped me to get to know my new country.'

Hook looked up from his notebook and said gently, 'But you have an English name. An English father.'

'I had not lived here since I was infant. This is new country to me.' The Croatian's eyes were almost black, their darkness emphasized by the fact that they were so deep-set, over high cheekbones and sallow skin. They looked defiantly at Hook, who had never worked outside this area, warning him that he would meet a fierce obstinacy if he chose to challenge these assertions.

But Hook was interested only in that thin, lifeless body he remembered upon the slab in Chepstow. He said, 'You must tell us about your meetings with Clare Mills, Mr Pimbury.'

'She was kind lady. She made me feel like a man.'

'How? Can you explain that, please?'

He looked around him, at the long furrows of red soil stretching away to the end of the field, at the stooped, unheeding figures, moving their baskets up beside them as they worked their way along the rows of strawberry plants. 'Is hard work, this. Long hours, very hard work. You never see woman. In evenings, sometimes, is nice to see woman, have drink. Have conversation. Clare, she help me with my English. Also help me to enjoy my life in England.'

Hook nodded, looking at the lean, hard body of the man in front of him, wondering just what lay behind those fierce warrior's features. And wondering also about the nature of this strange relationship between the English rose who had come through an unhappy marriage and embarked upon a degree and this enigmatic hard man from another culture and another land. 'How often did you meet Clare?'

Denis, slim and watchful, found himself warming to this well-fed Englishman with the countryman's features and the seeming willingness to understand and sympathize with him. The sergeant was less forceful than the taller man who had spoken at first, who had seemed to bring some of the intensity and tension Denis felt himself into the exchanges. He must be careful, though: he could not afford to be caught off his guard. 'I met her five or six times. Each time, we agree when we meet again before we part from each other.'

'You met in pubs?'

'Yes. Every time in pubs. Every time but one in the same

pub. I was there first, waiting for her. She said is not good for English ladies to go into pubs on their own, wanted me to be there when she got there.'

That tallied with the information the uniformed men had brought in. It was touchingly old-fashioned in a woman of twenty-five to feel that way about going into pubs, if it was true. But the pubs in question had been pretty rough ones, in the toughest part of Gloucester. And no one had been able to tell the police anything about what had passed between this strangely assorted pair. The people who had noted them had sniggered about them or shrugged their shoulders, but no one had heard anything significant in their conversation. Hook nodded understandingly, then said as casually as he could, 'And what did you talk about?'

'All sort of thing. She always asked me how I was getting on, how I was settling in. And she talked to me about her studies.' He wanted to tell them how they had laughed about some of her lecturers, how he too had been a student once and had told her about life in his university in Croatia. But he was determined to keep off that, to say as little as possible about his life before he came here. He did not want to be forced to talk about the English father he had claimed, this mysterious Mr Pimbury, nor about the mother who had taken him off to her homeland in his infancy. When you were lying, the less you had to say the better.

'And what did she say about her life at the university?'

He shrugged, feeling the tenseness in his shoulders as he did so, willing it to drop away with the gesture. 'We discussed psychology.' He articulated each syllable carefully, as if it were a completely new word for him. He wouldn't tell them of their lively exchanges, of how he had been able to help Clare, to give her one or two ideas from his own studies which she had not met before.

Instead, he said, 'Psychology is very difficult subject, I think. But we talked about Clare's mother, about the problems they had getting along with each other. And I think Clare was good student. Very intelligent. She was doing well at the university, getting good marks.'

'Yes, she was. Did you become lovers, Denis?'

Hook had thrown it in as if it were just another casual

question, as if it were no more important than the weather all these English loved to talk about. The dark eyes flashed before Denis said in carefully controlled tones. 'No. It was not that kind – not that kind of meeting. We were friends. We liked each other, I think. No, I know that we did. And I want you to catch the man who killed my friend.'

'We need to know these things, you see. Need to know everything we can about Clare, if we are to find who killed her.' Hook spoke earnestly, almost as if he had not heard the steel in Denis's voice.

'I understand.'

'When was the last time you saw Clare Mills?'

'Friday. Friday evening, before the Saturday she died.'

'How do you know when she died, Denis?'

In that moment of terror, he thought he had made an awful error, that they would clap the handcuffs on him now and lead him away to the car and an English prison. His mind was racing as he said, 'Was in newspaper that she died on Saturday. People talk about it. Talk here, when we eat our sandwiches.' He waved his arm desperately over the long field and the unheeding workers.

'Weekend was what it said in the papers, Denis. Not Saturday. We did not know for certain that Clare died on Saturday, when the news was released to the press.'

'Saturday,' he said stubbornly, making each syllable clear, as if by the careful repetition he could make things right. 'I assume Saturday. I think I hear other people say Saturday, when they talk about this.'

Lambert looked at him for long, heart-stopping seconds before he took up the questioning again. 'Tell us about that last meeting, Mr Pimbury. Tell us everything about it.'

Denis tried another shrug, found this time that his shoulders were too rigid to work themselves into the gesture. 'Not much to tell you. We talked about Clare's work, about the philosophy essay she had to write. I told her about my work here, about the books I was using to teach me better English.'

He couldn't tell them the other things. Couldn't tell them what had passed between them on that last night. Couldn't tell them about the things he had taken away with him from that last rendezvous with Clare. He kept his dark eyes on the grey, unblinking ones of the man who towered above him, as if to drop his gaze would be an admission of guilt, as if they would clap the handcuffs upon him if he failed in this childish contest of staring the man out.

It seemed a long time before Lambert said, 'Did you kill Clare Mills, Mr Pimbury?'

'No. Clare was my friend.'

Lambert considered the reply for a long time. The man's appearance was against him. He looked nervous and desperate. But if his background was what John Lambert suspected it was, if the passport he had offered so quickly was bogus, he had good reason to be nervous and desperate. He looked capable of killing, but what could Clare Mills have threatened him with, to make him take such drastic action? Or was this killing nothing to do with the man's background? Was it the old story of seduction gone wrong, of sexual favours refused and a violent male reaction? This foreigner, deprived of sex for many months, might have mistaken friendship for something more, and if Sara Green was right about Clare Mills having opted for same-sex relationships, she would certainly have rebuffed him.

'Then who do you think killed her?'

'I don't know. I would tell you if I did. I want you to get whoever did this.' He sought desperately for something beyond this bald denial, something which might convince them of his innocence, of his desire to help them. 'Someone at the university, I think. Something was worrying her, and it must have come from there.'

Later, when they had gone, he wondered why he had said this, whether anyone would hear of it and do him harm.

You had to keep out of things, at all costs.

Fourteen

Twelve and a half thousand miles away, as far away as you could get from the strawberry fields where Denis Pimbury worked, a man was looking out over a very different farm.

On the edge of the South Canterbury plain in New Zealand, the sheep run stretched for hundreds of acres, creeping up into the foothills of the mountains. The slopes were rolling rather than precipitous, and the man could reach most points of his ground in the Land Rover. It was winter here, but not the winter you endured in Britain. You got a little frost around this time of the year, but not the snows which buried sheep and the deep frosts which froze creatures to death in the occasional hard winters of Snowdonia or the Lake District.

This farmer, taking a little food out to his sheep to supplement the nourishment of the grass which scarcely stopped growing here, savoured the nip in the early-morning air and the clear sun which allowed you to see for miles towards the mountains in the west. Mount Cook had deep snows on its upper heights, but that was no more than a picturesque backdrop to his work, many kilometres away and many metres higher than these productive pastures. He was surprised how quickly he had grown accustomed to thinking in metrical terms, after his resistance to the idea in England.

He examined a dozen of his sheep. Their coats were good: there would be excellent shearings in the spring. And the beasts were sturdy and disease-free, a huge contrast to the rangy and tick-ridden sheep which Ian Walker herded in the Forest of Dean. This man had known sheep like that, and the memory enabled him to savour even more the health of his flock here.

There would be good profits by Christmas, and he would put them back into the farm. They would have over a thousand sheep next year, and he would take in more ground yet, in the years to come. He drove more slowly than he needed to on the way back to the farmhouse, relishing the sharp blue of this perfect winter's day and the different greens of the land stretching away towards Christchurch beneath the rising sun. He was reluctant to tear himself away from this life that he had grown so quickly to love.

The woman had seen the Land Rover ten minutes before it reached the house. She waited for him to come into the kitchen, gave him a welcoming smile before she said, 'You'd better get your breakfast. I got you a cheap local flight from Christchurch to Auckland. Gets you in an hour before the international flight leaves. You stop for three hours at Hong Kong before you board for London.'

'Thanks. That's about as quickly as you can do it.'

'It's a hell of a way.' It was the nearest she would get to expressing disapproval of his going. She wanted to say that there was nothing to be gained by this huge journey, that he was cutting himself off from her, connecting again with that former life which she felt, however unreasonably, was a threat to her.

He put his arms round her, a clumsy bear of a man, too tall for her to kiss without stretching up on her toes like the young girl she had long left behind her. She pressed him harder than usual to her, saying nothing, not trusting herself to words when her small hands could knead his back.

'I need to go,' was all he said, and that after several seconds.

'I know that.'

'It's all I can do for Clare now.' His big frame was suddenly rent by a sob, when he thought he had done with all that. 'She used to talk to me on the phone, you see. Told me I was the only one she could speak frankly to. Told me lots of things about the people who were close to her, the people she'd known for years and the new ones at the university. I might just be able to help the police.'

'If they haven't already made an arrest when you get there.' She hadn't meant it to be a rebuke, but it emerged like one.

He held her for long seconds before he spoke. 'And there's her mother, you see. The police might not understand her problems, might not be sympathetic.' He stopped: it was sounding too much like a statement of love for the woman he had long since forsaken. He hadn't meant it to be that.

She muttered almost inaudibly into his chest, 'They'll understand, when you tell them about it.' It came again like sarcasm, when she had intended it to be a statement of her love and confidence in him.

'And there's that woman she was planning to live with at the university. The police may not even know about that.'

'They'll know. It's their business to know.'

Ken Mills held her at arm's length, looking down into her small face with that intense seriousness which had made her love him. 'I have to go. She's my only child. Was my only child. I want to see whoever did this brought to justice.'

'Of course you do. And of course you must go.' She strove to put conviction into the words. 'I can keep things going all right here. It's a slack time of the year for us – well, as slack as it gets. And even if it is a long way, the world's a small place nowadays. You'll soon be back.'

They nodded earnestly at each other, the clichés the source of comfort that they often are in such situations.

On the other side of the world, Ian Walker was enjoying his Sunday.

He'd had a heavy Saturday night, with beer and whisky chasers and some rowdy singing. They'd had a skirmish and then very nearly a full-scale punch-up with some of the rugby-club toffs, but the police had driven up with their sirens screaming just when it was getting interesting.

Much better than the previous Saturday night. The less said about that the better. He pushed aside his thoughts about those events and got back to the safer present.

One of his mates had dropped him off last night; it must have been one or after when he got back to the caravan. But he'd slept late this morning, lying in until after eleven with a thick head and a mouth like sawdust. It had been after midday when he'd collected his *News of the World* and enjoyed the hair of the dog that bit him in the Rose and Crown. The Forest of Dean roads were busy with the Sunday drivers and the woods were full of picnicking families: he glared at them sourly as he came out of the pub into the sunlight.

Then he had a bit of luck. As he went back towards his caravan, a car a hundred yards in front of him hit one of the Forest's free-roaming sheep, which ran away in agony on three legs. Not one of his, was Ian's first thought. Stupid creatures, sheep. But tough buggers; they seemed to survive all kinds of hits. It was one of the jokes in the Forest that scarcely any of the sheep-badgers' free-roaming sheep had four legs intact. That was an exaggeration, of course, the kind of thing they used when they wanted to have a go at irresponsible motorists and get sympathy, but it was true that a lot of the sheep hobbled around and survived. And once they'd been through the abattoir, no one could tell on a butcher's slab which of them had been undamaged in life.

To his surprise, he saw that the car that had hit the sheep was stopping, drawing carefully into the side of the road where it broadened out a hundred yards ahead. The driver was a woman, easing herself reluctantly from the front seat of the car, looking fearfully back towards the spot where she had hit her woolly victim.

Ian Walker quickened his pace and went forward, his face suddenly full of indignation.

She wasn't as young as he'd thought at first. Forty maybe, with a tanned face and blonde hair, a little dishevelled by her distress. Bit long in the tooth for him, perhaps, but well preserved. He wouldn't kick her out of bed, for sure. And they said middle-class women went at it like knives when they got hold of a young bit of rough like him.

But there were more important things than fantasies, at the moment. He bristled with indignation. 'What the bloody 'ell d'yer think yer doing? Driving through 'ere like a maniac, when there's valuable livestock around!'

'I'm sorry! Your sheep came out right under my wheels, without warning. I wasn't really going very fast.'

Ian looked at the car. There was no man in it. But there were two children, about five or six, their round, fearful faces pressed against the back window of the car. This woman would want to get away as quickly as she could, before the kids got more upset. 'Too bloody fast, you were going, or you'd never 'ave 'it my beast. You bain't from round these parts, or you'd 'ave more sense.'

'I'm from Bristol, visiting my old aunt in Cinderford. Look, I don't want the poor creature to suffer. Is there anything to be done for it?'

He looked from her to the car, then over to the trees where the sheep had leapt for cover. 'Wait 'ere. Don't you drive away! I've got your number, see?'

He went away into the bracken, found the sheep licking its hind leg among its fellows. It was a spindly ram, not much meat on it. He felt the limb quickly, watched the animal bound away with an alarmed baaing beyond a copse of birches. The leg wasn't even broken; the animal would certainly survive, with or without a limp. And anyway, it certainly wasn't one of his.

He went back to the road with a face like thunder. 'Poor thing'll 'ave to be put down. In agony, 'er is. One of my best beasts too. I was looking forward to 'er lambs in the spring.'

She looked fearfully up and down the road as she stood before this angry-looking man in the stained clothes. His face seemed to be dominated by the scar on his temple. 'I'm sorry. I really didn't have much chance—'

'In agony, 'er is! 'Er'll need to be put down, right away, save 'er from further suffering.' He looked past her towards the two round white faces. 'You got room to take 'er in your car?'

'No! No, I couldn't do that! Not with the children, you see. They'd be terribly upset if they had to—'

'Shoulda thought about that before you ran the poor beast down, shouldn't you? I've lost one o' my best sheep, and now I'm going to have a vet's bill for putting 'er down on top of it.' He shook his head wretchedly.

'Look, I want to make whatever retribution I can. I haven't got much money on me, but I've got my cheque book in my bag.'

He mumbled and grumbled a little to disguise his elation. They settled for a hundred pounds for the sheep and twenty for the vet's bill to have the animal put down. He looked at the cheque doubtfully and said he'd rather have had cash, and she assured him that it wouldn't bounce.

Ian Walker stood perfectly still at the side of the road, watching the children's faces pressed against the rear window of the car until they passed slowly out of sight beneath the trees at the bend in the road. Then he flung a V-sign after his victim and threw his head back into a guffaw at the stupidity of city folk. He spat his satisfaction into the dusty grass beside him and turned back towards the caravan and the can of beans which would be his Sunday dinner.

The caravan smelt foetid in the hot sun. He opened the door and the one window he could still open without its falling out of its frame. The man who owned this land had told him he'd have to move on in the autumn if he couldn't tidy up the van: said it was lowering the tone of the place. He'd explained that he'd let things go because he was expecting delivery of a new one in a couple of months. Fat chance of that! The sheep weren't bringing in much at present. Criminal, the price of lamb was.

Still, he'd get back to his other business, as soon as this hornets' nest over the death of Clare had died down. Trust his bloody wife to interfere with his welfare, even when she was safely out of the way.

Ian Walker took two slices of bread from the wrapper and put them into his ancient toaster. They were a bit stale, but that wouldn't matter, when they were toasted. He put the can of beans by the pan, ready to open, then sat down with a can of lager on the chair outside in the sun. He'd let the van cool down for a bit, let the draught flow through it. Besides, he deserved another drink, to celebrate the cheque in the pocket of his shirt. He patted it contentedly and smiled again at the woman's credulity.

He turned to the sport in the *News of the World*. Hereford had lost again. Daft buggers! He belched a little after a couple of swallows from the can. A pleasant, relaxed, near-silent sort of belch. You learned to enjoy the simple pleasures, when you lived as he did. His head fell forward onto his chest and the newspaper slipped to the grass beside him. A couple of minutes later, a gentle, irregular snoring overtook him.

He did not hear the visitor arrive. The man came on silent, careful feet and stood for a full minute with his shadow over Walker's face, taking in the man and his surroundings, wondering if there was anything to be learned, any secret to be gleaned, from this squalid scene before the man at the centre of it was alerted to his presence.

The man in the flimsy garden chair was a countryman, despite his excesses, and presently the absence of the sun upon his face woke him from his doze. He started, feeling his vulnerability to the tall figure above him and so near to him. From his position near the ground, the figure against the sun looked immensely tall, black as night in its silhouette against the bright blue of the sky behind it.

As his vision slowly restored itself to something near normal, Ian realized that the shape was not black at all, but a dark blue for the most part, with the smart short-sleeved shirt a lighter shade than the sharply creased trousers below it. Ian struggled upright, setting the half-empty can down carefully upon the newspaper beside him. 'And who the bloody 'ell are you?' he said automatically.

The man did not move; he continued to stand very close to Walker, looking down coolly upon the dishevelled figure who presented such a contrast to his own neat appearance. Then he moved his hand unhurriedly down to his trousers, aware that a sudden movement might be misinterpreted as aggression by a man like this. 'Detective Inspector Rushton, Oldford CID.' He waved the warrant card swiftly across the unseeing eyes of the man in front of him. 'Here to ask you a few questions in connection with the murder of your late wife, Clare Mills.'

'I didn't kill the cow,' said Walker automatically.

'Glad to hear it, Mr Walker. With your record, I'll need to be convinced of that, though.'

'You coming in?' Walker moved automatically towards the caravan, needing to get further away from this man, whose closeness seemed to present a physical threat to him.

Chris Rushton's look took in the sordid scene he could see through the open door, with the slices of curling bread peeping from the toaster and the can of beans upon the tiny stove. 'I don't think so, Mr Walker. I wouldn't want to interfere with your domestic arrangements.'

'Suit yourself. I've nothing to tell you about bloody Clare, anyway. I've said everything I 'ave to say about 'er.'

'Not quite, Mr Walker. Not by a long chalk, perhaps. You've been telling us lies. Not a wise thing to do, that.'

Ian glared at him sullenly, wanting to hit him, knowing he

mustn't. 'I told you what I knew. Told it all to those other buggers I saw on Friday. I 'adn't spoken to the bloody cow for six months.'

Rushton looked at him with undisguised distaste now, hating his lack of grace, despising a man who could speak like this about a murdered wife, however fractured their relationship had been. He savoured the blow he was now going to deliver to him. 'That's not what her mobile phone says, Mr Walker.'

Ian's glance flicked automatically towards the door of the van and his own mobile in the jacket within it. 'Whad'yer mean?'

'When Superintendent Lambert and Detective Sergeant Hook spoke to you we didn't have Clare's mobile phone. We have it now. It shows that you rang her on the night before she died.'

'I didn't speak to her. Didn't get through.'

'Her phone has a memo option. You are listed under "Received Calls". You got through to Clare all right. What did you say to her?'

He glowered at this cool adversary, cursing modern technology and his own ignorance of it. Probably they even knew what he'd said. Probably this smug sod was just letting him tie himself in knots. 'I asked her to meet me.'

Rushton was too old a fox now to show in his face how excited he was. 'When?'

'Saturday night.'

'The night she died.'

'Yes. Except I didn't meet 'er, see?'

'And why not?'

'She wouldn't see me. Said she didn't want to meet me. That we'd nothing to say to each other.'

At least that last phrase sounded like one the dead woman rather than this lout might have used. But of course it might have been on any one of numerous previous occasions, not as a rejection of his request to meet her on that fateful Saturday. Rushton smiled grimly. 'But you saw her nonetheless. Saw her and killed her on that Saturday.'

'No! She wouldn't see me, like I told you!' Ian sought desperately for something which would deny the man's statement, and found nothing.

Rushton looked at the sheep-badger, this man whose life was such a contrast to his own carefully ordered existence, and did not trouble now to disguise his distaste. 'You have a vehicle.'

Ian tried to force his racing mind to work properly. He'd told the other two pigs, the lanky superintendent and his country-bumpkin sergeant, that he didn't have a vehicle, but this clever sod seemed to know he did. Better not deny it, then; at least the van was taxed and insured now. 'Yeah. I got a van. You need a van, to move your sheep about. People thinks we just take advantage of the free grazing, but there's—'

'I want to look at that van. Now.'

Well, you won't find anything, if you do, smart-ass. Not now. Aloud, Ian said, 'Invasion of privacy, this is.'

'Maybe it is, Walker. So sue me, if you like. You going to show me this vehicle?'

'It's down there. Behind the house.' Ian gestured with his head, then turned and walked out from where the caravan was parked among the birches. He led the way down the slope to the van, parked a hundred yards away, behind the house by the lane. Rushton looked from the scrawled note on the windscreen which said that the tax was in the post to the apprehensive face beside him. Ian Walker said, 'Tax disc will come tomorrow, I expect. I got the insurance certificate and the MOT in the caravan, if you want to see them.' Technically, it wasn't taxed at all, yet. He'd asked for the tax to run from the first of July, day after tomorrow; it hadn't seemed worth paying a month's tax for a couple of days. Good job the tax hadn't come yet, then: this pernickety sod would no doubt have picked him up on a little detail like that.

Rushton walked all round the van. It was white, or it had been, an ageing Fiesta diesel with a thick covering of grime and lines of rust around its seams. He touched the front offside tyre with the toe of his immaculate shoe. 'Surprised you got an MOT, with a tyre as bald as that.'

Ian looked at the dust around the wheels of the van and said nothing. Both of them knew that this was no more than a prologue, part of the initial softening-up process, prior to the inspection of the inside of the van which was the point of this visit.

Rushton said, 'Open the rear doors of the vehicle, please.'

Ian did that unhurriedly, trying not to smirk with the confidence he felt about this.

Chris Rushton peered into the interior of the van, shielding his eyes against the sun. It could hardly have presented a greater contrast with the exterior. It was spotlessly clean, its white metal gleaming softly, mockingly, in the shadows. There was not even a rug or a rag on the metal floor of the carrying space; they were a hundred yards away under the caravan, where Ian had carefully placed them with the brushes when he had finished the scouring.

'You've cleaned this out. Recently,' said Rushton. It was the nearest he could muster to an accusation.

'Couple of days ago, I should think. That was the last time.' Ian nodded, trying not to sound too truculent. He'd made the copper look a fool, but they could come back at you, these buggers.

'And why did you do that?'

'Routine procedure,' said Ian airily. He enjoyed that phrase: might have come from a pig itself, that might have.

'Not like the outside,' said Rushton.

'Outside don't matter. Inside's what matters, when you're moving sheep about,' said Walker, with the air of one educating a child.

'Smells of carbolic,' said Rushton, as if that in itself was a charge.

'Strong carbolic,' agreed Ian. 'Hygiene, you see. You need strong disinfectant, case of any diseases among your sheep. Don't 'spect you'd know about that.'

'You'd need to clean it out if you'd had a body in there, too. If you'd been transporting a body to dump in the Severn.'

' 'Ere, you'd better watch what you're saying, you know. Can't go round accusing people without evidence, even when they're 'umble sheep-badgers like me.' Ian knew he mustn't enjoy the moment too much, but he couldn't resist taunting this smug sod, who'd so obviously expected to catch him out.

'And how do you clean it?' asked Rushton.

Ian felt a spurt of alarm. Best be careful here. 'Plenty of disinfectant and a good stiff brush. Then I mops it out with old rags.'

'I'll need to take those away for analysis. Our forensic laboratory will be most interested to examine them in detail.'

'Rags have gone. Straight into a dustbin bag and away with the collection. Gone yesterday. Only use things that are ready for the rubbish tip, see. And I 'aven't got the brush: borrowed it from a mate, other side of Coleford. Don't know where it would be now. But it will have been used again since I cleaned the van. He works in the abattoir, see? Be all kinds of other things on it, I expect. But they put them under the 'osepipe, when they've finished, I should think.'

He enjoyed piling on the detail. The stiff brush was lying underneath his caravan, but this man couldn't know that.

DI Rushton was looking for a way to get out without too much loss of face. He still thought this man had killed Clare Mills, but it might need a search warrant before they could get into that stinking caravan and go through it the way he wanted to. In the meantime, he'd better not put this ruffian too much on his guard.

'I think that will do, for the moment,' he said stiffly. 'It may be that I or other members of the team allotted to this investigation will be back to speak to you again.'

But he'd got nothing, thought the sheep-badger, as he watched Rushton drive away. He went back to the *News of the World* and his baked beans feeling pretty secure.

It was another example of how wrong Ian Walker's judgements could be.

Fifteen

Judith Hudson looked exactly the same as when they had seen her two days earlier. From her impeccable ash-blonde hair to the tray with coffee and biscuits in the comfortable sitting room, everything seemed the same on this Monday morning as it had on Saturday. It was as if they had walked onto a film set after the continuity girl had been busy making sure everything matched.

'Have you found out who killed Clare?' Mrs Hudson might have been checking on the weather forecast, so scant was the animation behind the enquiry. They were back in the presence of the oddest mother of a murder victim whom either of them had ever encountered.

'No. I'm afraid we do not have any dramatic news for you, Mrs Hudson. But certain discrepancies have appeared in the information we have gathered. That is why we are here.' John Lambert looked in vain for some sign of apprehension in the woman. Indeed, any emotion would at that moment have been welcome.

She merely raised an eyebrow interrogatively at him, as if they were discussing some interesting puzzle from a news-paper. Lambert said, 'We are now in possession of your daughter's mobile phone. As there was no access to a phone line in the building where she lived, we can presume that most of her calls were made on her mobile.'

'Yes, I think that would be so. She made most of her calls to me on her mobile, and that was the only number I had for her.' She poured two cups of coffee for them from the tall pot, as if demonstrating how perfectly steady her hand was, how she was affected not at all by this visit.

Lambert tried not to show his irritation; however odd her behaviour, this was after all the mother of a girl struck down at twenty-five, with the world in front of her. 'The phone is a modern one with a call register. The memory option on that provides us with a record of the calls Clare made and received in the days before her death.'

'Really? I'm afraid the mysteries of modern technology leave me baffled. I'm sure these devices are very clever, but—'

'The memory option shows us several interesting things, which we are following up. That is why we are here this morning. The call register of Clare's phone shows that you have been lying to us.'

That was pitching it pretty strongly. Normally he would have started by talking of misunderstandings which needed to be cleared up. But this abnormally calm woman's version of the perfect hostess was getting to him.

'Lied to you?' She looked bewildered, as if this was a concept she found it difficult to deal with.

Lambert kept his temper, spoke calmly, as if outlining to a child how things stood. 'You said that she hadn't made her usual phone call home in the week before her death. That you hadn't spoken to her in that time. The "Dialled Numbers" section in her call register shows that she spoke to you on Thursday the nineteenth of June, at seven forty-five p.m. A mere two days before her death.'

If he had hoped to shake her, he was disappointed. She nodded slowly a couple of times, seeming to digest the information calmly before she said with just a trace of resentment, 'And does this call register tell you the content of our exchanges? Is that too recorded for posterity?'

He was tempted to let her think that it did, that they knew everything she was trying to conceal. Except that the woman seemed to have no burning desire to conceal anything, no great apprehension that she had been caught out in this. Lambert said, 'No, Mrs Hudson, we do not know what you and your daughter said to each other in that call. We are relying on you to tell us that now.'

She nodded thoughtfully, apparently quite unabashed to have been discovered lying during a murder investigation. 'It was nothing of great moment, Superintendent. I suggested that she might come home and see us. I think I also mentioned that she should try to cooperate with her stepfather.'

'Cooperate? In what respect would that be?'

For the first time, she looked a little ruffled, when he seized upon that word. But she did not hurry her response. 'That is probably the wrong expression to have used. I wanted the two of them to get on together. I wanted my new husband to be accepted by my daughter. That is what you would expect, isn't it?'

But even the tone of this was wrong. It sounded like a genuine enquiry, as if she was uncertain of it, rather than an assertion of her natural feelings as a mother and wife. Lambert studied her for a moment before he said, 'I suppose it is, yes. What was Clare's reaction to this suggestion?'

'She said that she would think about it. That there were other issues, issues which I did not understand.'

'And what do you think these issues were?'

'I have no idea.' Her ignorance seemed to give her great satisfaction.

'These issues, as you call them, might have a bearing on your daughter's death.'

'I suppose they might. But I cannot imagine what they might have been. I'm sorry about that.'

But she didn't look very sorry. Bert Hook looked up from his notes and said, 'Do you think Clare was thinking about her relationship with your husband, Mrs Hudson?'

She looked at him as if she was reassessing his function in these exchanges, then took away his empty coffee cup and put it carefully on the tray. 'I don't know. I'm not much good at analysing relationships, I'm afraid.'

We can certainly agree with that, thought Lambert.

It was a relief to get out into the bright sun of the last day of June, to glide beneath the dappled shade of the Forest of Dean as they drove slowly away from that chilling presence.

For the first time in their many years of experience of murder enquiries, they were confronting the possibility that the mother of a victim might be their killer.

Martin Carter was worried. Those detectives had been expert at concealing what they were really thinking when they had interviewed him; he supposed that that was part of their technique, a skill they had acquired over the years. But Martin had had the impression that they hadn't really believed him, that they had known that he was holding something back.

And now this. He could definitely have done without this.

'The boss isn't pleased with you.' The man who had burst into this quiet room without warning was big. He was older than Martin, and perhaps a little overweight, but he wasn't so much older or fatter that he wouldn't be fit enough to beat Martin up. The research assistant had no doubt at all about that. The man folded his arms, slid his buttocks insolently onto the edge of Martin's desk, and looked at his man with undisguised contempt.

They were all the same, these intellectuals: out of touch with the real world. Out of touch with the way you made money and got yourself on in life. Out of touch with the things you needed to do to make a living. Out of touch with the very idea that life was about the survival of the fittest, that you screwed people before they could screw you, thumped them before they could thump you. Living in ivory towers, thinking that the world owed them a living.

He looked at the weedy individual he had been sent to frighten and decided that this turd was typical of the breed. Dark red hair which should have been cut shorter, small-lensed glasses on the bridge of his thin, vulnerable nose, shirt clean and pressed, bright blue jeans which had never seen real work, room lined with more books than any bugger could ever read, nose stuck in some obscure article whilst other people were getting on with the real business of life.

What a fucking wimp!

He looked the puny frame up and down with contempt. 'You're a fucking wimp!' he said with conviction.

'If you've just come here to be gratuitously insulting, I don't think there's any further purpose in—'

'Shut it, mother's boy! Send you back home with a thick ear and a few broken ribs, if you don't!' Like most bullies, the big man grew more truculent when he smelt fear upon a victim.

Martin Carter made a belated attempt to assert himself. 'I've a student coming to see me in five minutes. You shouldn't really be seen here, you know. Be difficult for me to explain your presence – you must see that. I'm sure our employer wouldn't like it if he thought you were acquiring a high profile here.'

The man with his buttocks on the edge of the desk wanted to mock this natural victim, to repeat his own phrases menacingly back into his face while holding it two inches from his own, to feel the weak body trembling with fear in his grasp. But what this tosser said was true. The boss didn't want him hanging about here. In and out quickly, he'd said. Frighten him all you need to, but don't rough him up. Don't lay a finger on him, in fact. Not yet. He'd been quite clear about that. And you didn't take chances with the boss.

The enforcer fumbled for the phrases he'd been told to use. 'You got to increase your turnover, see? Otherwise he'll get in someone who will. And you'll be redundant. And you can't afford to be redundant in this trade, see.'

'No. I understand that, but will you tell him that—'

'You don't get severance pay when you're redundant, not in this game. You'd be too dangerous to leave around, see, the things you know. Boss wouldn't want you here when the pigs come snuffling, not with the things you know about the business. So anyone redundant is liquidated.' He pronounced the word carefully, syllable by syllable, producing it with the leer he had practised ever since he had seen *The Godfather* for the first of several times.

Martin tried desperately to be amused by this Hollywood heavy, this caricature of violence. In a film, you would have shrugged him off, used your superior brainpower to send him on his way with a sardonic dismissal in his ears. But it was different in real life, when you could smell the sweat beneath the massive arms and the bad breath from the curling lips, when this heavy man was sitting on the edge of your desk, twisting his fingers into fists, awaiting the excuse to use them as hammers. And Martin had an uncomfortable feeling that what this thug had said about eliminating surplus employees might be true. Martin had never felt himself to be that important before, but perhaps what the man said was correct. Perhaps he did know things about the organization which they wouldn't want him to reveal. Things which those anonymous men might see as a death warrant for him.

Martin Carter licked his lips and said, 'Tell the boss that things aren't easy at the moment. That I have to tread carefully after the murder of this girl Clare Mills. There's been police all over the campus for days now, and—'

'Bump 'er off yourself, did you? That tart who died last week? Understand you being shit-scared if you—'

'No! No, of course I didn't!' Martin could hear the panic rising towards a scream in his own voice. He'd got by with the police, even the senior ones who were directing the investigation. And now here was this thug accusing him of killing Clare! 'All I'm saying is that we have to go carefully. I really feel that you must tell the boss that at this moment he must trust my judgement about the local situation.'

' "Trust my judgement about the local situation".' This time the big man was able to repeat the phrase, delivering it sneeringly in a ridiculous, high-pitched voice. 'I'm not here to run messages for you, wimp! I'm here to tell you the boss isn't pleased. That you'd better improve your performance, or it will be the worse for you.' He leaned towards Martin, was encouraged when the slim frame instinctively flinched away from his belligerence.

The big man eased himself off the edge of the desk, reached out and grabbed a handful of shirt and tie, enjoying the tightening of the strip of fabric around the thin neck beneath the terrified face, looking straight into the bulging eyes behind the glasses. 'You'd better listen, Carter, and listen well. The boss ain't pleased, and that ain't good for you. I wouldn't like to be in your shoes, not one bit I wouldn't.' He looked down at the sandals Carter was wearing and sniggered, as if recognizing how inadequate such footwear was to protect this cowering victim from the situation he was in now. 'You got to increase your turnover, and increase it damned quick, see?'

He gave the man a final shake, then flung him backwards with a contemptuous gesture, so that Martin staggered a little and then sat down heavily and involuntarily in the chair beside the desk. The man gave him a final leer of contempt and then was gone, slamming the door behind him as his derisive farewell to this strange and feeble academic world.

Martin Carter loosened his tie and straightened his shirt, trying desperately to readdress himself towards the world of research and the student who would be coming to him for guidance any second now. He looked out on the calm, sunlit world of the campus beyond his window, with its carefree students strolling around and its dedication to the pursuit of knowledge.

It seemed a totally different world from the squalid and devious one in which he had involved himself, the world of dubious money and shady deals and terrifying enforcers, like the man who had so lately sat upon the edge of his desk and threatened him. Yet he knew that those two worlds were connected, that he had thought that he could straddle them and make easy money. It had been an illusion, but it was too late for him now to retreat and extricate himself.

For the hundredth time in the last few days, Martin Carter wished that he had never met the man who had sent this thug to frighten him. He needed something to calm his nerves now, even though he was trying to cut down. He slid open the bottom drawer of his desk and felt for the tablet of cocaine.

Sixteen

On this breathless Monday afternoon, Superintendent Lambert's room was one of the quieter places in Oldford police station. It was at the end of the building, with a window looking out over the new estates at the edge of the compact town to the country beyond it.

He had the window open on such a sweltering day, and the sounds of children in a school playground drifted up to them, an innocent, inappropriate accompaniment to murder. With the rest of the team checking leads in various parts of Gloucestershire and Herefordshire, DI Rushton and DS Hook met with the chief to digest the latest findings and pick each other's brains.

Chris Rushton had been exploring the avenues suggested by the call register on the dead woman's mobile phone. He was well aware of Lambert's insistence that they must concentrate always upon facts rather than speculation: the chief acknowledged freely that he could be a positive Gradgrind when it came to the assembling of facts. DI Rushton wasn't quite sure who Gradgrind was – someone out of Dickens, he'd been told – but he had got the message that you needed solid evidence to underpin any suggestions you might make.

'There are still a couple of people to be questioned about the call register, but I thought you'd want to see them yourself, John.' Rushton forced himself to use the forename which Lambert insisted upon, even though 'Sir' or 'Guv' would have come much more easily to him.

Lambert nodded. 'We saw Judith Hudson this morning. She didn't seem at all put out when we confronted her with a call she hadn't admitted to earlier. She claimed she was trying to persuade Clare to come home and see her, to re-establish some sort of relationship with her daughter.'

'And did you believe that?'

Lambert shrugged and looked at Hook, who was still shaken by the cold detachment of the woman they had recently left, who might from her attitude have lost a distant cousin rather than her only daughter. Bert said, 'Who knows what to believe with that woman? I've met her four times now, and I'm no nearer to decoding what makes her tick. She seems determined to set herself up as a possible suspect for the murder of her own daughter. I can't decide whether she's totally unbalanced, or very clever and having a quiet laugh at us when we've gone.'

Lambert nodded his agreement. 'We meet a lot of odd people in CID work, but I don't think I've ever met the mother of a murder victim who's odd in quite this way. Judith Hudson is either genuinely unbalanced or a consummate actress. I'm inclined to think the former. Which of course makes her more rather than less likely to have killed Clare Mills. There might be a diminished responsibility plea if it ever came to court, but that wouldn't make her less of a killer.'

Rushton nodded, trying to absorb this account of a woman he had never met. 'And what about her husband?'

'Roy Hudson's almost as much of an enigma as his wife, but in a different way. He's much more aware of the effects of the things he does and the things he says, but he's consciously keeping us at arm's length. He hasn't given us more than the sketchiest outline of his relationship with Clare Mills. I'm sure there's more to be learned about Mr Hudson, but I'm equally sure that he won't give it up easily.'

'He was trying to get hold of Clare in the days before she died. His name and number are listed under "Missed Calls" on her mobile register on both the Thursday and the Friday before her death. The ones from Roy Hudson are in fact the only missed calls on that register.'

'Which raises the possibility that Clare might have been refusing to take them, once she realized who the caller was. As she was available for all the other calls, that's quite likely.' Lambert watched Hook making a preparatory note in his round, clear hand before he said grimly, 'We'll need to have an account from the elusive Mr Hudson of what he intended to say in those calls.'

Rushton nodded, trying to conceal his impatience to get on to the one remaining relative of the dead woman. 'I went out to see Ian Walker yesterday afternoon, as we agreed. A thoroughly nasty piece of work.'

Lambert and Hook grimaced their agreement and the superintendent said, 'Ex-husbands are almost always in the frame, in a case like this. And Ian Walker seems determined to leave himself right there. He's an unsavoury character all right. But has he the guts to be a murderer?'

Rushton said firmly, 'I think so. He tried to arrange a meeting with her on the Saturday night when she died. He says that he never saw her, that she refused to meet him. But I think that he met her and killed her. Perhaps he didn't mean to. Perhaps they had some sort of argument and he lost his temper. Perhaps he demanded money and she couldn't or wouldn't give it to him. Perhaps she threw her lesbian liaison with Sara Green into his face. But I believe he met her and strangled her on that night, before dumping the body in the Severn.'

'But he denied that?'

'Of course he did. Said he was out drinking with his mates, the way he does most Saturdays. So far, we haven't found anyone to confirm that.' Rushton tried not to sound too satisfied as he reported this.

'Have we any idea yet where the body was put into the river?'

'No. And we may never find that out, unless we eventually get a confession. The team has looked at various possible places around Gloucester, but there are far too many possibilities. And if the corpse was dumped before the weather broke, the ground was bone hard at the end of a dry spell, so it's unlikely there'd be any footprints. And of course the thunder rain on that Saturday night probably removed even any vestigial traces.'

'So what else did you get out of our sheep-badger?' Lambert knew his inspector well enough by this time to deduce from his scarcely suppressed excitement that there was more to come.

'He told you and Bert that he didn't have a vehicle. In fact, he does. A battered Ford Fiesta van. Grimy white with rust trimmings.' This time Chris could not disguise his satisfaction. The chief had been deceived; his vigilant inspector had established the true situation.

'Which you plainly think he used to transport Clare Mills's body to the banks of the Severn on that Saturday night.'

'I do. But I recognize that we shall have to prove it.' Rushton tried to temper his smugness with realism.

'Did you inspect the interior of this van?'

'I did. It positively stank of carbolic. It had been very thoroughly cleaned out.'

'When?'

'Last Thursday, by Walker's own account. Five days after it was used to transport the body of Clare Mills to the river.'

'Five days after you think it was used for that purpose. Because I don't suppose Ian Walker has admitted any such thing.'

'No, of course he hasn't. Says he uses the van to transport his sheep. Says he regularly cleans it out, so that diseases won't be passed around among his flock. That's crap, in my view. I don't believe he regularly cleans the van at all. He cleaned it, probably much earlier than last Thursday, because he thought forensic might come looking at it.' DI Rushton was trying unsuccessfully not to sound prickly in the face of what he saw as Lambert's scepticism.

'Did you collect the brushes he used for the forensic boys?'

'No. He claims he borrowed stiff bushes from the abattoir, that they'll have been used there for lots of other purposes since. He also says that he dried out the interior with old rags, which had been conveniently removed by the refuse collectors by the time I got there. I certainly couldn't see any sign of cleaning implements in the caravan where he lives. The boys and girls from the lab are having a look at the white van this afternoon, but I haven't any great hopes that they'll find anything useful. I think Walker's done too thorough a job for that.'

Hook said quietly, 'Denis Pimbury's an interesting possibility.'

'The man you think is probably an illegal immigrant.' Rushton, clearly reluctant to relinquish the discussion of Ian Walker, flicked up Pimbury's file on his laptop.

'He obviously had some kind of relationship with Clare Mills. Perhaps a much closer one than he is admitting to at the moment.' Bert Hook, the Barnardo's boy who had rather warmed to the hard-working man in the strawberry fields of an alien country, was determined to be objective about him.

Lambert smiled. 'He says she was helping him with the language. That it was a non-sexual relationship between the two of them. We haven't found anyone else who can confirm or deny that. It's one of those instances where only the dead girl could give us the true picture.'

Rushton frowned. 'I thought we'd accepted that the girl was a lesbian.'

Lambert smiled. 'It's touching to meet such naivety in an experienced officer, Chris. Clare Mills could easily have been bisexual. She'd been married, however much we're told that it was a mistake, and Martin Carter claims that he thought he was in with a chance of establishing a relationship with her. We only have Sara Green's assertion that Clare was perfectly happy with a same-sex pairing.'

Bert Hook said, 'The girl's sexual orientation is emerging as very important. We all know sexual jealousy is a prime cause of sudden, unpremeditated violence. So this death may well be one that was completely unplanned. Sexual rejection might have prompted any one of Denis Pimbury, Martin Carter or Sara Green into a red mist of anger. And the sheep-badger, Ian Walker, talks as if he no longer cared for his ex-wife, but we only have his word for that.'

Lambert said, 'I'm quite sure we need to know more about the people who worked in the university. I'm not convinced that there wasn't more between Martin Carter and the dead girl than he's so far admitted. And because the affair between Sara Green and Clare was kept secret, no one has been able to confirm or deny whether it was as serious and long-term as Sara claims it was.'

Rushton said, 'Both of those two were in contact by phone with Clare in the days before her death. Clare made two calls to Sara Green: they're listed under the "Dialled Numbers" in the memory. Martin Carter is among the "Received Calls", so it was he who took the initiative and phoned her.'

114

'Thanks, Chris. Bert and I will be speaking to both of them in the next day or so.'

At that moment the phone shrilled suddenly on Lambert's desk.

The switchboard constable was apologetic. 'I know you said you weren't to be disturbed until four, sir. But Dr Cocker from the forensic laboratory is on the line. He says it's very urgent, and he wants to speak to you.'

'Put him through.'

All of them knew that this must be important. Inspector and sergeant, two very different men who were united now by their eagerness for new information, watched Lambert's lined grey face, searching it for any clue as to the content of the message he was receiving.

He paused for a second or two after he had put down the phone, not to heighten the tension, but to digest the import of what he had heard. 'It's those hairs we sent them from the body. The ones we thought wouldn't produce anything useful. They aren't human at all. They're sheep hairs. Cocker says it looks as if the body has rested on a surface where sheep had been carried.'

There was that moment of tremulous, silent excitement which always comes to CID men when there is a breakthrough in an investigation. Then John Lambert said to Rushton, 'It looks as if you were right about Ian Walker, Chris.'

Seventeen

The move to arrest Ian Walker was carefully organized. Lambert wanted to confront the man himself. The evidence was strong, but still circumstantial. The whole of CID might be privately convinced that the body of Clare Mills had been transported to the Severn in the back of the sheep-badger's van, but some sort of confession when Lambert and Hook had confronted and cautioned Walker would still be useful.

Two other cars with uniformed officers in them drove quietly behind Lambert's old Vauxhall Senator into the Forest of Dean as the long summer's day stretched towards its close. Walker was a man capable of violence, likely to become desperate when confronted with the reality of arrest. They would let him see that resistance to arrest was useless, that he had much better come quietly and wait to see what a lawyer could do for him at the station.

There was not a breath of wind as the sun disappeared in a blaze of fire beyond the western hills. The little convoy of cars moved past a lake which shone still as a mirror beneath the deepening blue of the sky. The newly burgeoned foliage on the Forest trees hung heavy and green in the heat. The sheep grazed on the common as if they had been carefully and formally distributed there to be part of a landscape painting.

A mission to arrest a murderer seemed totally out of place here.

There was as little sign of movement around the shabby caravan where Walker lived as there was in the houses below it. The scene seemed to be hanging around them as they arrived at the place, waiting for them to stir it into movement. Lambert motioned to the police cars behind him to stop whilst they were still hidden from the caravan by the houses on the road. Then he eased the big Vauxhall almost silently over the last few yards

116

to the spot where he planned to park, on the flat patch of grass twenty yards from the road. Beside the small, shabby white van which had taken Clare Mills on her last journey to the Severn.

He stood for a moment beside the rear wheels of the van. Rushton was right about the carbolic and the way the man had used disinfectant to wipe away the evidence of what had been carried. They could smell it clearly enough in the still, warm air, even with the back doors of the van shut.

There was still no movement from the caravan, which was now no more than eighty yards away from them. As he and Hook moved slowly up the gentle slope, John Lambert found himself willing their quarry to come through the door of his decrepit residence and meet them. An arrest in the open air suddenly seemed more attractive than one within the cramped metal confines of the caravan, where he would scarcely be able to stand upright.

They called Walker's name through the door, received no answer, tried it and found it open. Climbing stiffly up the steps and dipping his head to get through the door, Lambert half expected to be assaulted as he entered the caravan, so that he thrust his arms out in front of him and called a warning through the aperture, anticipating an invisible assailant.

There was no hostile presence within. A solitary fly, hovering above a half-open packet of sliced bread on the side of the sink, was the only movement in the oppressive heat of the caravan's interior. Yet the door had been unlocked, and the single window at the end of the battered residence was propped drunkenly open, stretched as wide as it would stretch by the use of a cardboard box.

The occupant could surely not be far away.

Lambert resisted the temptation to make an unofficial search of the few drawers and cupboards in these cramped living quarters, where any evidence of the occupant's guilt could surely not be concealed for long. There would be ample time for that when they had the man under arrest.

'He can't be far away,' he said unnecessarily to Bert Hook as he levered himself back down the steps and into the last of the evening light.

'I expect he'll be back in a few minutes,' said Hook, feeling his comment equally fatuous.

117

'It's almost as if he knew that we were coming here for him tonight,' said Lambert, looking back towards the road and the car he had left below him.

They were superfluous comments between men who did not normally waste words. But it was so still in that quiet place that each of them felt a need for speech, a desire for some sound to break the silence, which seemed suddenly too profound, as if the deepening of the warm twilight was making the quiet ominous rather than merely peaceful.

They kept close together as they moved up the slope and beneath the deepening shadows of the tall oaks, not from any sense of danger, but from some unvoiced sense of the smallness of humanity beneath these mighty sentinels, which had presided over this scene for two centuries and more.

Everything below them they could see. Even the sheep were lying quiet now, as if they too recognized the need to be part of the prevailing silence. Lambert turned upwards, away from the road and the caravan, not because he knew that that was where his quarry had gone, but because it seemed the only possible place where anyone might conceal himself.

The sun had dropped behind the ridge above them half an hour and more ago, and with its going the last of the birds had ceased to sing. The hush beneath the trees seemed tangible, like a living, waiting thing. They exchanged a few nervous, meaningless words as they moved, speculating on where Walker might be, reassuring each other with the sound of human voices in the brooding quiet.

It was beneath the tallest of the oaks that they came upon him.

He was lying on his back, with his right arm and leg twisted unnaturally beneath him. The white of an open eye glinted crazily at them, catching the very last of the light from the west. A single eye only, for more than half of the head which had contained it had been blown away.

A dark pool and then an awful splattering of grey and red, with large blue flies moving unhurriedly across it, stained the grass beyond the corpse. The shotgun had fallen across the left ankle, its muzzle pointing crazily at the men who were moving in upon the scene.

There would be no arrest of Ian Walker.

Eighteen

It was a quiet spot where Ian Walker had died, but by nine o'clock on Tuesday morning the news of his sensational death was passing quickly around the towns and villages of the Forest of Dean.

The rough square of the scene of the crime, defined by the blue-and-white-plastic ribbon which the police used to cordon it off, was visible from the road below the caravan. Even those commuters using this winding route to make maximum speed on their journeys to work in Gloucester and Cheltenham and Chepstow could not fail to notice the police cars parked by the road.

In Coleford and in Cinderford, the old mining towns of the Forest, people nodded their heads sagely in the shops and public houses, and reflected upon the sensational wickedness of the modern world. Sheep-badgers were not highly regarded residents in the Forest of Dean. The violence which this man had perpetrated was certainly extreme, but no more than what you might expect from one of those people.

The conclusion of this sorry saga with a suicide was shocking, but there was a certain logic about it. There was even an agreement among those discussing the local melodrama that there was justice in this latest death. Ian Walker had killed that poor woman in Gloucester who had made the unfortunate mistake of marrying him and divorcing him. It was a mercy really that the man had at least had the good sense to acknowledge his guilt and kill himself. By his final action, he had saved the public coffers from an expensive trial and then an even more expensive incarceration of the poor woman's killer.

In the CID section at Oldford police station, the satisfaction was more muted. No one liked to miss an arrest, and there

119

would be questions asked from outside the police service about why they had not got to Walker before he could kill himself.

Nevertheless, Detective Inspector Rushton could not disguise a sense of achievement. He had spotted Clare Mills's killer, from the moment when he had journeyed into the forest and confronted her ex-husband. He felt now that he had known who the murderer was from the moment when he had insisted on throwing open the back doors of that white van and revealing its spotless interior. Subsequent events had only illustrated the accuracy of his insight.

And Ian Walker, too, must have known from that moment that his game was up. He had pretended to be confident, even truculent, because his van had been cleaned out so thoroughly, but he must have known in his heart of hearts that the hunt was over, from the moment when Chris demanded that he open up his van for inspection.

It was a pity that they hadn't got their man and completed the process. If John Lambert had moved more quickly when Chris had offered him the capture, they might have had Walker under lock and key at this moment. Even after forensic had confirmed the presence of sheep hairs upon the clothing of the dead woman, the chief had wasted precious hours in setting up the back-up for an arrest before moving in on Walker's caravan.

It was true, Chris allowed reluctantly, that Ian Walker had scarcely seemed the suicidal type. And Lambert had pointed out the absence of any suicide note in the caravan. That was surely sour grapes: the superintendent would have to admit eventually that Chris had been right all along about the identity of Clare Mills's killer.

Apparently the pathologist hadn't said much at that lonely spot beneath the oaks of the Forest of Dean. He'd taken a few measurements, a rectal temperature from the corpse, let the police photographer shoot off a round of film, and had the body removed to the forensic laboratory at Chepstow for a full post-mortem.

The Scenes of Crime team had found the cartridge from the shotgun and identified the weapon. It belonged to Ian Walker and was kept in his caravan. No doubt it hadn't been stored as securely as it was supposed to be nowadays, but that would have been no more than par for the course with a man like Walker. There was a certain symmetry about the way he had arranged his death and the conclusion of the story. Good riddance, the public would say, and like most policemen Chris Rushton couldn't help nodding a silent agreement with them.

It was almost midday when the news came in. What John Lambert had felt from the moment when he had stood over the shattered body was confirmed by a preliminary call from the forensic laboratory. The nature of the wound and the position of the shotgun confirmed that Ian Walker hadn't killed himself.

They had a second murder on their hands.

They saw Roy Hudson at home this time. He had seemed strangely anxious to be seen separately from his wife, when most couples would have been looking to give each other mutual support. But Hook had announced firmly that they were coming to see him at his house, that no doubt in view of the circumstances Mr Hudson would not wish senior CID men to meet him again at his place of business, and thus set the tongues wagging anew among his employees.

When Lambert and Hook arrived at nine o'clock as arranged, Hudson had already reversed the big Mercedes out of the garage and left it prominently on the drive, signifying that he was a busy man who was cooperating with them but could scarcely afford the time to do so. He carried this brisk-ness into his curt greeting and his enquiry as to the nature of their business.

'Ian Walker,' said Lambert, equally laconically.

'That waster.' Hudson sighed theatrically. 'What's he been up to now?'

'He was brutally murdered last night.'

'Good heavens!'

Was the expression a little too conventional, the surprise a little too theatrical? Lambert had been watching his man closely, trying to see whether the information was genuinely news to him. He could not be sure. Hudson seemed perfectly confident of himself, depressingly so from the point of view of his visitors. 'Detective Sergeant Hook and I went out to his caravan last night to question him further in connection with the death of Clare Mills. We found that he had been killed with his own shotgun. The first estimate is that he died at around nine o'clock.'

'I know that shotgun. A well-worn double bore. But he kept it in good condition. Used to get himself a few illegal pheasants with it, during the winter. You're sure that he didn't despatch himself with it?'

'Quite sure.'

'Because I was coming round to the view that it was probably him that murdered Clare. He might have killed himself in a fit of remorse.'

Lambert didn't say that a senior police officer had offered exactly the same view. 'He may have killed Clare. That seems unlikely, in view of what's happened to him. Unless of course you take the view that this is a revenge killing. That someone who knows that Walker killed Clare took the law into his own hands and turned a shotgun on him.'

'You sound as if you don't buy that theory.' Hudson was curiously relaxed, as if determined to treat this as some intellectual puzzle in which he had no direct involvement.

Lambert found himself resenting the man's air of superiority, his confidence, even his tan and the neatly styled brown hair above the deep-set, mocking eyes. He said slowly, 'I don't accept the revenge theory. Anyone who knew that Ian Walker had killed Clare Mills had only to bring the information to us to have him arrested. Far more sensible than risking a life sentence for a revenge murder.'

'So who killed Walker?' Hudson was almost truculent now, knowing that if they knew the answer to that there would have been an arrest by now.

'Where were you last night, Mr Hudson?'

Hudson smiled, showing how unshaken he was by the sudden question. 'You surely can't believe that I—'

'You have no clear alibi for the time when your stepdaughter was killed. Can you account for your movements last night, at the time of this second murder?'

Roy Hudson paused, making even the silence a sort of insolence. 'I suppose if I object to this sort of questioning, I shall be told that this is merely routine, that you are just completing the formalities of eliminating me from your list of suspects.'

'You may object to my questioning if you think it out of order. There are channels of complaint which are well established. In the meantime, I require an answer.' For the first time since they had entered the house, Lambert found that he was enjoying the exchange. Yet he always told his juniors that they must not get involved, that they must eliminate personal feelings from any interrogations they conducted. He must be getting old, to let this suave businessman get under his skin like this. 'Where were you last night, Mr Hudson?'

'I was here. At home with my wife. Enjoying a quiet domestic evening at home. Mrs Hudson will confirm this, if you find that necessary.'

'I see.'

'Fact, Superintendent. Can't alter that.' The deep-set eyes seemed to mock his questioner as he gazed steadily at him.

'Indeed you can't. It's another fact that criminals offer their wives to provide a convenient alibi whenever they can provide no other witness to their whereabouts. Of course, in a small minority of cases, the information is perfectly genuine, whatever the police suspect.'

'And this is one such case. I think that if I had killed Ian Walker, I should have taken care to provide myself with a better alibi. Or perhaps I should say with an alibi which would be more acceptable to suspicious policemen.'

'Indeed? You could, of course, have employed someone else to kill him for you. That would have been the safest method of all.'

'It would have brought someone else into the affair, though, wouldn't it? Someone who would have had a hold over me for ever afterwards.' Hudson wrinkled his well-tanned forehead, considering the notion. 'If I were going in for such things, I don't think I should like that.'

'You would probably have employed a contract killer to do the job. Swift, efficient and anonymous. A man for whom silence is part of his trade, who takes his payment for a killing and moves on.'

'How intriguing. And how logical. I'm glad to hear that you are speaking quite hypothetically.' Roy Hudson allowed himself a small, mirthless grin, in recognition of a tiny point scored.

'Who do you think killed your stepdaughter?'

'I've no idea. Ian Walker, I should have thought, as I said a few minutes ago. But then I'm not privy to your investigations and what your extensive and expensive team have discovered, am I?'

'And who do you think shot Mr Walker last night?'

'This time I'm happy to say that I've no idea. Knowing a little of that man and the circles in which he moved, I should think there would be a wide range of suspects.'

Lambert reflected as they drove away that Roy Hudson certainly knew more than he was telling them. And if that was true, he'd moved from being blandly unhelpful to being positively obstructive. And once again he had met them without his wife at his side.

Back at Oldford police station, DI Rushton was filing a new set of information about this second murder into his computer. Deciding that the deaths were almost certainly related, he enjoyed setting up an elaborate system of cross-referencing between the two crimes. When he was able to show some obscure but significant connection among the people involved in the investigations, that would show that old dinosaur Lambert the benefits of modern technology.

He was disappointed with the early information coming in from the routine enquiries. A call from the pathology laboratory confirmed that Ian Walker had probably died some forty to eighty minutes before Lambert and Hook had found the corpse. That was hardly news, since Bert Hook had already told him that the body was still warm when they discovered it. Some time around nine o'clock, then. Probably just after sundown on that long summer day.

But there were as yet no reports of cars seen parked in the area or leaving it hurriedly at that time. Chris had hoped that enquiries made in the region by the uniformed officers would have come up with a vehicle already familiar to them, perhaps belonging to one of the people involved in the Clare Mills enquiry. He would have liked to be able to wave a registration number triumphantly in the face of the chief when he came back from seeing the dead woman's stepfather.

The inspector worked away quietly, recording the information, most of it negative, which was now coming in rapidly from the house-to-house and other enquiries being made around the spot where Ian Walker had died in the Forest of Dean. Chris still clung to his notion that the sheep-badger had killed his former wife Clare Mills, but he was having to accept that his death wasn't a suicide, in view of what forensic said about the death-wound and the position of the shotgun.

The man who came to the desk in the early afternoon would normally have had to deliver his thoughts to the station sergeant, but when he said he wanted to speak to the man in charge of the Clare Mills murder investigation, he was shown through to DI Rushton immediately. Murder opens many doors.

He was a man in his early fifties, Chris reckoned, tall and lean, with his hair cut short and a tan which suggested he worked abroad, perhaps in Africa. Rushton was surprised to find him speaking with a local accent, more surprised to find that he was a resident of South Canterbury, in New Zealand.

He was even more surprised when the man announced that he was the father of Clare Mills.

Nineteen

Denis Pimbury had grown used to his new name. It had seemed a strange and difficult name when he had decided to adopt it. Now other people seemed to have accepted it, and it sat more happily on his sinewy shoulders than he would ever have expected.

Everyone at work knew him now as Denis, and if they weren't even aware of his surname, he couldn't see how that mattered. He felt more at home on the farm with each passing day. He was on the official payroll now, and he gave value for money. That was the best way of bedding yourself into this new life, which was so very different from what he had known in Croatia. Even his employer seemed to trust him now to get on with the job without supervision. As he worked his way along the long, back-breaking rows of strawberries, the farmer appeared less often at his shoulder. There had even been a suggestion from his employer yesterday that Denis Pimbury would be here many months ahead, that he might be given responsibility for other, more temporary, workers.

It was a mark of his new status that he was taking an official day off. Mr Martin had insisted upon it, now that he was an official employee. Because Denis didn't mind working at weekends, enjoyed it indeed, he was taking his day off on a Tuesday. And much to his surprise, he was rather enjoying it.

He had been here many times before, but only during the hours of darkness. Wandering round the familiar streets of Gloucester when everyone else was at work was a new experience for him. He was able to enjoy the sun of a balmy afternoon without the grinding toil which characterized most of his days.

For the first time since he had slipped into this strange,

exciting new country, Denis felt relaxed, very nearly at ease with himself and the world around him.

There had been brief half-hours of happiness when Clare had been alive, snatched interludes when she had managed to convince him that all would be well for him. But he had known even at the time that they were transitory, that once he was out of her presence he would become a creature of the underworld again, a man watching his back and steering clear of any official recognition.

That had all changed with his acquisition of the passport, with his addition to the official workforce at the farm, and with the recognition of Denis Pimbury as a person.

He wandered unhurriedly round the shops, making himself move deliberately slowly, marvelling at the richness and diversity of the merchandise available in this prosperous world. It added to his pleasure that these were the streets where once he had moved only by night, slinking along with an eye always on what was happening behind him. For the first time in many months, he thrust his hands into the pockets of his trousers and strolled deliberately along, an Englishman at ease in his ancient city.

In the pedestrian precinct, he stopped for a moment to watch the buskers, standing with a woman police officer at his elbow, making that a test of his nerve in his new-found security. Then he stood looking at the plants outside a gardening shop, pretending that he had borders to fill and a house to maintain. One day, perhaps . . .

It was all an illusion, of course. A pleasant illusion, but an illusion nonetheless. He was glad that he had proved himself with the policewoman, that he was able to move at leisure among the shops like this. But he was not here simply for pleasure: he had something to do, a mission to complete. It was a routine transaction, he told himself, a thing which would excite no attention among the huge and unheeding public around him. Yet all his assurances to himself did not succeed in stopping the thumping of Denis Pimbury's heart.

The shop was hidden away from the main thoroughfares, down one of the narrow old streets on the cathedral side of the town. It looked from the end of the alley like an ordinary house, sandwiched as it was between other narrow stone cottages which had ceased to trade as shops. Only the three brass balls, so tight against the lintel above its door as to seem almost an apology, denoted the nature of the business transacted here.

There were such places all over the world, Denis told himself firmly. They provided a necessary service, nothing more and nothing less. There had even been such places in his native country. But he had never before set foot inside one of them. The man serving him must not get to know that.

It was not a man but a woman. He almost turned round and left the shop when she came out through the beaded curtain from the rear and stood expectantly at the counter. But retreat would invite suspicion, and that was the thing Denis had learned to fear most of all. And why shouldn't he deal with a woman, after all? This was just a straightforward commercial transaction, the way in which this place made its living. He couldn't explain that he had expected not a woman scarcely older than himself but a hunched and bespectacled old Jew, probably wheezing and certainly grasping: that would merely show his prejudice in all its raw ugliness.

The woman watched the man with the sallow face and the black, hunted eyes as he stood just inside the door. Such diffidence was familiar to her; it came into this tiny shop in a variety of guises. Sometimes it brought with it surprising things. She said as brightly as she could, 'How may we be of help, sir?'

He sprang forward, reaching the narrow counter too quickly, almost losing his balance and falling with the abruptness of his movement. 'I want to sell these.'

The ring and the brooch tumbled from the tissue paper onto the glass tray in front of him, tinkling unnaturally loud in that quiet place. Away from the old Georgian window at the front of the shop, there was little natural light; the stones gleamed softly in the semi-darkness, blinking like an accusation at him.

She said coolly, 'How did you come by these, sir?' Then, when he did not immediately reply, she added more softly, 'We have to ask, sir. It is required of us by the authorities. There is a lot of stolen jewellery around, you see.'

'They were my mother's.' Denis found it hard to deliver the phrases he had planned. He had meant to give a fuller explanation, but he found that the simple terse statement was all he could make himself deliver.

It was a familiar enough explanation. The woman at the counter did not give much heed to it. She had asked the question; the answer was not particularly important to her. She flicked on a small, fierce white light and shone it down onto the two pieces whilst she looked at them through her eyeglass. A single diamond in the ring, emeralds in the brooch. Good quality, both of them.

She said, 'I'll need to consult with my colleague. He's more of an expert than I am on jewellery.'

Denis gave her the briefest of nods, not trusting himself to speak. He was wishing now that he had not come here: it smelt dangerous, and he still had a sharp nose for danger. But he needed the money, after what had happened last night. Money allowed you options.

She picked up the tray and took it back with her through the beaded curtain. She shouldn't really have done that: the proper procedure was to bring any expertise forward to the counter, not remove the goods from the sight of the owner. Once the goods were out of sight, you could do switches, swindle the customer by substituting worthless trinkets and swearing that they were what he had offered to you for valuation. But this man was a foreigner: she knew that from the few words he had uttered. More importantly, he was much too desperate to insist upon the niceties of the trade.

Denis listened to a whispered exchange; he had no chance of distinguishing any of the words. It seemed to him to go on for a long time, though in fact it took no more than a minute and a half. He resisted the urge to turn and flee, to leave his treasures and to indulge the simple, overwhelming instinct to escape.

The woman came back to the counter. 'It's a nice brooch: antique. There's not as much demand for emeralds as there was a few years ago, but it's attractive enough. And the diamond in the ring is—'

'How much?'

She could smell the staleness of the man's breath, smell the desperation upon him. She was no more than thirty, but because of her trade she had smelt that desperation hundreds of times before. 'Five hundred, for the two of them.'

They were worth much more, but she had divined correctly that he wasn't in the frame of mind to bargain. He looked at her with those wild dark eyes beneath the lank black hair, and she moved her foot nearer to the alarm bell on the floor, fearing for a moment that he might physically attack her. She realized in that instant that he knew that she had undervalued the pieces, that he was more intelligent than she had taken him for.

But all he said was, 'All right. I need cash, please.' The accent he had struggled to lose returned now when he least wanted it, harsh and guttural with his tension.

She smiled at his naivety. 'We don't do cash, I'm afraid. I'll give you a cheque. It's the normal terms of the trade. You'll find that—'

'I need cash. I do not sell if it is not cash.' His teeth flashed white in the half-light. In his desperation, he looked like a hungry jackal.

She wondered whether to put all the arguments to him, to point out that it wasn't safe these days to carry large amounts of cash, especially in a pawnshop. But he looked very determined. And at five hundred, the items were a steal. She said, 'Wait a moment, please,' and went back through the curtain, taking the brooch and the ring with her again. He surely wouldn't take flight without his booty.

She came back within thirty seconds this time, and said, 'The owner is prepared to make an exception for you. You are very lucky. We'll need your name, of course.' Then she counted out five hundred pounds for him in twenty-pound notes and explained carefully that he was depositing the items with them for a set period, that he could redeem them for the standard charge by producing the ticket she was giving him at any time during that period, that the shop would be entitled to sell the goods for whatever they would realize if he did not redeem them in the time allowed.

He scarcely heard the terms of the transaction. His eyes never left the notes as they passed beneath her practised, manicured fingers. It was only a supreme effort of self-control which prevented him from snatching the money from beneath her professionally smiling face.

That did not surprise the woman. She was used to people

not heeding the terms of business. But she felt legally bound to deliver them, even though they were outlined in small print on the back of the pawn ticket. Not many people listened, and even fewer came back to redeem things, these days.

When he had gone, she made the phone call she had always planned. You had to keep on the right side of the law, in this business.

'It's good of you to come in here so promptly, Mr Mills. I'm very sorry it has to be in these circumstances,' said Lambert. His real thought was that it was a relief to have someone in this baffling case who actually seemed anxious to help them, but he could hardly say that.

'I landed at Heathrow this morning and drove straight down here in a hire car. It seemed the least I could do for Clare.'

'Since you've taken the trouble to come from the other side of the world to offer us your thoughts, I feel I owe it to you to be completely honest. I have to tell you that we'll be grateful for any help you can give us.'

The big tanned figure in the chair opposite him nodded. 'You're not getting much help from the immediate family.' It was more a statement of fact than a question.

Lambert raised his eyebrows. 'You expected that?'

Ken Mills frowned. 'I suppose I did, for a variety of reasons. That's why I'm here. The New Zealand police said they'd relay whatever I had to say to you, but I felt I wanted to be personally involved in this. I owe it to Clare to see that whoever did this to her is brought to justice.'

Beneath his surface health, he was taut with anxiety. No doubt it owed something to the long flight and the time change, but both John Lambert and Bert Hook thought that there was something more than that, that he wanted to deliver himself of something which was troubling him. Lambert said quietly, 'You had better tell us why you think that those who were closest to your daughter are not likely to be very helpful to us.'

He sighed. 'I've had hours to think about it on the plane. The words came to me easily, when I was just sitting and thinking on my own. Now that I'm here, I feel much more confused.'

'Your daughter is dead, Mr Mills, and I've just virtually admitted to you that ten days later, we aren't even close to an arrest. This is no time for being squeamish about voicing your thoughts. We shall certainly respect any confidences you offer to us.'

'All right. Let's begin with the easy one. That wretched husband of Clare's. Ex-husband, I suppose I should say. The sheep-badger, or whatever he calls himself now. I expect you've talked to him and formed your own impressions. He's no good, Superintendent. He was a disaster as a husband and from what I was able to gather from Clare he's been a disaster ever since.'

Lambert nodded at Hook, who said quietly, 'Ian Walker is dead, Mr Mills. He died last night.'

Ken Mills's brown eyes opened wide in horror. 'Strewth! Look, I didn't like the bloke, and I'm not back-tracking on that. But I'd no idea that—'

'He was murdered, Mr Mills. Killed beside his caravan with his own shotgun.'

Both CID men were watching their man intently. They had no idea of Mills's background, whether he was the kind of man who would have had the inclination and the knowledge to employ a contract killer, if he thought the man he had just confessed to hating had killed his daughter.

Mills's surprise at the news of this second death seemed complete and genuine. He seemed quite dazed as he said, 'And you think this second death is connected with my Clare's?'

Lambert said, 'We don't know that for certain, as yet. I should be very surprised if there wasn't any sort of connection.'

Mills stared unseeingly at Lambert's desk. This world of murderous intrigue and secret hates was as far removed from his new life in the wide spaces of New Zealand as it was possible to get. For a moment, he wondered why he was here. He wanted to throw off this tight Gloucester world of his youth and his failed first marriage, to stand up and storm out of this claustrophobic police station and into the open air.

Yet he owed it to his daughter to stay here, to do whatever he could to pin down her killer. He dragged his thoughts back to another of the people he had been directed to talk about and said dully, 'Roy Hudson. He didn't feel anything for Clare. Didn't want her in the house.'

There was a pause before Bert Hook looked up from the note he was making and said, 'How well do you know Roy Hudson, Mr Mills?'

Mills gave a short, mirthless laugh, which emerged as almost a bark. It was the first audible evidence of the strain he was feeling. 'You wouldn't expect me to be objective, would you? Not about the man who crept into my bed and took over my family.'

Hook smiled, trying to take the tension out of the air. 'I don't think we would anticipate a balanced view, certainly. Nevertheless, your thoughts would be interesting for us to hear.'

'I'm not as bitter as you might imagine. My marriage was finished long before Roy Hudson came along. If you want the truth, I think that at the time I was quite glad to have someone to take the responsibility for Judith off my hands. I still felt a duty towards her, you see.'

'But you weren't happy about Mr Hudson's relationship with your daughter.'

'No. I don't think he wanted to make a home for her.' He paused, looking out towards the park, hearing for the first time the shrill voices of the distant children through the open window of the superintendent's office. 'No doubt there were faults on both sides. Clare was an adolescent at the time, with everything that goes with that. And she was still very attached to me. She'd always been closer to me than to her mother.'

His voice cracked a little on that thought, and it seemed for a moment as if this tough outdoor man would dissolve into tears. Then he gathered himself together and spoke evenly. 'I felt Hudson wanted Clare out of the house. I only got Clare's side of things, of course – I was still in this country in the early years of Judith's remarriage. But I don't think Roy Hudson offered her much sympathy or understanding, or even tried to keep going any sort of relationship between Clare and her mother. Rightly or wrongly, I felt he was to blame for Clare's marriage to Ian Walker. Everyone from the outside could see that it was going to be a disaster, but I think she wanted more than anything to get out of the house and establish a new life for herself.'

'How well did Roy Hudson know Ian Walker?' Lambert slipped the question in as unobtrusively as he could. Mills had come round the world to talk about his daughter's death, but they had a second murder on their hands, a second network of relationships to establish and investigate.

'I don't know. I was still here for Clare's marriage to Walker, but I left for New Zealand a fortnight later. I've married again out there, quite unexpectedly. We're very happy.'

For a moment, they had a glimpse of his very different Antipodean world, of the effort it had taken him to turn back the clock and come here as a last duty to the dead daughter he had loved. Lambert said very quietly, 'Do you have any reason to think Roy Hudson might have killed Clare?'

'No. I can't pretend to like the bloke, and I think he could have been a better stepfather and friend to my daughter than he was. But that's very different from saying I think he killed her. I can't see any reason why he would do that.'

'Or why he should kill Ian Walker?'

'No.' He gave a sour smile. 'I said I didn't wish that man dead. But I can't grieve much for him. He made Clare's life a misery for a couple of years, and even after they were divorced he was trying to sponge off her. I recognize that you have to try to catch his killer, but I shan't be losing much sleep over his death. It's Clare's murderer I want you to arrest.'

'I can understand that, but as we've already indicated, it's highly probable that the same person killed both of them.'

Ken Mills looked at Lambert for a moment, weighing that notion. Then he nodded and said, 'You say "person". Does that mean that you think a woman might have killed Clare?'

'She was strangled before her body was put into the Severn: probably with a ligature. That means no great strength was necessary and it would have been perfectly possible for a woman to be our killer. And Ian Walker was killed with his own shotgun; again it is quite feasible that it was a woman who pulled the trigger.'

Mills nodded his acceptance of the logic of this, then said suddenly, 'I wanted to talk to you about Judith.'

'I wish you would. I don't mind admitting to you that your ex-wife is one of the enigmas of the case so far. Mrs Hudson is proving the strangest mother of a murder victim I have come across in a quarter of a century of murder investigations.'

Mills nodded, seemingly not at all surprised by this frank declaration. 'I struggled with that personality for fifteen years before I gave up on her. Clare has struggled with it throughout her life. I suppose it was even more difficult for a daughter than a husband. When Clare was a child, she simply didn't understand it. She saw other mothers continually demonstrating their affection for their children, when hers didn't seem to care for her. It must have been very hard.'

'Are you saying that there was a psychological basis for this situation?' Like almost all policemen, Lambert distrusted psychologists and psychiatrists, who seemed too often to provide the let-out for criminals whom it had taken many man-hours to outwit and arrest.

Ken Mills sighed. 'I'm saying I'm not certain how responsible she is for her own actions. I never was and never will be. It's the reason why our marriage broke up. Perhaps we should never have tried. I'd be interested to know what Roy Hudson thinks about his marriage, after a few years with her. You think this might have a bearing on Clare's death?'

Lambert smiled ruefully. 'I've no idea what's relevant and what isn't at the moment. We shan't know much more about that until we have a murderer under lock and key. That's always the case when we have no obvious suspect immediately after a murder. We have to gather every scrap of information we can and pool our knowledge. With luck and a little expertise, significant connections will emerge.' He wondered if he sounded as tired as he felt as he offered this familiar explanation.

Ken Mills decided that he liked this intelligent, rather intense man, who was so unlike any policeman he had previously met. He would trust him to find out who had killed Clare. He said, 'It's difficult to know where to begin with Judith. You've heard of autism?'

A grim smile, a quick glance at Bert Hook. 'We've heard of it, yes. Come up against it, sometimes. But we're strictly amateurs. You're saying that your ex-wife is autistic?'

Mills shook his head sharply from side to side in a flash of irritation at the oversimplification he had met so often over the years. 'As with every sort of psychological condition, there are infinite shades of affliction. At the time I married Judith, we hoped that she would be able to lead a normal life. Whatever that might be.'

He smiled bitterly at the treetops beyond the window and uncomplicated world outside. 'Autism derives from the Greek word for self. But that doesn't mean that autists are selfish. Their sense of self is almost as rudimentary as their sense of other people. Judith didn't put her desires in front of those of other people; she simply didn't understand that other people had desires.'

He spoke like one in a dream, voicing ideas which were once familiar, but which he thought he had long since put behind him. 'When autism was first identified in the nineteen-forties, it was described as "extreme aloneness". That still seems to me the simplest description of it.'

Bert Hook, struggling to relate these generalities to the woman who was a suspect in a murder investigation, said with a feeling of inadequacy, 'You think your wife is lonely?'

Mills smiled wearily at the familiar mistake. 'No. Alone, not lonely. She feels no need to make the kind of connections which help the rest of us to make sense of the world. Asperger's syndrome, the medics suggested. She's highly intelligent, but incapable of an unthinking, altruistic act. The kind of instinctive love and concern which would come naturally for most mothers. That made life very difficult for Clare.' Again that bitter smile, that unspoken recollection of past sufferings and frustrations.

'And difficult for you as well.' Hook was suddenly full of sympathy for this man struggling to bare his soul in the interests of his murdered child.

'I coped all right at first. We coped, I should say. Sex wasn't a problem. Many autists live through their senses. Judith sometimes seemed to exist in the here and now, to have no sense of past or future. But I was prepared for that; the diagnosis when she was twenty was that her severest problems might be over. Unfortunately, when she had a child, the problems really set in again. My wife didn't see herself as a member of a family, as a mother of a daughter who needed her affection. She didn't even understand what affection was.'

136

Bert Hook, struggling to relate all this to his own boisterous pubescent boys and their very sane and loving mother, Eleanor, said, 'This must have made your married life a struggle. It sounds as if you gave her every support you could.'

Mills carried on almost as if he had not heard Hook. 'Judith didn't seek comfort. She never turned to me or to anyone else near her for solace or support. Autists lack the instinct to do that.'

Lambert said, 'I'm sure this hasn't been easy for you. But it's very valuable for us. It helps us to see a woman and a situation more clearly, within this case. I'll be as frank with you as you've tried to be with us: Judith Hudson was baffling us by her non-involvement, by her failure to grieve for her daughter. I'm sure we understand her behaviour a lot better now.'

'Is she a suspect for either of these killings?'

'I can't comment on that.'

'Which means you haven't ruled her out.'

'We haven't been able to eliminate her from the enquiry yet. That's a bit of jargon. In this case, it means no more and no less than it says.'

Ken Mills was gazing past them into the middle distance outside the window again. He said slowly, 'There's an innocence about autistics. Everyone says that. There is also a lack of moral responsibility. They don't feel guilt and other emotions in the way ordinary people do.'

It was a sentence which kept coming back to John Lambert during the long hours of his evening at home. It was an accurate description of several murderers he had known in the past.

Twenty

Christine Lambert watched her husband secretly, glancing at his face only when she was sure that he was watching the television.

Cases took more out of him these days. There were times when she wished the Home Office hadn't allowed the chief constable's special request to have John's service extended. But she knew that he got his kicks from taking villains, and there were other times when she wondered what on earth he would do when he was suddenly deprived of the adrenaline which coursed through his veins when he fought serious crime. He liked his garden, but she couldn't see the roses which were the traditional policeman's retirement pastime being enough for John Lambert.

At least he didn't shut her out of his life nowadays. When he was a young inspector in CID, he had worked eighteen-hour days without her knowing when he was coming home, without ever letting her know his movements or his slightest thoughts on a particular case. Those were the days when she had almost walked out with her two young daughters and ended this marriage, which now seemed so solid to his younger colleagues.

She looked at the lined, intense face beneath the still plentiful but now grizzled hair, wondering what effect the strain he had never felt as a young man was having upon him now. Bert Hook assured her that John worked as hard as ever and was as effective as he had always been in their CID work. But good old Bert (who was in fact five years younger than John) was biased, and she wasn't in touch with any other of her husband's colleagues, these days.

She did not think he was conscious of her attention, but he said suddenly, without looking away from the television

138

screen, 'We're very lucky with our kids, Christine. And it's all down to you!'

'We are lucky, yes. They're both good girls. And very fond of you, for some reason I can't fathom.'

It drew the ghost of a smile. 'You were the one who was there when they were growing up. You were the one who shaped them.'

'I did my best. You were busy at work. You didn't have much option.' She could say that now, could give him the benefit of the doubt. She hadn't felt it at the time, when she had been dealing with childish and adolescent tantrums on her own, after the strains of teaching during the day.

'You've always been my prop.' Still he didn't look at her. Still he stared steadily at the play he was not watching on the television screen. 'I never really appreciated you properly, until I thought I might lose you.'

It was a reference to the heart bypass she had needed eighteen months ago. 'Perhaps I didn't appreciate you either. Perhaps I didn't know how much you cared for us, even when you weren't there.'

This was quite absurd. They both knew it, but neither of them felt confident enough to break out of it. They had been brought up not to show physical passion, to believe that public demonstration of affection was not just in bad taste but a sign of weakness. If she went over and put her arms round him now, it might break the spell, and the simple statements which were coded declarations of love between them might dry up. And Christine didn't want that to happen.

She said softly, 'I worry about you, you know. Much more than I used to. Worry that the job will be too much for you, sometimes.'

His smile this time was of genuine pleasure, though still he did not look at her. 'I'll be all right. I've got young, keen blokes like Chris Rushton to run about after me and organize the leg work.'

'You make sure you do, then. Age catches up with all of us eventually. Even you.'

She thought the cliché had ended the little exchange of affection. Then, after several minutes, he said, 'She was the same generation as our two, that girl whose body was dumped in the Severn last week.'

'I know. It makes you thankful that ours are so well adjusted, so safe. Well, as safe as anyone is, these days.' She made that instinctive maternal qualification, as if it would invite disaster if she did not recite that small, automatic caveat.

'And now the sheep-badger's been killed. The one who was married to her once. The one everyone seemed to think was our prime suspect for the girl's killing.'

She wanted to tell him that she knew how that increased the pressure on him, that she knew how a second murder with the first one still unresolved brought unwelcome publicity, much of it critical. Already one or two of the papers had begun the familiar mutterings about police bafflement. But she knew he didn't want her to voice her sympathy. It wouldn't be snarled away, as it might have been in the bad old years, but it would be seen as pointless and unwelcome.

Five minutes later, long after she thought the exchange was closed, he said, 'There's a tutor at the university who claims to have had a lesbian relationship with Clare Mills. How jealous do you think people like that get?'

It was a confession of failure. He knew the answer to his own question, but weariness was making him uncertain, was making him seek reassurance for his thoughts. Christine said gently, 'Homosexuals can be as unbalanced and extreme as heterosexuals, when love is at stake. It depends on the individual whether she becomes deranged. You can't rule out a violent reaction.'

He nodded, still looking at the television screen, not the wife who was his sounding board. 'No. Any more than I can rule out violence from the male research student who claims to have had a thing about our dead girl. Or the illegal immigrant whom she befriended. Or the stepfather who claimed he wasn't in touch with her when he was.'

His voice rose as he catalogued his suspects, until he concluded in a quiet fury of irritation. It was as if he was accusing the wife who had never seen these people of adding to his frustration. She understood perfectly that she was an Aunt Sally for his impotence, even secretly rejoiced in this strange and bitter closeness between them, where once she would have been shut out.

140

Again she thought the strange conversation was concluded. And again after several minutes he said, 'You must have taught children with various degrees of autism, in your time in schools.'

It sounded inconsequential, but she knew it could not be. She said slowly, 'One or two. Asperger's syndrome was the most we had to deal with.' She thought immediately of the most extreme case, a boy who had needed to be watched in the playground and the laboratories, who had needed to be supervised throughout the day, because his actions and reactions were not those of other children. She said, simply because she knew he needed her to say something, 'It's a difficult thing to handle. In extreme cases, people like that need constant supervision.'

He nodded, staring fixedly at the television screen, whose flickering messages he had long since ceased to register. 'And would you say a person like that would be capable of murder?'

She wanted to say that she had no idea, that it would need a specialist to answer such questions. But she knew that that was not the answer that he wanted, that this exchange was about trying to bring a kind of order into his own thoughts, not a straightforward quest for information. 'Yes, I think he would. He would probably be deemed to have diminished responsibility, as soon as a psychiatrist was brought in, because people like that exist in an isolated world, where they don't operate by normal moral standards.'

He nodded, then looked at her and smiled for the first time, acknowledging the bond between them. She couldn't know, of course, that he had been thinking about a woman and a mother.

Martin Carter had rehearsed the words and the phrases he needed many times. It had seemed easy, then. He had been both coherent and firm, when he had planned these things in the privacy of his own flat.

Now, in the older man's formidable physical presence, everything was much more difficult. Roy Hudson was tanned, urbane, experienced. Martin Carter was pale, uncertain and naive, and at this moment he felt acutely conscious of all these things. He said, 'It's been difficult, these last few months. In all truth, I have to say that I've found that I'm not really cut out for this.' He forced a wan smile, running a nervous hand through his dark red hair.

He had spent a sleepless night after that gorilla of a man had threatened him with such relish in his room at the university yesterday. The thug must have reported back his unhappiness to the hierarchy, for he had been summoned tonight to this rendezvous with the man who had recruited him, paid him and directed him. The man who seemed so effortlessly to control his destiny. Martin felt that the velvet glove might at any moment be removed from the iron hand.

They were in a high-roomed Victorian house on the outskirts of Cheltenham, a place where he had never been before. A place where Roy Hudson felt comfortable and Martin Carter emphatically did not. This room at the front of the house was fully furnished and yet curiously anonymous, as if no one actually lived here. There were no ornaments, and just a single undistinguished picture on the longest wall. Martin wondered what part this house played in the organization.

But he could not afford irrelevant speculations like that.

There were just the two of them in the room. Hudson sat in a deep armchair with his legs crossed, whilst Martin sat on the edge of an upright chair eight feet from him, trying and conspicuously failing to look relaxed. He knew that he had been summoned here because Hudson chose not to be seen anywhere more public with him, because he wanted their association kept secret.

Martin wanted that too. But most of all he wanted to be out of it all.

Yet this was the moment when he realized what he had always known subconsciously but hadn't dared to acknowledge to himself: he wasn't going to be allowed to go. He tried to keep the panic out of his voice as he said, 'It was my mistake that I ever got involved. I haven't the personality or the—'

'Forget it.' Hudson didn't even accord him the status of annoyance. The older man was perfectly calm, almost avuncular, as he said, 'You should have thought about this much earlier, Martin. There's no going back now, I'm afraid. Not for you. You know too much.'

That flat final statement, with its four hammering mono-syllables, would reverberate in Martin's mind long after he had left this place. He looked desperately at the heavy blue curtains which masked the window. 'I'm just not very good at this business, am I? I need to face the fact that I'm an academic, pure and simple. I might even become quite a respectable academic. I'll work away at my books, do a little research, get it published, and make my way as a university teacher. I should have stuck to that in the first place, instead of thinking I could be a capitalist.'

He had pressed on, becoming ever more inconsequential, expecting with every second to be interrupted, wanting to be interrupted, in the end. Instead, Roy Hudson had let this drivel run its course, until it came to a halt with a nervous giggle from the younger man. Now he said with cold menace, 'You don't seem to be listening, Martin. I said leaving our organi-zation is not an option. Improving your efficiency is the only option you have.'

'But I thought I'd made it clear that—'

'And I thought my representative had made it clear to you yesterday that you needed to do better. When he visited you in your ivory tower. Where you should have felt at home, in the middle of your customer base.' Hudson threw in the last phrase with his lips curling in contempt, flinging the bit of jargon at his man like a dart.

'But I'm sure you'll agree that if I'm not very good at this you're better without me.' Martin conjured up a sickly smile from somewhere, but it was not answered by the man sitting in the armchair.

'I thought you were an intelligent man. The message doesn't seem to be getting through to you. Perhaps the messenger I sent yesterday wasn't direct enough for you. Perhaps I should have let him rough you up a little. He'd have liked that, and he's quite good at it.'

Martin thrust a hand through his bright red hair. 'Look, Mr Hudson, isn't there room for some sort of compromise here? I should never have got myself into this, and I'm sorry that I haven't done more for you than I have.'

He looked up to see if this was too sycophantic, but Hudson's expression hadn't changed one iota, and Martin found that more chilling than anger would have been. He licked lips that were like paper and plunged on. 'I'm not much use to you, but I'm perfectly trustworthy. I'm sure you'll agree that you've no reason to doubt me when I say that.'

'Trust isn't a thing we go in for. You know too much, Carter.'

Martin noticed the switch to his surname, the sudden hardening of the tone, and tried to ignore them. 'I know very little, really.'

'You know me. That's enough. As well as certain other things. And you know the rules, Carter: you don't quit. We don't leave people who quit around to tell tales. It's quite simple, really.' He smiled, but it wasn't a smile anyone would respond to.

Martin said desperately, 'My lips are sealed. I've more sense than to talk, haven't I? And I'll hand over whatever contacts I have to whoever it is you send to take over from me. And he or she will be welcome to the little knowledge of the patch that I've picked up over the last few months, and—'

'You don't seem to be listening to me. You'd better start listening very hard now.' Hudson spoke slowly, as if delivering instructions to a child. 'You go away from here and you set about increasing your turnover. The police have left the campus now and the rumpus over the Clare Mills murder is over. Things are getting back to normal.'

Martin tried not to notice that this man spoke of the dead woman who had been his stepdaughter as if he had never known her, tried to concentrate fiercely upon his own situation. 'The students are going off for the summer vacation. There won't be many around for the next three months. It's not the time for expansion.'

'Good local base of students round here, though. And others will be coming home for the summer from other universities. Looking for the exciting range of products we can supply.' Hudson smiled; he enjoyed throwing these orthodox retail phrases in, enjoyed the ironic ring they gave to his pronouncements. 'And no one said you had to confine yourself to students. We're very liberal about these things.'

He made it sound easy and straightforward. For an instant, Martin was beguiled anew by the man, by the prospect of vast sums of easy money, by the world of excitement which he had never known before he involved himself in this. He thrust down the gambler in his make-up that wanted to put his very life into the stakes. 'But my patch, the university campus which I know, will be very quiet. You don't want me to take unnecessary risks.'

That was true enough. But to admit it to this petrified man would be seen as a sign of weakness. Roy Hudson spread his expansive smile across his features, became the experienced man encouraging his protégé to develop his potential. 'Ideal time to strengthen and extend your network, then. Be ready to go when the new term starts. We'll be watching you and monitoring your progress. I'm sure you'll do very well, with the stuff we can now supply, and with the strength of our organization to back you up.'

Hudson now made an elaborate performance of taking a cigar from the box on the table beside him and deciding not to offer one to Martin Carter. He cut and lit the cigar in a slow, elaborate ritual, savouring the way the man's eyes followed his every movement, like those of a rabbit caught in a headlight. 'I hope you enjoy more success in the next year than in the last one, Mr Carter. Failure would be most unfortunate. And do remember that leaving us isn't an option.'

He blew a smoke-ring at the ceiling and watched it as Martin Carter left the room uncertainly, on legs which refused to work normally.

Twenty-One

Judith Hudson was waiting for them on the top step of the four which led up to the front door of the now familiar stone house in the Forest of Dean village.

'My husband isn't here. He had to go into work early today,' she said. She smiled at them. Perhaps she divined their thought that they had still not seen how husband and wife behaved together. They couldn't be certain of anything with this woman. She took them into a sitting room they had not seen before, with prints of nineteenth-century Weston-super-Mare and sixteenth-century Bristol on the walls and an etching of open-cast Forest of Dean mineworkers in a vanished age.

Mrs Hudson had the same coffee pot they had seen before, the same cups, even what might have been the same home-made gingerbread. And her hand was as steady as ever as she poured.

But this time they felt that they knew a little more about this affluent middle-class woman who had struck them as so strange, this mother who seemed not at all affected by the murder of her only daughter. Her first husband's description of her autism made sense of her actions; what they did not know, what no one could be sure of, was the extent of the condition, in this human being who seemed sometimes to exist in a different world from those around her.

'Have you found out who killed Clare?' she asked, as she consigned a delicate china plate into Bert Hook's large, careful hands. She might have been making polite conversation about the weather.

'Not yet, Mrs Hudson. We will, though. Quite soon now, I expect.' He watched her carefully, automatically studying her face for a reaction to this thought. But she merely nodded understandingly, as if accepting an expected answer to a routine query.

Lambert said sharply, 'And now your daughter's ex-husband is dead. Murdered, as Clare was murdered.'

His repetition of the word which normally brought an automatic chill to members of the public elicited no frisson in this woman. She said merely, 'I'm not really surprised,' as if congratulating herself on forecasting a passing shower. Then, having attended to her guests, she picked up her own cup and saucer and sat down unhurriedly in the armchair opposite them.

Lambert knew now that the niceties of conversational politeness had no meaning with this lady. He said with brutal abruptness, 'What do you know about the death of Ian Walker?'

'Nothing. Why should I know anything?' She seemed genuinely puzzled that he should make such an enquiry.

Lambert said, 'Detective Sergeant Hook can give you one good reason,' and nodded at Hook, who flicked open his notebook.

'On the first occasion we interviewed you, Mrs Hudson, you told us that Mr Walker had treated your daughter very badly, in your opinion. You said that he was a "sponger" who continued to give problems, even after they had been divorced. And you said, "I could cheerfully murder the man myself!" '

'Did I? I suppose I must have done, if you say so.' They had been hoping to shake even this woman with her damning statement about the dead man, but she seemed not at all abashed, even slightly amused. 'But it's understandable that I should feel like that, isn't it? I mean, Walker was no good to anyone. And worse than no good to Clare. That man took everything he could from her whilst they were married, and he kept trying to get money from her, even after they'd been divorced. No, I can't say I'm sorry he's dead.' She nodded quietly to herself, as if confirming the logic of her opinion on some minor matter, and took a sip of her coffee.

Lambert said, 'You do not seem particularly anxious to help us to discover who killed your only daughter, Mrs Hudson.'

'Is that how it appears to you, Superintendent? Well, Clare and I weren't as close as we might have been, you know. She'd disappointed us, several times, especially in the years since I married Roy. Did I tell you that she still seemed very attached to my first husband?'

147

'You did, yes.' He wanted to say that this was hardly surprising, in the circumstances, but he sensed that there was no point in going down that road. 'You also said that you wanted her to be more cooperative with your second husband. What exactly did you mean by that?'

For the first time, she seemed discomforted. 'I don't know. I can't think what I might have meant.'

'You weren't talking just about them getting on better together, were you? You had something specific in mind. Some issue on which she was resisting Mr Hudson, was refusing to do what the two of you wanted.'

'I don't know. You'll have to ask Roy about that.' She had passed in a moment from unnatural calmness into something more disturbed. She looked out of the window at the roses outside, as if she expected salvation of some sort to emerge from the bright colours of the neat beds.

Lambert let the moment stretch, until she looked back at him in wide-eyed, almost childish panic. This was not a well woman, and he felt his irritation turning with that thought into compassion. But he had to be cruel, if he was to squeeze all he could from this unyielding source. 'Where were you on the night of Saturday the twenty-first of June, when your daughter was killed, Mrs Hudson?'

'I was here. Here in this house.'

'Alone?' He tried to put a wealth of scepticism into the single word.

'Yes.'

'So there is no one who can vouch for your presence here.'

'No. Well, yes, there is really.' Her hand flew to her mouth, and he was reminded again of a small child who has made a mistake. 'I've got that wrong, you see. Roy was here with me. All through the evening.'

This time he let his sceptical silence show his reluctance to accept her word. Then he said, 'So the two of you are providing alibis for each other on that night.'

'Yes.' Then, far too late, she added, 'Not that we need alibis for Clare's death. You should be out catching the person who killed her, not questioning me.' But it was said automatically, like a bad actor reading wooden lines in a play, rather than with real outrage.

Lambert said quietly, 'Where were you on Monday night, Mrs Hudson?'

'This Monday? I was here again, I think.'

'I wish you would. It's only thirty-six hours ago.'

It seemed impossible to provoke anger in her. She ignored the cutting edge in his voice as she said, 'Yes, I was here. I remember. I was watching the television. Is it important?'

'Ian Walker was killed on Monday night. Someone blew half his head away, with his own shotgun.'

'Yes, of course. It wasn't me, though. I was here.'

'And no doubt your husband was here with you again on this occasion.'

'No. I was alone. Roy was out on business. He often is, on a Monday night.'

'What kind of business would that be?'

'I don't know. You'd need to ask Roy.'

'And we shall, in due course. Mrs Hudson, have you any idea who killed either your daughter or Ian Walker?'

This time it was she who paused, and they thought for a split second of intense excitement that she was going to give them something vital. But then she said, as dully and evenly as an automaton, 'No. I don't know who might have done these things.'

'Then please carry on thinking about them. I need hardly say that it is your duty to communicate any thoughts you might have on either of these killings to us immediately.'

She nodded earnestly, and they were reminded yet again of a dutiful child.

Chris Rushton was pleased with himself.

His trawl through the records had produced nothing for either Roy Hudson or his wife. Young Martin Carter had an unblemished record in his previous life, as might have been expected. He put Denis Pimbury into his computer, and the name produced nothing, as he had expected.

But now the detective inspector had come up with something which made all his patient work worthwhile. It was unexpected, but that made it even more valuable. This would show that hidebound John Lambert the value of modern technology. This might even turn out to be the turning point in the case after ten days of stalemate.

DI Rushton had turned up something very interesting and very surprising about Clare Mills's sexual partner Sara Green.

While Chris Rushton was getting excited about Sara Green, Roy Hudson was taking delivery of his new Mercedes.

Cars were one of his weaknesses. He didn't really need a new Merc. The old one had clocked up barely thirty thousand, and these vehicles were built to last. But he fancied the new model, and he could afford the sixty thousand it cost. Business was booming and expanding, so why stint yourself?

He enjoyed the deference of the salesman as he showed the new owner the few changes in the controls. Then he eased the sleek new maroon machine out of the Cheltenham show-room and indulged himself with a little run in his new toy. The three-litre engine kicked him agreeably in the back when he put his foot down. He joined the M5 and let the new car sweep him effortlessly and gracefully northwards, past Tewkesbury and up to the outskirts of Worcester, enjoying the power beneath his foot, feeling at one with the machine in which he would move for the next two years, gliding effort-lessly past Jaguars and Volvos as he let the needle creep up over the hundred mile an hour mark.

He kept his eye on his rear-view mirror as he stayed in the outside lane: it would be silly to be pinched for speeding, when the police hadn't a clue about other things which might be of much more interest to them.

He turned back at Junction 6, enjoying the view of the long ridge of the Malvern Hills on his right as he drove south down the motorway. He visited one of his dealers in his own house near Evesham, savouring the privacy accorded by the high hedges of the house in the narrow lane. The man had done well for himself: that much was apparent from the fittings and the garden of this spacious house. Roy recalled the narrow modern terraced house in Chepstow where the man had resided when he had first employed him. It was good to see people get on. Roy Hudson didn't mind his staff enjoying the pros-perity which success brought to them. They deserved to enjoy the benefits of hard work in a dangerous trade.

He tried to phone his wife on the car mobile as he drove down the M50 towards Ross-on-Wye. She did not answer. It didn't really matter. He was sure nothing could have gone wrong. But he would have liked to have Judith's reassurance on that. He tried again, ten minutes later, but there was still no reply.

He frowned his annoyance, then eased the speedo needle up over ninety again. He had better go home.

Judith was in the garden. She had finished weeding around the perennials in the long border; now she was removing the spent blooms from the roses, which were even more dazzling as the sun moved temporarily behind a slowly moving white cloud. 'They've been wonderful this year, haven't they?' she said, as he moved over the weedless grass carpet to join her.

'There's no need for you to do that, you know. Joe will be in tomorrow.' They had a gardener for two days a week now.

'Oh, I enjoy it. It's so uncomplicated, gardening. Takes me out of myself. I think I'll work with Joe when he comes tomorrow. I enjoy that, and I think he does.'

'You didn't answer your mobile.'

'No. It's inside the house. I wouldn't hear it, out here.'

He tried not to let his irritation show. There was no point, he told himself: he should know that by now. 'How did you get on?'

'Get on?'

He wondered if she was being deliberately obtuse, to annoy him, then decided that she wasn't. Judith wasn't like that. 'With the police. They were coming to see you this morning, weren't they?'

'Oh yes. It's hours ago now. They didn't stay long.'

He didn't let her see his impatience. It wouldn't do to accord this visit any real importance. 'I expect it was just routine, was it?'

'Oh yes, I think so. He's quite a nice man, that Superintendent Lambert. And that sergeant came with him again. He's very quiet and friendly. But he likes my ginger-bread. I could see that.'

'What did they ask you about?'

'Oh, about Clare again. They seemed to find it odd that I wasn't more agitated about her death. But I explained that she'd done a lot to upset us. They seemed to understand that, this time.'

151

'Ken Mills has come back from Australia. Did they tell you that?'

'No. Why would he do that?'

She was round-eyed with wonder, so that he wanted to shake her, to tell her that it was obvious that a man who had loved his daughter would want to be involved in the investigation of her death. But the feeling passed in an instant; he was used to coping with her reactions by now. Or rather with her lack of reactions. That was part of the package you took on when you lived with Judith. So he said merely, 'I expect it was for old times' sake. We both know that he was very fond of Clare, and she of him.'

'Yes. Ken enjoyed having a child, even when she was young. I found it hard work.'

'Did the police give you any idea whether they were planning to arrest someone for Clare's murder?' He bent and sniffed a perfectly formed hybrid-tea bloom, studiously unconcerned.

'No. They asked me where I was when she was killed, though.'

'And what did you tell them?'

'What we agreed. That I was here with you all through that Saturday night. That's correct, isn't it?' She was anxious only to please him, seemingly totally unaware of the implications of this for the CID enquiry.

'Yes, that's what we agreed. Because it's right, isn't it? It's the truth, it's what really happened.' He tried not to be too vehement. It was like checking things off with a child. Yet this was a highly intelligent woman, when the circumstances were right. That only made it more difficult for those close to her. Affection welled within him, overcoming his irritation. He put his arm round her shoulder and said, 'We'll get through this, Judith. I don't want you to worry about it.'

She nodded sagely, like a serious child, as she put more spent roses into the barrow beside her. The one thing she did not seem was worried. 'Have you time for a sandwich? I'll get you some lunch now.'

He watched her quick, expert hands as she cut the bread and slipped ham and cheese within it in the kitchen. How competent she was, in most things! And how carefully you needed to supervise her in others. He let her make the tea, knowing how she resented interference in her kitchen, then followed her into her favourite room, the small one at the back of the house which looked out over the garden. He took his plate with the sandwiches, smiled affectionately, and said as casually as he could, 'Did those policemen ask you about Ian Walker?'

'Yes.' She gave a small, brittle laugh. 'Apparently I'd told them that I wouldn't mind killing him myself, when they talked to me about Clare's death! They raised that with me today. I said it was quite true, but as it happens I hadn't killed the man!'

'And they accepted that?'

'Oh, I think so. I told them I was here on Monday night, when it happened.'

'That's right! And that I was here with you. That way, we both account for each other, as we said.'

She frowned, her small teeth very white as she bit into a sandwich. He knew from her face that there was something wrong, but she made him wait until she had swallowed and her mouth was empty, like a well-mannered child. 'No. I told him I was here on my own. I'm afraid I got a bit confused about what we'd agreed on that. They'd just been asking me about Clare and I—'

'Where did you say I was on Monday night?'

'Out on business, I think I said. Yes, I'm sure I did.'

'Where? Where was I supposed to be working?' He wondered if she would catch the tension in his voice.

'Oh, I didn't tell them that. I knew you wouldn't want them knowing what you were doing. It's none of their business, is it? I remember you saying that before.' She looked quite pleased with herself for that recollection.

'Did they ask you anything more about me?'

'No, I don't think so. I think I told them you were usually out on a Monday, so they probably accepted that.'

He watched her as she poured the tea unhurriedly, her face as open and uncomplicated as a child's. But not as innocent, he thought. 'Do you think they accepted that neither of us killed Walker?'

'Oh, I should think so. They seemed quite satisfied with what they had heard from me, when they left.'

But Judith wasn't the best judge of that, he thought. When a woman had no sense of danger, it was impossible to instil one into her. If he hadn't known that from the start, he certainly realized it now.

153

Twenty-Two

Chris Rushton said as casually as he could, 'A couple of things have come up whilst you were out. One of them at least seems likely to be relevant to the Clare Mills case.'

His shirt was as immaculately pressed as usual, the cuffs just the right length on his steely wrists. You couldn't let things go, just because you were divorced. The ironing board was as meticulously maintained as everything else in his uncluttered, sterile house. He spoke now as modestly as he could, but his body language told the real story.

John Lambert thought sourly that his detective inspector was positively preening himself. If a man sitting staring at a computer screen for much of the day could ever be said to be preening. Chris Rushton was getting altogether too pleased with himself. They must do something to keep the world in perspective for him. Something which would really cut him down to size.

Perhaps they should persuade him to take up golf.

Lambert was not usually as cruel as this. His escapist reverie was interrupted by Rushton saying carefully and precisely, 'Denis Pimbury.'

'What about him?'

'He's been pawning jewellery. In Gloucester. Reported to us as routine. I picked it up because I was cross-referencing the name on my computer.' Rushton tried unsuccessfully not to sound smug about that.

Bert Hook said thoughtfully, 'Pimbury didn't seem the kind of man who would have jewellery to pawn.'

'A diamond ring and an emerald brooch.' Rushton gazed unnecessarily at the entry he had recently made on his computer file for Pimbury.

'We'll have further words with him about that. See what

his story is. Be interesting to know where a man like that acquired a ring and a brooch.' Lambert wondered why he could not sound more grateful for the information. Rushton had done the job allotted to him, and done it well. 'What was the other thing you had to report, Chris?'

'Sara Green.'

Lambert was irritated by the way he produced the information, doling it out in answer to a series of questions rather than coming straight out with it. He wondered what Rushton had learned about that rather intense young woman who taught at the university. He was pretty sure that Rushton had never seen her, but he said hopefully, 'Not another of the women you fancy, is she, Chris?'

Rushton, who was nursing a secret passion for Clare Mills's former flatmate Anne Jackson, felt himself blushing like an adolescent. These two older men could always get him going, when he should have been proof against their barbs after years of experience. He said stiffly, 'I would remind you that I have meticulously recorded the findings of your interviews, sir. So I am well aware that Ms Green prefers liaisons with her own sex. I am interested in her only as a murder suspect.'

'Quite. And what have you discovered about her?'

'That she has a history of violence. Serious violence.'

'How recent?'

'Nine years ago. She was twenty-four at the time.' Not a child, Chris Rushton wanted to say. An adult, responsible for her own actions and the consequences. A fact which made the discovery especially relevant to the present enquiry.

'If she has a criminal record, why has it taken so long to come to light?' Lambert was aware that he was being unfair, that there was sure to be a good reason, but he didn't feel like being fair to his priggish inspector at this moment.

'She hasn't got a record. Charges were never brought. The person concerned refused to go into the witness box against her.'

The old story with violence. If it was domestic, the parties made up, at least for the time being, and didn't want to proceed with charges. If it wasn't domestic, there were often more sinister reasons why no charges were brought: the victim was bought off, or more likely intimidated with threats of further brutality. Lambert nodded and said gloomily, 'Let's have the details.'

'Sara Green was in a lesbian affair with a woman of twenty-two, who evidently decided that she was heterosexual after all and shacked up with a boy of the same age. Ms Green did not react kindly to that.'

'She assaulted the woman?'

'Yes. She threatened her with a shotgun when she discovered what was going on. Two days later, she attacked her with a kitchen knife.'

'With what result?'

'The woman was hospitalized. Two stab wounds in the chest and quite severe bleeding, apparently. It's not clear how life-threatening it was, because the woman concerned eventually refused to take her to court, or even to appear as a witness in any case the Thames Valley Police chose to bring against Sara Green. She subsequently married the man concerned and emigrated to Canada.'

'Pity about that. It would have been interesting to have her views on Sara Green's temperament. As it is, we shall have to explore the detail of this incident with Ms Green herself.'

Superintendent Lambert spoke with some relish about the prospect of disturbing that composed lady.

Martin Carter was doing his best to save his skin.

Fear is rarely the best way to get results from people, but drugs were an industry which ran on fear. You couldn't afford to ignore what the people above you in the hierarchy directed you to do, and you were perpetually aware of those vaguer and darker forces beyond them. Forces which could eliminate you without you even knowing who had killed you, without you leaving more than a swiftly disappearing ripple behind in the dark pool of crime.

Fear is the worst, most dangerous, motivation.

And Wednesday night certainly wasn't the best time. But Martin wanted to make some effect, to achieve something which would show that he had taken note of the warning which Roy Hudson had delivered to him. So he put on his dark blue anorak, filled the pockets with some of the best and most sinister of his new supplies, and went out into the town.

It wasn't the wisest or the most considered action to move so quickly, but Martin Carter wasn't as experienced as he should have been to be operating at this level. Nor was he very efficient in this trade: as he had tried to explain to Roy Hudson, he was not cut out for it. Hudson might have been better advised to heed Martin's estimate of himself, but Hudson was driven by greed. And greed unbalances judgement more quickly than any other failing.

With a boss driven by greed and an operative driven by fear, the omens were not good.

It was still warm when Martin left his house, still light on what was still very nearly the longest day of the year. It was after half-past nine on his watch, and yet the western sky over the Severn was a brilliant crimson, still and almost cloudless, betokening more fine, hot weather to come. Martin stared at it glumly as his feet carried him unwillingly over the familiar streets. He would have preferred rain and the cloak of a Stygian darkness for the work he had to conduct tonight.

People seemed to his oversensitive eyes to be looking at him curiously as he passed them. Perhaps he should not have worn the anorak. Even at this time of night, people were still walking in T-shirts and jeans; there was scarcely a sweater or a jacket in view. He was overdressed in the navy anorak. Worse than overdressed: he was conspicuous. Martin walked past the pub he had meant to enter, moving on, through streets where he had not walked before, streets which had come down in the world from their Victorian heyday, with high elevations diminishing the light from the darkening blue sky.

It was darker when he returned. The bright orange lights of the pub and the sounds of laughter from within it seemed to emphasize the gloom outside. He went in and ordered himself a pint of bitter, resisting the impulse to give himself the swift infusion of Dutch courage which spirits might have provided. He stood with an elbow on the bar, forcing himself to turn casually and slowly, to conduct a detached assessment of the scene around him.

It didn't look quite right. He would have liked more people around. In a busy pub, where people were crowded enough to brush against each other, where there was perpetual movement in and out and to and from the toilets, it seemed that nothing you did was noticed in the general mayhem. This wasn't anything like as busy as that. About normal for a Wednesday evening, he supposed.

He had been served very promptly, which was not a good sign, from his point of view. There were plenty of people around, but in no way could you say that the place was crowded. There was plenty of banter going on between different groups, but they were aware of each other, aware of who else was in the place. They might even remember that he had been there, if anyone asked them later.

He had intended to drink his beer unhurriedly, to sip it, to estimate the situation coolly, to watch for the right moment. Now he found that three-quarters of his pint had gone without his even realizing it. Watch it, Martin. Keep a grip on yourself. You're an experienced drug dealer now, not a novice. You could have a lucrative future in this business, if you keep your head and play things right.

Roy Hudson said so.

Martin had seen two of his agents, but he didn't do any more than acknowledge them with his eyes, not even nodding his head at them. It was part of the training; you never knew who might be watching you, even in unlikely places. Better safe than sorry: Martin rolled out another of the meaningless clichés to himself and found that he had finished his beer.

He ordered another pint, leaning on the bar as nonchalantly as he could. He acknowledged a couple of students who knew him from the university, but took care not to be drawn into their conversation. The period he liked least of all was this lengthy spell of inactivity, where you sized up the situation and decided whether it was safe to make a move. Some people seemed actually to enjoy the smell of danger, sniffed it like hounds on a scent. He'd never been like that: the feeling of peril almost made him physically sick at times. He felt the stale bile of the beer at the back of his throat now.

At twenty-five to eleven, he went out to the small outside toilet, the one not visited by many of the clients, except when the place was crowded and there was a queue at the indoor ones. It was cooler now out here, and he could see the first stars in the clear sky. He relieved himself in the urinal, trying to welcome the strong scent of ammonia which overcame the traces of other, more unpleasant scents, trying to pretend that he was not waiting here for an assignation.

It could not have been more than two minutes until his man came out from the pub, looking studiously at the night sky until he was sure that they were alone here. He was a student from the university. But because he was not in Martin's department, they had had no dealings with each other in that other, more innocent world.

'Did you shift the stuff?' asked Martin Carter. He stood ridiculously beside the urinating young man in the darkness.

'Most of it.'

'You want more? I've got good stuff. At good prices.'

'No. I only sell to students. You know that. The next two months will be a slack period for me.'

It was so exactly what Martin had told Roy Hudson about his own situation that he could scarcely raise the will to argue, but he tried. 'There'll be others home from the holidays, from other universities and colleges. And you shouldn't confine yourself to students, you know. There are plenty of other people out there who want what we can give them. They won't beat our prices.'

The boy shook his head in the darkness. 'I'm not making much out of this. Not for the risks I take. I'm only selling pot. My people don't seem to want anything but grass. And there are too many people offering that. There's not much profit in it, unless you can move bigger quantities than I can.'

'You want to get them onto coke and ecstasy. That's where the big profits are to be made. I can get you quality stuff and—'

'I can't move coke. Not in any quantity. I've tried. I'm not making enough to warrant taking the risks I take. I was hoping I'd have cleared my student loan by now, but I'm nowhere near doing that.' He paused, blew out a long breath, which drifted the sweet scent of cannabis over the man next to him. 'I think I want out, Martin.'

Martin knew that he should pressurize him, that he must lean hard on him, the way Roy Hudson had leaned on him when he had suggested quitting. He tried, but his heart wasn't in it. And he had no real threat to offer. This lad knew nothing: he wasn't important. No one would have thought it worth liquidating a part-time, amateur dabbler in the trade like him.

Martin told him that he had done the hard work, that once he had learned the rudiments of selling there was easier money to be made, that he had a foothold in the market which he could now develop. But he was no salesman himself, he realized now, and his blandishments to the younger man rang hollow. In three minutes more, he was alone again, contemplating the prospect of losing a member of his diminishing and ineffective sales force, when he had been hoping to expand it.

He waited in vain for the other contact he had seen inside the pub to present himself out here, feeling an involuntary shiver shake his chest, which had earlier in the evening been so overheated in his anorak. He wondered bleakly if Roy Hudson had been bluffing, if he would simply have accepted Martin's departure from the organization if he had insisted upon carrying it through.

Martin wasn't good at judging people, he was realizing belatedly, so he wasn't sure. But he wouldn't fancy testing out the idea that Hudson was bluffing. Those anonymous people behind him dealt out violence without a thought. His shiver turned into an unambiguous shudder of horror.

Martin was trying to compose himself to go back into the pub when another man came out. He did not seem very old, though with the light from the pub behind him Martin Carter could see little more than an outline. He had an anorak on, like Martin; it was the first one he had seen tonight apart from his own.

Martin had been about to re-enter the pub when the door opened and this man came out. He glanced at Martin, called a greeting, went into the urinal, carried on a desultory conversation about the sweltering evening as he performed in there. It was quite ridiculous, but Martin found that he could not leave him there without seeming rude.

And suddenly, he did not want to leave the man. Perhaps it was the fellowship of the anoraks: Martin's nervous giggle on that thought told him how much on edge he was, should have been a warning to him. But he could think only of what Hudson had told him about developing new markets. This might be an opportunity to move outside the university ambience and into new and richer markets. This man surely couldn't have come out here by chance.

As if responding to that thought, the man said through the darkness, 'Smell of pot in here, if I'm not mistaken.'

'Oh, I don't think you are. The fellow who was out here just now had been smoking grass, I'm sure.'

The man finished his leisurely evacuation, shook himself unhurriedly, said amiably, 'Bit of an expert on that sort of thing, are you?'

'I suppose you could say that.' The giggle came again, too loudly through the darkness. Martin worked his brain furiously. This man must surely be in the market for drugs, or he wouldn't have come out here and begun to talk like this. And you had to speculate to accumulate: that meaningless phrase bounced into his head from some forgotten evening of gambling. 'I can supply pot, if you're interested. And other, much more interesting things.'

'Can you, indeed? I'd certainly be very interested to see what you have to offer.'

It was strange, indirect phrasing. Most people were straight in with questions about price and quality. But they were both feeling their way, weren't they? It would be good to have someone working for him who was a little older than his previous operatives, who would exercise an appropriate caution like this. Martin had the feeling that this might be the beginning of a productive relationship.

'I can do horse, coke and ecstasy. All at good prices. Even better prices, if you can shift certain quantities.'

'Crack?'

'As much as you want. And better quality than you'll get anywhere else round here.'

'LSD?'

'Sure. You name it, we can do it. What sort of quantities are you thinking of?' Martin could feel the excitement rising within him. He leant a little nearer to the man's face, saw that he was unshaven, with the kind of lean face which often sat upon a heroin addict. 'We can even do Rohypnol. That's in short supply, but we can do it for you.'

The date-rape drug. They all wanted that. You could shift that without trying: it said something about the decadence of modern society, but there was unlimited money in Rohypnol, if you could get hold of it. Perhaps he imagined it, but he thought he caught a sharp, excited intake of breath from his new companion when he mentioned it. This might be the clincher in his recruitment.

The man said, 'I'll need to see the goods. Need to have evidence of the quality you can offer.'

Martin nodded, telling himself that they were almost there, that the man was hooked. Perhaps now he should back off a little, should seem a little less eager, if he was to drive the best bargain with this new member of his sales force. There was a low wall beside him, the remnants of what had once been a wash-house behind the pub. He dug deep into the pockets of his anorak, produced examples of everything he had named. 'These are only samples, mind. We'll discuss the quantities you think you can shift. Then we'll agree a price and I'll see you here on Friday. You bring the cash, I bring the drugs. Cash on delivery, that's the way we work.'

He felt in control of himself and the situation, now, as he issued this series of orders. It had been much easier than he could ever have anticipated. He felt in his bones that this man was going to be a serious dealer, was going to shift the quantities Martin needed to move if he was going to appease Roy Hudson. He produced the tiny torch he carried in his pocket, flicked its beam over the array of drugs he had set out on the little strip of felt on the wall. In the sudden bright light, they looked like jewels displayed on velvet.

Martin did not think of the misery this array could usher into the world, of the lives he would never see ruined by this lethal array. He thought not of the victims but of the man who had threatened him, of Roy Hudson and the warnings he had issued so unequivocally.

Fear is always the worst, most dangerous motivation.

His new recruit bent to examine the wares, noting each of the drugs but saying nothing as Martin conducted his sales pitch. The words came more easily now. He was gathering the confidence he needed at last. Perhaps, as Hudson had implied, it was just a matter of perseverance. Perhaps in a few months' time he would be grateful to the man whom he had begun to hate.

And then, as if he spoke from some echoing cave, the man beside him was pronouncing the formal words of arrest, telling Martin that he had no need to say anything but that it might prejudice his defence if he did not state facts which he would later rely upon for his defence in court.

Martin found a second man at his elbow, restraining him gently, even though he could not summon into his limbs the faintest impulse to escape. He was led past the white-faced student who had said he wanted out, through a pub lined with curious faces, outside to a police car whose blue light winked silently, mockingly at him as he approached.

Martin had never been in a police car before. He sat on the rear seat, needlessly handcuffed to the plain-clothes officer beside him, seeing but scarcely hearing the city as they drove slowly through it. A car horn seemed to sound from some remote distance; it took him a long time to realize that the faint, melancholy sound he could hear was a church clock tolling eleven.

They made him sign for the few pounds he had in his pockets and the torch, as well as the drugs. Then they took away the shoelaces from his trainers and sent him shuffling to the cells.

The first sound which Martin Carter had heard clearly since he had been arrested was the harsh clang of the steel door of the cell closing upon him.

Twenty-Three

Geoff Harrison, the farmer who employed Denis Pimbury, was not at ease with the police.

He had been in trouble in earlier years for employing illegal immigrants, for not checking closely enough on the backgrounds of his workers. Now, when a chief superintendent and a detective sergeant asked to see him in private, he was shrewd and experienced enough to realize that something serious was in hand.

'You people just don't recognize the difficulties of recruiting seasonal labour,' he grumbled automatically. 'You can't just go into the job centres and recruit a hundred people to pick fruit for a month, you know.'

Lambert said dryly, 'We try to make sure the law is observed, Mr Harrison. That's what a police service has to do.' He had some sympathy for Harrison, but didn't want to get into arguments about casual labour when he had bigger fish to fry.

'Sometimes I think some of these busybodies would rather watch good food rot in the ground than see it picked and taken to market. I pay the proper rates and provide the proper breaks, unlike some I could name. No one seems to take any account of that!' Harrison looked out over his sheds and the long, impeccably straight rows of strawberries and raspberries, nodding his resentment.

'We're not here to check on the details of your working practices,' said Lambert stiffly. He wanted to say that they were here in pursuit of something much more important: a murder enquiry. But the man they wanted to question already had enough things stacked against him in life. If in the end he proved not to be a murderer, he could do without the residual slur of being an alien suspected of the worst crime of all.

Lambert said to Harrison, 'We need to speak to you in confidence about one of your workers, Denis Pimbury.'

'I've offered Denis a permanent job. He's a bona-fide worker, with his card properly stamped.' Harrison's mind was immediately on his own situation, not that of the man working outside beneath the baking sun.

Bert Hook smiled at the farmer, his countryman's face pulsing with sympathy for rural industry, festooned with red tape by bureaucrats in city offices. 'Good worker, is he, your Mr Pimbury?'

'Excellent worker. I wouldn't have offered him permanent employment otherwise. As a matter of fact, I'm thinking of putting him in charge of a gang when it comes to apple-picking later in the year.'

'Honest, then, I expect.'

'Honest as the day is long.' Harrison wasn't a man who threw out compliments lightly; not many farmers do. But it was a relief to be talking about someone else, to find that his own employment practices did not seem to be the issue here. 'You'll understand that with a casual workforce recruited from a lot of different backgrounds, I have to give a lot of attention to these things.' He spoke a little portentously, delivering a sentence he had prepared for officious councillors: you hadn't to mention foreigners, or some of them would accuse you of prejudice. 'Denis not only won't rob his fellow-workers, he won't rob his employer. You can leave him to work on his own, without coming back to find that he's been slacking.' Finding that he was enjoying the unaccustomed pleasure of praising one of his workers like this, he allowed himself to be carried even further than he had intended. 'I'd trust him with my life, Denis.'

So the ring and the brooch the man had taken to the pawnshop hadn't been acquired round here. Lambert said heavily, 'Thank you for being so frank with us, Mr Harrison. And please don't allow any of this discussion to reach your other workers. Now, if you'll be kind enough to allow us the use of this room, we'll see Mr Pimbury in here immediately, please.'

The man who had told them he was Denis Pimbury came into the room with his normal sharp-eyed air of suspicion and sat uncomfortably on the wooden chair in front of Harrison's battered and paper-strewn desk. He had never been into the boss's office before, but he had eyes not for his surroundings but only for the two men who had brought him into the room for questioning. The dark, deep-set eyes watched them unblinkingly; when his lank black hair dropped momentarily over his forehead, he brushed it angrily aside, as if it was affecting his vision when it needed to be at its sharpest.

He said, 'I know nothing. Nothing which can be of any use to you. What is it that you want me to tell you?' He folded his thin arms resolutely across his chest, as if stilling his too mobile body by a fierce effort of will.

'You could start by telling us your real name.' Lambert's tone was friendly, not hostile. He knew that he held all the cards in the strange game he had to play against this nervous opponent.

'My name is Denis Pimbury.' He pronounced it carefully, throwing all the conviction he could muster behind each syllable.

Lambert remained amiable as he said firmly, 'Whatever your name is, it isn't Pimbury. You made an unwise choice there.'

'I do not understand what you mean. I have passport. My name is Denis Pimbury.' He reiterated the words slowly, like a mantra, as if with sufficient repetition he could make them into the truth.

'No, Denis. We shall call you Denis, if you wish it: it suits us to call you something. But we shall not call you Pimbury. The only living holder of that name was seventy-three last month. That is such a curious fact that it was reported in the newspapers – on the front page of *The Times*, to be precise. I don't know how you picked up the name, but it was a most unfortunate choice. I hope you did not pay too much for that bogus passport.'

Denis saw his world disintegrating before his eyes, glimpsed his ruin in the calm, compassionate face of this senior policeman, who spoke so quietly and sympathetically to him. He said woodenly, 'I am British. My mother lived abroad since I was infant. I come back here to work. To make a living. To make my life here.' He could feel hysteria rising in his voice on the successive phrases. Perhaps that did not matter now. Perhaps it was all over. As suddenly as this. When he had thought that things were coming right at last, were falling into place for him.

Lambert glanced at Bert Hook, who said, 'Maybe that is still possible. Maybe you can still make a life here.'

'But you do not believe me. You say passport no good.' He did not trust these strange policemen who came in ordinary clothes and offered false hopes. Policemen were not like this. At worst they were instruments of darkness, who snuffed out your life and went on their way. At best, they were harsh figures, instruments of government, who cast you into prison and left you there to rot without trial whilst the world forgot you. These men must have their own agenda, must be playing him like a fish on the end of a line for their own ends.

Hook saw the desperation in the narrow features and understood most of the fear behind them. He said, 'I'm afraid that passport won't be much use to you, as you say. But Superintendent Lambert and I aren't concerned with illegal immigration into the country. Someone else will be following that up, in due course. But Mr Harrison says that you have been a model worker here, Denis. He is willing to offer you permanent employment, if your entry into this country can be regularized.'

Denis had a facility for languages, and he had picked up English very quickly. But now, with his world crashing about his ears and his mind reeling, he understood little of Hook's formal, guarded language, and trusted even less. He repeated blankly, 'I good worker. I give no trouble here. Mr Harrison will speak for me.'

Lambert said quietly, 'We need to ask you some questions about another matter altogether. We are CID officers, investigating murder.'

So that was it. They had been softening him up with all the illegal-immigrant stuff, telling him that he had no hope, that he might as well confess and get it over with. Denis looked into the long, lined face and mustered all the conviction he could summon into this strange new language as he said, 'I not kill anyone.'

'Perhaps not. But you'll need to convince us of that. There

are certain factors which are not in your favour.' What a stupid, roundabout phrase that was, Lambert thought, what a pitiful substitute for direct accusation. He realized that his desire to study this man and his reactions had taken over, when bluntness would be more effective on both sides. He said, 'You took certain items to a pawnshop in Gloucester. A brooch and a ring, both of considerable value.'

He had accepted too little for them. He knew even at the time that he should have demanded more, but he had been able to think only of getting out of that claustrophobic shop and away from that calm, assessing woman, who had seemed to read his every thought. Denis spoke softly, trying to pick his words and avoid other things they could use against him. 'They were mine, those things. I thought I should have the money from them. I had no one to give them to.'

There was a whole world of heartbreak in that last pathetic confession. Lambert nodded his acceptance of the logic of this disposal, studied the tortured young face for a second or two before he said, 'A valuable diamond ring and an emerald brooch. Where did you get these things, Denis?'

He wondered whether to say they had come from his mother, that mythical mother who had taken him abroad as an infant. But they had already told him that they did not believe the myth; probably they knew exactly where these things had come from and were just trying to trap him into lies. He said in a voice they could scarcely hear, 'I got them from Clare.'

'From Clare Mills?'

'Yes.'

'After she had been killed.'

'No. Clare gave them to me.'

'That doesn't ring true, Denis. You removed the ring and the brooch from Clare Mills's body after she had been killed, didn't you?'

'No. She gave them to me.' He wanted to say that she had given them to him when she had been a living, affectionate, smiling girl, that she had wanted him to have them. But all he could produce was this stubborn denial, these few poor monosyllables which sat like ashes on his tongue, and told these men whose task was to be suspicious that he had killed Clare.

Bert Hook said gently, almost cajolingly, 'You'll need to convince us of that, Denis. You must see how it looks, to anyone viewing the situation from outside.'

Denis stared at him, trying to work out why he was offering him such understanding, thinking that this man with the earnest, weather-beaten face was so unlike any other policeman he had met. 'I didn't want to take them. You not believe that, but it is true. Clare said that she did not want them, that there were reasons why she did not want them.'

'And can you tell us what these reasons were?'

Denis wanted to thank Hook for not dismissing his protestations out of hand, wanted to come up with a convincing reason why Clare had given him such an unlikely gift. But his English wasn't up to delivering the invention, even if his racing mind could have produced one. 'No. I not ask her. I think Clare did not want to talk about it.'

Lambert thought that Bert Hook had offered too much sympathy to this man who was in the frame for murder, that he should have gone hard for him, been cynical, forced him into whatever justification of his conduct he could offer. But he had worked with Hook for a long time now, and he had seen him successful so often in drawing out unlikely facts that he trusted his intuition, trusted him to build bridges when he knew that he himself would have been altogether more harsh. Lambert now said sceptically, 'You're asking us to believe that Clare Mills gave these valuable items to you whilst she was still alive, and without any pressure from you?'

'Yes. Is the truth.' His Eastern European accent came out strongly, more guttural than he had heard it for months, telling him that the strain of his sudden downfall was getting to him.

'And why would she do that?'

'I not know. She just did.' He had held himself rigid with tension, but on this simple, hopeless statement he forced a shrug, and he was so little in control of his body that the sudden violent movement of his shoulders threw him off balance and almost deposited him in a heap on the floor. He had to clutch the wood beneath his knees to preserve his position upon the edge of the wooden chair.

Lambert thrust in the steel which Hook had eschewed. 'You must see that the logical conclusion for us as CID men is that you killed the girl, then removed the jewellery from her body before consigning the corpse to the river. You deny that this is what actually happened, but you provide us with no reasons to believe you.'

Denis stared at him, his deep-set eyes widening in their sockets. Were they really prepared to listen to him? Or was it all an elaborate charade, inviting him to condemn himself from his own mouth? He said, 'Clare did not tell me why she wanted to be rid of those two things. I do not think she wanted me to ask her about that.' He paused, searching for words which would not come to him. 'She said I would need money, if I was to stay here.'

'Because of the way you had come here, you mean? Clare knew that you were an illegal immigrant?'

He sought desperately for a way out, but could see none. They had told him they knew all about this, that the elaborate precautions he had taken to establish himself here had all been torn away like so much highly expensive tissue paper. 'Yes, Clare knew that. But she was sympathetic. She wanted to help me. She said she had no use for these two pieces of jewellery, that I should have them to help me to make a proper life for myself here.'

It was just possible, Lambert supposed, but desperately thin. 'When did she give you the ring and the brooch?'

'On the tenth of June.'

Surprisingly precise. He wouldn't speculate about the reasons for the precision, at the moment. 'So why didn't you take them and sell them immediately? You say that she invited you to do that.'

'I didn't want to take them. I kept trying to give them back to her.' He scratched at his brain for anything which would add substance to this unlikely thought, could come up only with a pathetic, 'Clare was my friend.'

'But you took them to the pawnshop on Tuesday, ten days after Clare Mills was killed.'

'Yes. Clare wasn't here any more to take them back. Those things reminded me of my dead friend, the first person in England who really tried to help me. I didn't want to see them in my room for any longer.'

'What did you want the money for? What were you planning

to buy with it? Because you weren't planning to redeem the goods from that pawnshop, were you?'

'No.' The reasons he had to give were so vague, so unlikely, that he wondered if he should even begin the struggle to put them into words. 'In my own country, before the war in Kosovo, I was medical student. I was going to be doctor. I talked to Clare about her mother, about what I knew about autism and Asperger's syndrome. I thought when I was established here, I would see if I could try again to be doctor.'

He stared at the floor, unwilling to look into his questioner's eyes after this bizarre suggestion. Lambert let long seconds drag by before he said, 'Did you know Ian Walker?'

'Yes. Clare's husband. Ex-husband. He not nice man.'

'Why do you say that?'

'He threaten Clare. He try to get money from her, when she did not have money to give him. Walker bad man.'

'He's dead now, Denis.'

'I know. I'm not sorry.'

'Did you kill him?'

'No.' But he did not seem at all surprised at the suggestion.

'He died on Monday night.'

'Yes. I read about it. He was shot.'

'Did you shoot him, Denis?'

'No.'

'Where were you on Monday evening?'

'At home. At my room in Gloucester.'

'On your own?'

'Yes.'

'And you didn't go out during the evening?'

'No.'

Lambert nodded, watching Hook make notes in his round, clear hand. 'You come to work here on a bicycle each day, I believe.'

'Yes. That is correct.'

'So you could easily have ridden out into the Forest of Dean on that evening and killed Ian Walker. It's only half the distance you ride to come to this farm each day.'

'Yes, I could have done that. But I did not do it.' Denis was beyond caring whether they believed him any more. His situation in this strange, desirable country, which he had so quickly come to love, seemed hopeless. He couldn't understand why they did not arrest him.

Instead, they noted his address in Gloucester, told him to carry on with his work on the farm for the moment. Other policemen would be coming to see him about his situation, which couldn't be allowed to continue. They told him that almost as though they regretted it.

John Lambert did not reply when Bert Hook offered his opinion on the road back to Oldford that the man known as Denis hadn't done either of their murders. It was perhaps his silence as they drove through the Herefordshire lanes that drew from Hook the proposition that Denis might make rather a good doctor.

Lambert thought that was perhaps the most unlikely thought so far in this whole unlikely case.

Twenty-Four

DI Rushton had heard all about Judith Hudson. He switched
to the Internet, put up Asperger's syndrome on his
computer and read a little about it before venturing out into
the Forest of Dean to see this woman who was such a puzzle
to the CID team.

It was a strange meeting, this one between the handsome
policeman with few of the social graces and the woman who
seemed to become more and more locked into her own world
as the stress of events increased around her.

Chris said with stiff apology, 'I'm sorry to come here with
questions at this time. I know you will feel that you have had
quite enough of questions.'

'It is a busy time in the garden. You would not think it,
perhaps, but as we approach the end of spring and move into
high summer, everything grows apace. You have difficulty
keeping up with things. The grass needs mowing twice a
week.'

She spoke like a gardening page in the local paper. He
looked at her closely for the first time. She did not seem as
though she was being wilfully oblique. Chris sought desperately to establish some sort of link with her. 'The death of
your daughter must have been a great shock for you.'

'It's well worth mowing frequently, mind you. The fine
grasses like it, you see, and the coarse ones don't. The meadow
grasses mow out, in time, and you get a much more closely
knit turf, if you cut it often.'

The way she ignored what he had said disconcerted him.
He found himself saying, 'Yes. I've lived in a small flat, since
I was divorced. I don't have much of a garden. But then I
don't seem to have much time for it, these days.'

'The dahlias will be out soon. I start them in the greenhouse, you see. We've got a few flowers already, and lots of buds. I was looking at them this morning.' She was looking past him, through the long window of the old stone house and down the length of the garden. She hadn't looked into his face since he had come into the room, but he didn't feel that there was anything personal in her evasion.

'Were you very close to your daughter, Mrs Hudson?'

'Not recently, no. Not during the last few years.' She nodded to herself, as if that was a perfectly satisfactory summary of their relationship, and then said, trying genuinely to be helpful, 'We each led our own lives, you see, Clare and I. I expect you come across that quite a lot.'

'Not as often as you might think. Did your husband like Clare?' Chris Rushton had meant to be subtle, understanding, prising confidences from her where others had failed. Now he was driven into a clumsy directness.

'Roy?' She took her gaze from the garden and stared at the Persian carpet, as if contemplating the relationship for the first time. 'Oh, Roy liked her well enough. But Clare didn't like him very much, I think.'

'And why was that?' Chris tried not to show his excitement, sensing he might elicit some strange, abrupt revelation here.

'Oh, you'd really have to ask him about that. She wouldn't give him what he wanted. And he likes his own way, my husband. My second husband, that is.'

A strange suggestion from a very strange woman. She surely couldn't mean that Roy Hudson had been pursuing her daughter sexually? Surely even this woman would have been more affected than this by anything of that nature? 'What was it that Clare was refusing to do, Mrs Hudson?'

'Oh, I don't know. You'd have to ask Roy about that. I just know that he used to get frustrated with her. I didn't think it was worth bothering, myself. I didn't have a lot to do with her after she married Ian Walker, you know.'

'I see. You didn't like Ian Walker, did you?'

'No.' She shook her head emphatically and looked him in the face for the first time, as if glad to find something they could agree upon wholeheartedly. 'No one liked Ian Walker. No one in our family, I mean.'

'Who do you think killed him, Mrs Hudson?'

'Oh, I don't know that. That's your business, isn't it? But I can't say that I'm sorry that he's dead. He didn't make Clare happy, you know. We told her he wouldn't, but she wouldn't take any notice of us.'

'I see. And where was your husband last Monday night?'

'Out on business. The others asked me that. I'm sure that they did.'

Rushton didn't tell her that he was checking whether her story had changed. It seemed to him quite possible that it would have, with this brittle, unpredictable woman. On the other hand, he felt now that lies would not come naturally to her. He said, 'Can you tell me the nature of that business?'

'No. You should ask him yourself.'

'Lead separate lives, do you, Mrs Hudson?' It felt rather like leading a child, but Chris Rushton was desperate to discover something new about this strange partnership.

'No, I wouldn't say that. Roy needed my money, didn't he, in the early days? But I suppose I don't show any great interest in his business activities, nowadays.' She looked as if that reflection came as a surprise to her. 'I'm really more interested in my garden here, you see. I could show you round, if you like.'

'I'm afraid I haven't the time at the moment. Have to get back to the station and serious crime, you see!' He gave her a ritual little laugh at the policeman's lot, but she merely nodded her acceptance. 'You say your husband needed your money to help him in the early days of your marriage?'

She didn't take offence at the question, as he had thought she might. 'Yes. I didn't mind. I inherited a little money, and I came out of my first marriage with quite a good settlement. Share and share alike, what's mine is yours, and that sort of thing.' This time it was she who gave the little giggle, and Rushton had a feeling that she was quoting phrases which Roy Hudson had used to convince her that she should help him.

'But the business has picked up since then.'

'Oh, yes. I'd never have thought there was so much money in office supplies! He's doing very well now. Came home in a new Mercedes on Tuesday.'

Rushton would have suspected irony with other women, but

Judith Hudson seemed incapable of irony. He had learned something from this visit, anyway. Roy Hudson had used her money, had perhaps married her for it. That might explain both the curious marriage itself and the daughter's animosity to her stepfather.

'Have you ever handled a shotgun, Mrs Hudson?'

She did not seem to be annoyed by his sudden change of tack, did not seem to resent the implications of the question. Perhaps she did not even see those implications: there was no sign of tension in the open, unlined face beneath the ash-blonde hair. She turned her clear brown eyes upon his face as she said, 'I used to be quite a good shot, when I was young. Rabbits and hares, mostly. My father taught me. But I haven't shot for years, now. I decided I didn't really like killing things.'

Judith Hudson's last sentence rang through DI Rushton's mind as he drove beneath the green canopies of the Forest. A woman with no sense of irony.

Sara Green couldn't be certain what they wanted to speak to her about, and that made her nervous. That Detective Sergeant Hook had been very polite when he rang, but very insistent. They needed to talk to her again. They could see her at the university if she preferred it, but he thought it would probably be more private for her to see them at her home. Sara wondered why this needed privacy.

She could have met them any time during the day, because her lecturing commitments were finished for the year and she was marking summer examination scripts at home. But she had been allowed to specify the hour for this meeting, and it had seemed a wise precaution to give herself an interval of two hours before it took place. That would give her the opportunity to compose herself and prepare for it. But she was used to formal meetings in the university, where you knew what you were going to talk about. How did you prepare when no one had given you an agenda for a meeting? How did you compose yourself when you did not know what arguments you would have to meet?

She had always scorned housework, but now she found herself completing a series of minor domestic chores, seeking to occupy herself as she waited for the CID men to arrive.

Her small, high-ceilinged cottage was part of the conversion of an old church, where in the nineteenth century Sunday school children had listened rapt to simple tales with simple morals, recited to them by women like Sara. For them, this voluntary, unpaid instruction had then been the nearest thing to a fulfilling career.

Now that things had moved on, the present mistress of this little kingdom had a fulfilling career of her own, a love-life which defied the conventions which had once prevailed in this high-windowed stone temple. No children ever came here now, and Sara Green's modest, impeccably tasteful abode was never really untidy.

Yet she found herself vacuuming the floor, putting the crockery which she normally left to drain into the kitchen cupboards, even dusting the window-sills and the surfaces of the perfectly arranged furniture in her sitting room. Dusting! That was an activity for mothers and ancient aunts, in Sara's view. She could not believe that she even possessed a duster, still less that she was now diligently applying its livid yellow softness to the picture frames and plates on her walls.

And inevitably, when they eventually came, she did not feel prepared for them. How could she be, when Hook had given her no intimation of the reason for this visit?

The two big men looked unhurriedly round the room before they sat down in the armchairs she offered them. It was almost as though they were checking on her cleaning, Sara thought resentfully. But perhaps it was just a CID habit. Perhaps these people were trained to look at the detail of any place they entered, in case it could tell them something about the person who lived or worked there.

She knew that she should wait for them to take the initiative, should force them to make the running. Instead, she found herself saying with a directness she had never intended, 'Have you discovered who killed Clare yet?'

Lambert smiled, understanding this anxiety in one who had been so closely involved with the dead woman. But it was an infuriating smile to Sara, because it seemed to her patronizing. He said, 'I think I can tell you that we are much nearer to an arrest than we were when we last spoke.'

She wondered exactly what that meant. And most of all

what it meant for her. Had they found out what had happened in her last days with Clare? She couldn't see how they could have done that. But then she couldn't be certain that Clare hadn't spoken to anyone, and they were clever, these people. They spoke to everyone, even to people you least expected to be involved. She knew that from talking to Martin Carter: that pale, red-headed, callow young man had been really scared when she had last spoken to him at the university. It must be because of the prying that these people and the rest of their team had been doing over the last ten days.

Sara had thought they would have been quizzing her by now, launching straight into whatever it was they had come here to tax her with. Instead, both of them continued to look around the room, studying her curtains, her wallpaper, her pictures and ornaments, as if a detailed study of the decor and furnishings could conjure up the life she had conducted here with Clare Mills. She could think of nothing other to say than a banal, 'It was good of you to come out here to see me.'

'Not at all. Frank discussions are better conducted as privately as possible.' She did not like either the phrase or the smile with which Lambert accompanied it. Then he did ask her a question, more shocking for its abruptness after the prologue of harmless courtesy. 'Will you tell us again where you were on the night of Saturday the twenty-first of June, please?'

It was so sudden that she couldn't remember what she had said the first time, or even if they had asked her the question in this direct way. She told herself that she must keep calm: she had only to stick to what she had worked out a week and more ago and all would be well. 'I was here. Watching TV. There was the usual Saturday-night rubbish on. I watched the highlights of the cricket at some point during the evening. I have a weakness for the game, you see – I blame my father for that. I follow Middlesex, though I've never lived in London. But it was Freddy Flintoff who had a big innings that day. I recorded the highlights and watched them twice.'

She knew that she was talking too much, giving too much detail, but once she had embarked on the tale she did not see a way of shortening it. She knew also that it was a useless defence, that anyone could have mugged up the little she was giving about what had been on the box that night. Lambert seemed to her to imply as much when he said, 'Was there anyone else with you at any point during the evening?'

'No. If I'd been – well, been involved in the death of Clare, I'd have made sure I had someone to support my story, wouldn't I?'

He looked at her face for a long second before he spoke. 'Would you? It's true that sometimes it's the most innocent people who leave themselves without an alibi. Did anyone ring you during that evening?'

'No.' She was aware that the answer was out too promptly, right on the heels of the question, that she had not given herself the time to think which an innocent person should have taken. And this time she could think of no way of elaborating words to disguise her gaffe. She felt her lips setting like those of a stubborn child as she stared at this irritating man defiantly. Did he never blink? The grey eyes seemed to be looking into the secrets of her mind, the long, lined face to embody a wealth of experience, which would take in her petty traumas and range them alongside more serious evils.

It was the man she had almost forgotten beside him who said, 'I watched Freddy Flintoff's innings on that Saturday night. I don't blame you for recording it: it was well worth a re-run.'

She smiled weakly, not knowing how to react to this, trying to realign her attention to him. This was the man who had carried the Herefordshire attack in the Minor Counties league for many years, she had been told. Detective Sergeant Hook looked an unlikely figure for a fast bowler, with his slightly overweight frame and his fatherly, benevolent air. She said, 'I've played women's cricket a little myself, but I don't appreciate all the subtleties. Dad used to say there was more to batting than giving the ball a bash, but I must admit I enjoy seeing it hit hard.'

'Everyone does. Was Clare Mills a cricket fan?'

'No. I was trying to educate her to the game.'

'But you weren't together on that night.'

'No. I've already said we weren't.'

'Yes, you did. I just thought that if you were as close as you said you were, you might have been together, on a

Saturday night.' Hook was concerned, thoughtful, as if he wished his quiet manner to take away the undoubted sting from his suggestion.

'We weren't joined at the hip, you know.'

'No. But it's surprising that you didn't know where she was planning to be on that evening.'

He had put his finger on the weakness in her account of things, this man with the friendly, avuncular air. He spoke as if he were slightly puzzled, as if he wished to understand more clearly for her sake, not his. Sara said in a low voice, 'Normally we would have been together. Clare had other things on that weekend. I'm not sure what. She may just have been anxious to revise for her end of year examinations. She was a conscientious student, you know.'

'Yes, we do; everyone has emphasized that to us. But she had already taken the important papers. I should have thought you'd have known that, being as close to her as you were.'

His broad brow furrowed a little in perplexity. Sara Green was realizing how easy it was to underestimate this man with the village-bobby exterior. She said, 'I do remember that, now that you mention it. I was merely trying to think of what she might have been doing on that night.'

'Do you think she might have been meeting Ian Walker?'

She wondered if there was a trap here. But she couldn't see one. She said carefully, 'She might have been, I suppose. She knew that I didn't approve of her seeing that man at all, so it's conceivable that she wouldn't have told me, if she was planning to meet him.'

'Why would she have been seeing him, do you think?'

'He kept trying to get money out of her. Walker was a sponger. Clare was too soft-hearted to deal with him. I'd have sent him on his way.'

'I see. You don't think there was any residual affection between them?'

'There shouldn't have been. He was a bad lot. Clare shouldn't have had anything more to do with him.'

'But she did.'

'I told you, she was soft-hearted. Too much so for her own good.'

'And on his side?'

180

'I don't say he wouldn't have fancied getting her into bed again. "A quick shag for old times' sake", he'd have called it, I've no doubt.' She was aware that her anger was colouring her face, that she was supposed to be objective, even detached. But she was still too animated as she went on, 'There was no real affection on his part. Maybe a bit of lust, an eye for the chance of sex. No more than that. Clare should have sent him packing!'

'Someone did, of course. Someone sent him permanently packing, last Monday night.'

'Yes.'

'Someone with a real dislike of him, presumably. A hatred, even.'

'Someone like me, you mean.' She glowered at him, this traitor who had led her so unwittingly into these declarations. 'Except it wasn't me, you see.'

'Yes. I see that you're telling us that. Where were you on Monday night, Miss Green?'

'I was here. I wasn't out in the Forest of Dean, shooting Ian Walker outside his caravan.' She could hear her voice rising towards hysteria, feel how her breathing was lurching out of control.

'And alone, I presume?' Hook was studiously neutral, taking care not to imply the scepticism the question might suggest.

'Yes. And I didn't have any phone calls. Not that I can remember. And that's not evidence of guilt.' Sara stared at Hook, challenging him to deny it.

Instead, it was Lambert who said quietly, 'You must expect us to ask about these things. Especially when you have just declared your feelings about a man who was brutally murdered three days ago.'

'Perhaps. But I didn't shoot the damned man. The very idea is ridiculous!'

Lambert studied her unsmilingly for a few seconds. 'No doubt you recall a young woman named Anne Redmond. Or Anne Grayson, when you knew her.'

Sara felt as if she had received a blow to her solar plexus, doubling her up, depriving her of the breath to speak. She told herself now that she should have been prepared for this. She had thought with Anne safely in Canada they would not

181

discover it, but they must keep records of some kind, or have some sort of police grapevine which relayed things about their suspects. Because there was no doubt now that she was a suspect, that these men had come here to study her reactions. She struggled eventually into speech, managing to say, 'What happened between Anne and me has nothing to do with either of these killings.'

'Perhaps not. But you will see that it is bound to interest us. We know that statistically a person who has offered serious violence once is likely to do so again, particularly under the stress of extreme emotion.'

'It was a long time ago.'

'Nine years. Not so very long. And you stabbed a woman of very nearly the same age as Clare Mills twice with a lethal weapon. Shortly after threatening her with a shotgun: the implement with which Ian Walker was killed. Are you surprised that we think these facts might be significant? Especially when they are things which you have carefully concealed from us.'

'I didn't carefully conceal them. I didn't volunteer them, that's all. What happened with Anne isn't something I'm proud of, surprisingly enough.' The man had sounded like a prosecuting counsel, she thought bitterly, twisting his new information, making it sound as bad as he could for her.

And in that moment, she almost blurted out the facts of that furious break-up she had had with Clare, two nights before her death. They must surely know about it, must surely be waiting to throw it in as the clinching argument before they took her in to the station with them. Did you ask for a lawyer at the moment of arrest, or did you wait until they detailed the charges against you and put you in a cell? It was so exactly a repeat of the break-up she had had with Anne all those years ago that they must be laughing up their sleeves at her, these two, as they waited to add the clinching details of the fracturing of her relationship with Clare.

But they did not raise it. Miraculously, they did not seem to know of it. Lambert said evenly, 'Did you kill Clare Mills, Miss Green?'

'No.' Her voice was so strained that for an instant she could not believe the word had come from her.

'Or Ian Walker?'

'No.'

A pause. She did not dare to look up into those all-seeing grey eyes. Then he said, 'Have you any idea who might have been involved in either of these murders?'

'No.'

'Please do not leave the area without giving details of your movements to Oldford CID. And please ring me immediately if you have any further thoughts on these matters.'

And then, miraculously, they were gone, and she was alone in the quiet, spotless little house, with her familiar things around her. They did not know.

Twenty-Five

Even on a murder case, policemen cannot work all the time. Senior officers like Chief Superintendent John Lambert have to have a little amusement; long-serving detective sergeants like Bert Hook are surely entitled to a little ribald laughter amidst the rigours of the job.

To provide this necessary relief, Detective Inspector Christopher Rushton was being introduced to the game of golf.

It was just after eight o'clock on a perfect English summer evening, with the motionless shadows of the oak trees at Ross-on-Wye golf course lengthening and the golden light of early July deepening into an evening amber. At this time, there was no one on the first tee. Rushton would be spared an audience for his first steps in this game, which he was assured would teach him lessons about life and provide him with much healthy exercise and friendly competition.

That is to say, he would have no audience save Lambert and Hook. The attention of the Glasgow Empire would have been a merciful alternative.

There was evidence in the dress of the three men of the way in which the game reflects character. Lambert had long held the view that it was a waste of good clothing to use it for sport. Only when garments were too old for work or respectable social settings should they be used for golf. You could usually get a good couple of years out of clothes beyond these uses before they were on the point of disintegration and you finally consigned them to gardening.

John Lambert wore what had once been a navy leisure shirt, which long hours in the Herefordshire sun at Ross had bleached to more indeterminate and varied shades of blue, above trousers which shone a little at the seat and had long since lost all but the most unplanned of creases. His golf shoes were serviceable still, but could now most charitably be described as off-white.

Hook had been introduced to the game three years earlier by Lambert, and as in professional life he followed the tenets of his mentor. He had found a use for his discarded white cricket shirts on the golf course. The snag with this splendid economy was that he had put on weight in the years since he had relinquished fast bowling. This meant that his impressive torso threatened with every movement to burst dramatically through its cotton covering.

Bert's grey trousers fitted well enough, having been worn for work until three months previously. But they now bore indisputable evidence of Bert's apprentice status in the game. His erratic driving took him into some strange places, and green smears were accompanied by clear evidence of hawthorn and bramble on the rear of his legwear. He wore a cap which he had acquired with some second-hand clubs, which carried prominently the legend 'Taylor Made'. This was unfortunately the name of the headgear's American manufacturer rather than any guide to the fit of the cap, which was so large that it tended to remain stationary when Hook turned his head violently. This produced an effect which would have pleased only a slapstick comedian.

The strictly utilitarian nature of Lambert and Hook's apparel was emphasized by the meticulous attention given to his appearance by their pupil for the evening. Everything Christopher Rushton wore was brand new, bought specially for the occasion and this new development in his life. His tan leather shoes gleamed in the evening sun, his dark green trousers were impeccably creased. His lemon shirt fitted his slim frame perfectly, its effect in no way diminished by the Pringle logo at his breast.

The DS's mentors exchanged glances which anyone at Oldford CID would have interpreted as ominous.

Rushton looked from his companions' workaday shabbiness to his own peacock brilliance, sensed his first error of the evening, and said a little nervously, 'I thought I might as well look the part!'

'You're sure you're not tempting fate?' said Lambert innocently.

'Tiger Woods always looks smart,' said Rushton defensively.

'Indeed!' said Hook encouragingly. 'And of course we hope the analogy will be carried into your playing of the game.'

Rushton was nettled into the most unwise thing he would say that year. 'Golf surely can't be so difficult, when you've played other games. You approach a dead ball, and hit it in your own time. No one gives you an impossible serve to deal with, no one bowls you an unplayable ball.' He looked edgily at the impassive Hook. 'You can't even get a bad decision from an umpire or a referee.'

Rushton had been quite a good footballer and tennis player. The ones who had played other games usually came most heavily to grief in their early golfing days. Hook said with grim relish, 'Shall we get started, then?'

Chris hadn't thought that silence could ever be quite so intimidating. He was conscious of the intense attention of the two big men on his right as he teed up the ball. When he took his stance to hit it, he was almost sure that there were ghoulish faces in the doorway of the clubhouse, but he thought he had better not glance behind him and be certain of that.

He concentrated fiercely on the small white ball, which suddenly seemed a long way below him. He found that the precepts he had absorbed from his weekend reading of instruction manuals had fled his brain like racing pigeons. He was about to hit it when Lambert's voice came into his ears, as from an immense distance, 'Eye on the ball now, club slowly back.'

Chris shuffled his feet, fixed his eyes on the ball in bulging concentration, swung his driver back with easy grace, then lunged downwards in a desperate quest for the ball. He looked to see it soaring down the wide green acres of fairway, prepared to shoulder his bag and move quickly to some more private place upon the course.

'Often happens, that.' Bert Hook's quiet assurance came from six feet away to his right, restoring him to the real world.

The hateful real world. It took him a moment to realize that the white ball still teed so immaculately in front of him was his, that all his effort had failed even to establish the most minimal of contacts. 'Counts a shot, that, in golf,' said Lambert. 'Other sports, you get away with an air shot, but in golf they all count.' Rushton thought darkly that he seemed to relish giving that information, in a manner which was quite unbecoming to a chief superintendent.

Chris got his club on the ball at the fourth attempt, sending it a hundred yards towards merciful oblivion and producing a ragged cheer from the clubhouse behind him. He whirled in malevolent fury, but there was not a face to be seen in either the empty doorway or the blank stretches of glass which flanked it.

They played six holes, during which his tutors displayed to him what seemed an impossible level of competence and Chris's apparel descended steadily towards that of his companions. There were more trees than he had ever thought possible on a golf course. He emerged from each sortie into them with a new range of flies around his head. Thorns tore at his expensive attire. Brambles wrapped themselves around his shining new clubs. His beautiful lemon shirt stuck on the branch of a birch as he thrashed wildly at the ball, and the horseflies so prominent at this hour on a summer's evening bit three times into the flesh exposed in the small of his back. He could not understand why it was so impossibly hot at this late stage of the day.

'Perfect temperature for golf, isn't it?' observed Lambert, as he despatched a short iron into the very centre of the green which had just eluded Rushton. Chris wondered if a disembowelling would represent justifiable homicide.

Christine Lambert was pleased to see her husband looking much more relaxed when he came into their bungalow at ten o'clock that evening. It was a good thing that he had enjoyed an hour or two at the golf course, getting a little relaxation. It seemed to have been a particularly good break, to judge from his air of mellow content. 'Good game?' she asked as the kettle boiled.

'We only played a few holes. We were introducing Chris Rushton to the game.' John smiled like a lion digesting a particularly tender antelope.

'That was good of you and Bert.'

He glanced sharply at her, but there seemed to be no hint of irony. His wife was an innocent soul, who didn't play the game herself. He said contentedly, with the air of a man who had successfully addressed a problem, 'He's been getting a bit above himself lately, has Chris.'

*　　*　　*

Roy Hudson decided that he would be at his most urbane.

He had considered when Hook rang to make the appointment whether he should be prickly about this, should take the view that he'd offered them all the help he could and it was time they stopped coming to see him at work. But that wouldn't serve any useful purpose. The CID had been perfectly polite so far, if a little terse on their last meeting at his house, so there was no reason why he should not observe the courtesies towards them. Better that way, in fact. Play an impeccably straight bat until they got tired of it and went away.

He didn't realize that Bert Hook was a cricketer, who had outwitted a lot of straight bats in his time.

Hudson greeted them affably and said, 'I can easily rustle up some coffee for you, if you think this is going to take long.'

'No need for coffee, thank you. Too early in the morning for that. And this shouldn't take very long, if you give us honest answers to our questions.' Lambert as usual was watching his man closely and showing not a trace of embarrassment about doing so.

'Of course I shall. I'm as anxious as you are that you discover who killed poor Clare. And although Ian Walker wasn't my favourite man, we can't let people get away with murder, can we?'

'Where were you between eight p.m. and midnight on the night of the twenty-first of June, Mr Hudson?'

'That's the night when Clare was killed. I was at home with my wife. I'm sure I've told you that before.'

'And Mrs Hudson has confirmed the fact. Can anyone else do so?'

He smiled, refusing to be ruffled by this more aggressive line of questioning. 'No, I don't think so. But the innocent don't need cast-iron proof of things, do they?'

'And your wife was with you throughout the evening?'

'Yes. But you surely wouldn't be suggesting that Judith might have been out killing her own daughter.' He smiled at the absurdity of the suggestion. Bert Hook was thinking that this was the first woman he had met who might just have been capable of killing her only daughter.

'And last Monday night?'

He took his time. They had caught him out in a lie here,

but at least he was prepared for it. 'I think I told you when we last met that I was at home. That wasn't in fact the case.'

'So why tell us it was?'

'Because I was foolish. Because I wished to give my wife an alibi for the time when Ian Walker was killed.'

'You're saying that she shot him on that night?'

'No. Of course I'm not. But she'd already told you that she sometimes felt like killing him, because of what he'd done to Clare. I wanted to protect her.' It sounded thin, even thinner than it had when he had prepared it. But it was the best he could do. And he would do anything to protect Judith: that at least was true.

Lambert studied him dispassionately for long seconds before he said, 'So where were you on Monday evening?'

'I was out on business. Judith was at home on her own.'

'We shall have to press you about your exact whereabouts between eight and ten on that evening.'

'And if I am unable to provide you with anything more exact than I have already given you?'

'Then we shall be unable to eliminate you from the enquiry into the murder of Mr Walker.'

'Which is not to say that I killed him, of course.'

'Of course. But your failure to cooperate with us in our enquiries would have to be noted.' Lambert tried not to show his impatience with a man who seemed to be playing games with them in the course of a homicide investigation.

Roy Hudson smiled. 'I was in Cheltenham, Mr Lambert. And in anticipation of your next question, I shall give you a name. Mark Jolly.'

'This is a man who can confirm your whereabouts during the hours I mentioned?'

'Indeed he can. He was with me throughout the evening, Superintendent. In Cheltenham. I should like you to note that, DS Hook. The best part of thirty miles away from the spot where Ian Walker died.'

Hook looked up from his notebook. 'This Mr Jolly. Is he a friend? A drinking companion, perhaps?'

'You could probably best describe him as a business associate. But he will confirm that I was with him throughout the evening.'

'What sort of business would that be, Mr Hudson?'

He hadn't expected that question. He realized now that he should have done, but he tried not to let that ruffle him. He smiled and said, 'In a small company like this, there is a need for a versatile workforce. You need salespeople, of course, but you need also someone who will keep you in touch with your suppliers. And someone who has his finger on the pulse of demand, so that one can anticipate traits. It's a strange world, the world of office equipment. Mr Jolly is well versed in it. He is useful to me in all kinds of ways. He does a lot of running about, a lot of unglamorous but very necessary dogsbodying. I prefer to think of him as a general business associate.'

It was flannel, and he fancied they knew that as well as he did. But for some reason they did not press him about Jolly, did not follow up on exactly what kind of business he had been conducting that night. That should have reassured him, but in fact it made him more uneasy. Lambert said, 'We shall need to speak to Mr Jolly. But no doubt you would expect that.'

He gave them the details of Jolly's address, making a note to himself to go over what the man should say yet again as soon as they left him this morning. He was thick but reliable, Mark. He wouldn't let him down.

But Hook was getting something out of the briefcase he had set down beside his chair. He produced a polythene envelope, extracted the contents carefully, unwrapped blue tissue paper as if he were a conjurer producing something remarkable; Hudson had a sudden shaft of irritation at the painstaking slowness of this stolid man. 'What have you there?'

Hook did not reply until he had the contents displayed on Hudson's desk. Then he said, 'I wonder if you recognize these items, sir.'

Roy Hudson looked down at the innocent trinkets. A diamond ring and an emerald brooch. He recognized them all right, but the sight of them set his brain racing. Why were they here? Where had they come from, and what would be the implications of identifying them?

He picked up each of them in turn, then revolved them carefully between his fingers, playing for time. The key thing was

190

where they had been found, how they had come into the possession of these senior policemen. But they weren't going to tell him that, unless it suited them to do so. He forced a smile and said, 'Of course I recognize them. They belonged to Clare Mills, didn't they? I should know: it was me who gave them to her.'

The full name dropped oddly from his lips. They would have expected 'Clare', or at least 'my stepdaughter' from him. Bert Hook, ball-pen poised now over his notes, said, 'When did you give them to her, Mr Hudson?'

He took his time, checking in his mind that each statement could do him no harm. 'I gave her the brooch when Judith and I told her that we were going to get married. I knew how attached she still was to her father. I hoped the gift would act as a goodwill gesture, smooth the way for her mother's remarriage.'

'And did it do that?'

He wanted to say that it was none of their business. But he knew that he and Judith had kept these men at arm's length until now, that they couldn't go on doing that for ever. And they'd already caught him out in one lie. Besides, he needed to give them the best possible version of his relationship with Clare, to get himself off the hook. 'It did, yes, to a certain extent. Clare wore the brooch at our wedding, so that had to be a good thing.' He was pretty sure that she hadn't, but no one was going to be able to disprove it, at this distance in time.

'And the ring?'

He took his time again, wondering how he could make the best capital of this. 'That was later. I couldn't be precise.'

'It looks like an engagement ring.'

'It does, rather, doesn't it?' He laughed, pleased with himself for being able to relax like this. 'That isn't an accident. When Ian Walker proposed to Clare, he produced an awful glass thing which might have come out of a Christmas cracker. We tried to persuade her not to marry him. When it became clear that she was determined to do just that, I wanted her to have a proper ring.'

It didn't seem particularly likely, but they'd never be able to expose it as a lie. Hook wrote it down dutifully, taking what seemed to the man opposite him an age over it. Roy Hudson said, 'Was Clare wearing these things when she was pulled out of the river?'

Hook looked at Lambert, wondering how much he wanted to reveal of the manner in which these things had come into police hands. The superintendent said quietly, 'Both these items were taken to a pawnshop on Tuesday by a man who had known your stepdaughter, Mr Hudson.'

Roy tried not to shout out his triumph. This took him off the hook all right. He had always known that it would be so. He could not keep the elation out of his voice as he said, 'That's it, then, isn't it? This man killed Clare and removed her jewellery. I can assure you that those were the only two items she possessed which were of any value. And now he's no more sense than to go pawning them, only ten days after her death. He's delivered himself into your hands, surely?'

Lambert said, 'He's certainly delivered himself into our hands, yes. We haven't yet established that he killed Clare Mills.'

Bert Hook, who had thought privately that he was probably the only man who didn't believe that the man who called himself Denis Pimbury was their killer, was delighted to hear his chief speak with such conviction. Lambert picked his words as carefully as the man in front of them was doing as he said, 'We have not so far been able to disprove the man's account of where he was on the Saturday night when Clare died. We need evidence before we can charge a man.'

'Evidence which will be forthcoming, I am sure.' Roy tried not to sound too smug or sycophantic, tried not to show the immensity of his relief, which at that moment was surprising even him. 'With the efficiency of the police machine, it's only a matter of time, I'm sure.'

Lambert answered his smile. 'I'm sure it is, Mr Hudson. Whether the man who pawned these items is the man eventually arrested for the murders of Clare and of Ian Walker, only time will tell. In the meantime, it is possible, even probable, that we shall need to speak to you again.'

'Always at your service. Always anxious to be of help to the forces of law and order!'

Roy Hudson tried not to sound too dismissive as he showed them to his door.

Twenty-Six

Thirty-six hours in custody had not improved Martin Carter's appearance.

His hair was still a bright young man's red, but the face beneath it was unnaturally white; the once bright blue eyes had lost their lustre and there were dark hollows beneath them; and the wide mouth drooped in what seemed permanent despair.

A night in a cell usually has a pronounced effect on anyone who has not been there before. It had softened Carter up nicely for the Drugs Squad officers, who were now convinced that he had given them everything he had to give about the organization he was working for. As they had feared, he did not know very much: little more than the name of the man immediately above him in the chain and the person who had recruited him and supplied him. The barons who made the millions out of illegal drugs kept themselves well insulated from the dealers who took the risks on the streets. The man at the top of the pyramid above Carter was not even in the country for most of the time, though his Swiss bank account was kept regularly supplied.

Martin Carter had been charged with dealing in Class A drugs and then led back to collapse limply into his cell. The Drugs Squad superintendent intended to ask for him to be remanded in custody, but that would be more to protect him from the wolves above him in the hierarchy of the evil industry than because he represented any further danger to the public.

The Drugs Squad enjoy a high degree of autonomy within the police service, and their superintendent was a powerful man. It was not until he had a phone conversation with Superintendent John Lambert that he knew that Carter was a suspect in a murder enquiry.

Lambert had let him stew for another night in the cells before he came with DS Hook to interview him. They studied the pathetic figure unhurriedly before they began to question him; there is rarely need for haste when a man is in the cells. Eventually Martin could stand their scrutiny no longer. He said wearily, 'I've told those Drugs Squad officers all I know. I've nothing left to say.'

'I doubt that. We're here about something even more serious than drugs. Murder, Mr Carter.' The pitiful figure in front of him excited feelings of compassion in John Lambert, but this was no time for mercy. This was the time to have the truth out of a man: people with no resources left lost the capacity to deceive.

Carter did not look up, even at the mention of that oldest and worst of crimes. He was a man at the end of his resources, who had not even examined the drab surroundings of the interview room to which they had brought him for this exchange. 'I don't know anything about Clare's killing. I can't be of any help to you on that.' He delivered his monosyllables slowly and evenly, like a man speaking in a dream.

'You won't expect us to take that at face value, Mr Carter. You're a criminal now, charged and awaiting trial.'

His face winced on that, but still he did not look up. He lifted his hands from his sides and put them on the square table in front of him, as if to demonstrate that they contained nothing. They were small, delicate hands, as pale as the rest of him. The fingers began to twine and untwine, very gently, as if someone had pushed the slow-motion button on a video. 'I'm a criminal and my career's gone. Clare Mills wouldn't think much of me now, would she?'

'You told us when we spoke to you last week that you fancied Clare. That you were hoping at one time to develop a relationship with her.'

A nod, scarcely perceptible. No words.

'That wasn't true, was it? Or perhaps I should say it wasn't the whole story.'

A pause, when it seemed as if he might deny it. Then another, more definite nod.

'I think we know why you contacted her so persistently in the months before her death. But I'd like you to tell us about it, Martin. I hope you can see that your best policy now is to be completely frank with us.'

He had looked up for the first time on the mention of his forename. 'Yes. I've nothing left to hide, have I? I was trying to recruit her to sell drugs for me. Trying to build up my sales network.' He delivered the last phrase with a bitter irony, so that they knew that it was not his own.

'That wasn't your idea, though, was it? Someone else was pressing you to recruit Clare into the organization.'

He should deny it. He knew that well enough. It had been drilled into him from the start. You didn't give anything away about the people above you, if you wanted to stay alive. But it was too late for that: he'd told everything he knew to those persistent drugs detectives, who had seemed to know so much already. 'Yes. They wanted Clare in. I'm not quite sure why.'

'And that is why you kept arranging meetings with her.'

He nodded his acceptance of that and then, as if snatching at the last shreds of his integrity, added, 'I did fancy Clare Mills, though. I'd like to have been her boyfriend, if she'd have had me.'

He stared at the slowly turning cassette in the tape recorder, not looking up at them, fearing the mockery he would see in their eyes. It was Bert Hook who pointed out gently, 'But she was in a lesbian relationship, Martin.'

'Yes. I didn't know that at first. But she told me. To stop me making a fool of myself, she said. She told me that was in strict confidence and I hadn't to talk about it to others. And I didn't; I kept her secret.' A tiny morsel of pride stirred in him at that thought.

'And kept your feelings alive for her, I expect. In spite of the sexual preferences she told you about.'

'Yes. I even thought we might get together, after she'd walked out on Sara Green.'

They were disciplined by long years of CID questioning. Neither of them showed the slightest reaction to this; neither of them suggested that they were hearing this news for the first time. Hook said in the same even, sympathetic tone, 'And when was this, Martin?'

'Two days before she died, wasn't it? I saw her on the day she died. Tried to say I'd support her, be a shoulder to cry on.

195

I should have left it at that, let her recover a bit before I tried to get together with her, but I was silly enough to let Clare know that I wanted to be her lover.' His lips curled in a bitter contempt for his own naivety, but still he did not look up at them.

'And what did she tell you about her break-up with Sara Green?'

'Just that it was final. That they'd had a tremendous bust-up, on that Thursday night before she died. That she'd made a great mistake in planning to live with Sara. That she wasn't a lesbian at all.'

Hook glanced across the bowed head of Carter at Lambert. They had only the word of this exhausted, defeated man that this was an accurate report. He might be putting his own slant on what had happened between the two women. Even if he was being honest, he might be remembering the situation in the way he had wanted to see it rather than recounting what the dead woman had actually said.

But if even the bare facts of what he said were true, this gave Sara Green a motive for murder. Sexual jealousy is perhaps the commonest of all causes of domestic killings, and that is essentially what this would have been. This fracturing of the relationship had occurred just two days before the woman leaving it had been murdered. And the most significant fact of all was that Sara Green had deliberately concealed this break-up from them.

'She wouldn't have me.' Oblivious of the thoughts of the two men who were interrogating him, the man with his head bowed over the small square table continued his account of his own agony.

'What did she say to you, Martin?' Hook prompted gently.

'She was polite enough. She said she didn't want to get into another relationship immediately. Of any kind.'

'And did she give you any hope for the future?'

This time the pause was so long that they thought he was not going to reply at all. But at length he said, 'No. She said that she couldn't see herself having a one-to-one relationship with me. That she hoped we could always be friends!' He looked up sharply on that last phrase, as if he expected to catch them laughing at his misery. 'They always say that, don't they? That they want to be bloody friends with you!'

196

'Only when they want to be kind, Martin. I doubt if Clare would have said it unless she really wanted you as a friend.' Hook watched the abject figure in front of them, well aware that he too was a murder suspect, that this latest development increased rather than decreased the chances that he might have killed Clare Mills. He said quietly, 'Did you try to get her to sell drugs again?'

'No. I didn't get the chance. She brought the matter up herself. She warned me that I should get out of the trade, should stop dealing before it was too late.'

'And why do you think she raised that?'

'I don't know.' A huge, racking sigh shuddered through the slim body. 'I wish to hell I'd listened to her.'

As if in answer to this movement, Lambert's harder voice rang again in his ears. 'How did you react when she turned you down, Mr Carter? Because that is in effect what happened, isn't it?'

He nodded, his wan face cast down again towards the scratched surface of the table. He said abjectly, 'I accepted it, didn't I? That's what I do, accept things.'

This was more than self-pity. This man was looking at himself and what he had come to, and loathing what he saw. Lambert said, 'Are you sure that there wasn't a more violent reaction?'

'What do you mean?'

'Here was a girl who had repeatedly refused to work for you, who was now refusing point-blank to have any emotional dealings with you. Did your temper snap at this point? Did you in fact strangle Clare Mills?'

'No. I didn't kill her. I don't know who did.' But he had no energy left to add vehemence to his denials. He sounded as if he did not expect them to believe him.

Lambert let the seconds stretch out agonizingly in the quiet little box of a room, but Carter said no more. Eventually the chief superintendent said, 'You knew Ian Walker, didn't you?'

'Yes. I didn't like him. He was nothing but trouble for Clare.'

'And he'd been in her bed, hadn't he? The place you wanted to be, but were being refused access to.'

'Yes. Walker kept coming back and bothering her. He wouldn't get out of her life.'

'And he'd have come back again, once he knew she'd finished with Sara Green, wouldn't he?'

Another pause. And then, 'I expect he would. He wasn't one to miss an opportunity.'

'He might even have got some sort of relationship going with Clare Mills again, don't you think? She still had some feelings for him, from what we hear from other people.'

'He'd have tried.' His voice was so low that they could only just hear it above the quiet whirring of the tape machine.

'Did you shoot Ian Walker last Monday night, after you'd got rid of Clare?'

He glanced up at them again, looking from one to the other. 'No. I don't do that sort of thing, do I? I'm not man enough for that.'

There was a curious combination of self-contempt and challenge in the statement. He was in a state of near-collapse as he was taken back to his cell. Lambert and Hook said nothing to each other. But each of them knew enough about weak personalities to realize that they could be dangerous.

A man like Martin Carter could kill, if he was driven to the point of desperation.

The man wore a dark suit, of good quality but well worn, fraying a little at the cuffs. He looked round him nervously in the police station, as if he felt that this was not where he should be. The station sergeant had seen this sort of unease too often before to take any particular account of it. But when the man came to the desk and said he wanted to see the officer in charge of the Clare Mills murder investigation, he was fast-tracked through to Lambert's office.

'It may be nothing,' he said nervously. 'Probably is nothing, in fact.' He grinned apologetically for his presence here.

Lambert had seen such diffidence too often to be surprised or irritated by it. 'You've done the right thing coming here. We're grateful for any information. Don't you worry about the relevance: it's our job to see where it fits into the general picture. First of all, you'd better give Detective Sergeant Hook your name, please.'

'Tillcock. Chris Tillcock. I used to work for Roy Hudson.' He looked at the long, lined face of the chief superintendent for any sign of excitement at that news, but Lambert was too old a hand to offer him more than a nod of recognition. 'I was in the accounts department. I am a certified accountant.' He offered the information nervously, as if he expected the fact that he was not chartered to be queried.

Instead, Lambert said, 'You say you used to work for Mr Hudson. How long ago was this?'

'My employment was terminated three years ago.'

'By Mr Hudson?'

A hesitation. 'Yes. You could almost say by mutual consent, I suppose. But he got rid of me all right. Paid me my redundancy money and sent me on my way.'

They watched him without speaking for a moment. This might be just a man with a grudge against an employer who had fired him. Tillcock might be a man who was legitimately sent on his way for inefficiency, who now wanted to get a little of his own back on a former employer.

Lambert said carefully, 'But you asked to see the officer in charge of a murder enquiry. So you believe you have some information which could be of interest to us.'

'Yes. But you may already be in possession of it, for all I know.' His confidence was draining with each passing minute.

'Let's have it, shall we? It will go no further, if it has no bearing on the case. You needn't fear that you'll be embarrassed.'

'His business was making a loss!' He'd blurted it out suddenly, in the end, reddening as he did so.

Lambert smiled at him, not wanting to discourage him when he had made the effort to come in and do his duty. 'Let's have a few more details, shall we, Mr Tillcock? Hudson Office Supplies wouldn't be the first business to struggle, but you obviously feel there are some suspicious circumstances about these particular financial difficulties.'

'Yes. It was making a loss when he married Judith. He took her money and poured it in to keep the firm going.'

Lambert shrugged. 'So he used his wife's money to turn a struggling business into a prosperous one. It's not the first time that's happened. You could even say that it reflects credit on him, shows how as an entrepreneur he just needed capital to realize the potential of his ideas.'

He was trying to provoke Tillcock into a reaction, and he succeeded. 'Hudson didn't revive the firm as he claims. He frittered away his wife's money. It was still making a loss when that was gone. He wanted me to disguise it, to cook the figures for the auditors. I said I couldn't continue to do that. So he got rid of me.'

This was undoubtedly a bitter man. Everything he said and did now bore witness to that. But if there was substance in what he said, it might still have a connection with a murder or murders three years later. Lambert said, 'You're sure of this? Sure that business did not pick up after you'd left?'

'I'm absolutely sure. It's a small firm. I've kept in touch with what's happening there. Most of the people who work there don't want to ask too many questions about the viability of the concern. So long as their pay cheques arrive on time and there's no threat of redundancy, that's good enough. That's understandable, but it's helping to hide what's really going on there.'

'Which is what?'

Chris Tillcock leaned forward. Now that he was animated and assured of an audience, he seemed a much more incisive man. His small brown eyes glistened with excitement, his hands clasped together in a gesture of urgency. 'It's my belief that he's running Hudson Office Supplies as a front for something more sinister.'

'Using a loss-making firm as a money-laundering agency, you mean?'

He nodded eagerly, delighted that a senior policeman had put into words the accusation that as an accountant he had hesitated to make. 'That's exactly it. I'm sure he's involved in something much more sinister, making money he could not legitimately disclose. Big money.'

Drugs. Tillcock didn't want to say the word, but that's what he meant. And they already knew from talking to Martin Carter and others that he was probably right. Lambert said quietly, 'Can you substantiate what you say about the finances of the firm?'

'I can up to the time when I left it. I've kept my records from then, and I can provide detailed chapter and verse. It's vaguer after that, but I can still give you pointers: his bank credits will represent far more than is being generated through Hudson Office Supplies.'

Lambert nodded. 'Keep this information and these views strictly to yourself at present.'

'Yes. I won't give him the chance to plan any cover-ups beyond what he's done already.'

Lambert hadn't been thinking of that, but of Tillcock's personal safety. It was probably better not to emphasize that. Roy Hudson was becoming a more unsavoury character with every new fact they learned about him.

But was there a direct link with the deaths of Clare Mills and Ian Walker?

Twenty-Seven

Eleanor Hook was having trouble with her husband.

She could not recall him ever having asked her to help him like this before. 'I can't do it myself,' he explained patiently. 'It wouldn't be right. After all, the man is still a leading suspect in a murder investigation.'

'But you want me to do it. I see.' Her lips set in a thin line of the resentment which she did not feel: she enjoyed teasing Bert when he became earnest. And he was secretly very proud of her work for Amnesty International, though he affected to find it a professional embarrassment. The ways of partners are strange, unfathomable to outsiders, even a little touching.

'He's a good case.'

'But a murder suspect. And I don't even know him.'

Bert knew now that it was going to be all right. No stranger would have understood the marital code, but Bert knew even at this stage that Eleanor was prepared to help him. She trusted his judgement. He said happily, 'You'd like him if you did. You'd think him well worthy of your support.'

Eleanor sighed resignedly. 'What's his name?'

Bert gave her an apologetic grin. 'He calls himself Denis Pimbury. But that's not his real name. He spun us a wild story about having been born in this country and then brought up in Croatia, where his mother hailed from, but that's patently untrue. He's got himself a passport through some dubious source; those unscrupulous people will have overcharged him fiercely for it, poor bugger. It's a bogus document that's completely useless to him, of course.'

'So he's an illegal immigrant, trying to defraud the system, and a suspect for two murders.' Eleanor counted off the offences on her fingers. 'And you want me to help him.'

Hook grinned. 'That's about it, yes.'

'Can you give me any good reason why I should?'

Both of them were enjoying the fencing now, knowing that she was going to help, knowing that if necessary she would do it on no more than his say-so, knowing that in the end this business would only bring them even closer together.

Hook did his best. 'I'm pretty sure he's been through some dire times during the war in Kosovo, but he can't talk about that, of course. Can't even admit that he's been in the fighting, you see. But I'm privately certain that he'll be in danger of his life if he's sent back there. And he's a hell of a good worker on the farm where he's employed, so he won't be a drain on the state. He'd done three years of medical studies when the war ended all that. He might even become a doctor here, if we can sort out his residence.'

'And "we" means me.'

Bert's smile got wider. 'You and whatever formidable resources you can muster to help you, yes.'

'Because Detective Sergeant Bert Hook can't be seen to be helping a murder suspect who is also an illegal immigrant to the UK.'

'That's about it, yes.'

'And why on earth should the gullible Mrs Hook get involved?'

'Because she's a wonderful woman. Because he's a deserving case. There's something about him. You'd agree with that, if you saw him. Oh, and by the way, he didn't do either of those murders.'

'Who says he didn't?'

'Detective Sergeant Bert Hook. Relying on many years of CID experience.'

'And what does Chief Superintendent John Lambert think? With the benefit of even more years of CID experience?'

'You're a very acute woman, Eleanor Hook. You always spot the technical weakness in a case. Denis Pimbury needs a woman like you on his side, whatever his real name is.'

'So John Lambert thinks he might well have killed that woman. And the man who used to be her husband.'

Bert pursed his lips, as though weighing the facts of the matter. 'He hasn't committed himself yet. He's a cautious old bird, John. But then with his rank, he has to set the example, you see, show other people lower down the hierarchy that you mustn't jump to conclusions without proper evidence.'

'He doesn't allow himself to be swayed by sentiment, you mean.'

'Perhaps. But you can take it from me that Denis Pimbury didn't commit these murders.' Bert found that he was suddenly not quite as sure as he sounded.

'So who did?'

'Remains to be seen. Perhaps even the woman's mother. She's got Asperger's syndrome, I think, and she's difficult to work out. She doesn't seem to have any normal moral sense about her actions, and she admits she wasn't on good terms with her daughter. Still less with the man who used to be her husband.'

'There's a stepfather, isn't there?'

'Yes. Dubious character, involved in illegal drugs. And almost certainly in money-laundering, to disguise the profits from the drugs trading. Was in touch with his daughter in the weeks before her death, though he denied it at first. Appears at the moment to have alibis for both deaths.'

'Any others?'

'Two, I'd say.' Bert hastened to reduce the odds on Denis Pimbury. 'There's a female tutor at the university, who was conducting a lesbian affair with the dead woman. We've just found that they had a big separation two days before the woman was murdered. Apparently a final one.'

'But it's a big step from separation to murder.'

'Agreed. But this woman has a previous record of violence in similar circumstances. And she concealed the bust-up with Clare Mills from us when we spoke to her.'

'Probably didn't want to broadcast her humiliation.'

'Maybe. But there's another candidate as well. Young man we caught dealing drugs. He'd been keen on Clare for years and he tried to take up with her when she said same-sex relationships weren't for her after all. He admits he didn't take kindly to her rejecting him. And also that he was jealous of her first husband, a waster who he thinks still had a hold over Clare.' Bert was working hard to see the pale-faced Martin Carter as a killer, conjuring up the vision of his vivid red hair as an assurance that he must have a quick temper.

'In view of this array of villains, I suppose I'd better do what I can for your Mr Pimbury.'

Bert searched her face for irony, and eventually his anxiety brought an instinctive smile from her. It seemed as though that intense, fierce, hard-working man on the farm had a staunch advocate on his side now.

An hour later, DS Hook was thinking that Mark Jolly might be the most inappropriately named man he had ever met.

He had huge arms, the lower parts of which bulged out of the shirt sleeves which were supposed to contain them. The hairy forearms had tattoos of Union Jacks and crowns, though any monarchist would surely be disturbed to have this man for a supporter. There was a recent scar on the forehead above the small, close-set eyes, which were made to seem even tinier by the size of the coarse features which surrounded them. The man's hair was cut very close, and yet contrived to look both greasy and in need of a wash. His T-shirt with the beer advert stretched across its chest looked as if it had not been washed for weeks. Even with a desk to keep you apart from him, you could catch the smell of onions upon the man's breath, the scent of stale sweat from beneath those huge arms.

Anything less jolly would have been difficult to imagine.

'I got nothing to say to you.' The man's attitude chimed perfectly with his appearance.

'You will have.' Lambert smiled grimly at him, perfectly at home with his belligerence. He had dealt with thousands of Jollys in thirty years of police work; this was like coming home to familiar territory. In the game of bluff and counter-bluff that he was about to embark upon, he was confident that they could outwit this dangerous oaf. In a dark alley with a cosh or a knife, Jolly would have been favourite. In this war of words and minds, he might play a negative game for a while and refuse to cooperate, but he had no decent cards in the hand he had to play.

'You need to talk to Mr Hudson. He's my employer. I've nothing to say.' Mark Jolly repeated the phrases he had prepared as if they were some sort of formula.

'Worked long for him, have you?'

Jolly considered the question for a moment, prepared to

block it with a surly 'No comment.' But there couldn't be any harm in answering a question like that. Even a brief would tell you to answer that, to offer the trappings of cooperation to the pigs. 'Three years.'

'And what is your job description?'

He glared at them suspiciously. He'd never had anything as official as that. 'I do whatever Mr Hudson asks me to. Help out around here. Drive him, sometimes. Make sure people are available when he needs to speak to them.'

'You must be invaluable to him.'

He glared at the long watchful face. He'd like to put a fist into it, to feel the grinding of bone and gristle under his knuckles, to watch the blood spurt from the nose and hear the yell of pain. That would show the clever sod who was boss. But he knew he couldn't do that. Not here, anyway. Not now. 'Mr Hudson uses me quite a lot. You could say he relies on me.' No harm in building your job up a bit, the boss had said, so long as you don't give them any details.

'Relies on you to frighten people, I expect.' Lambert nodded repeatedly, as if this thug had confirmed something they knew already. 'I expect you can be quite good at that.'

Mark Jolly was suddenly uneasy. He hadn't said that. They were twisting what little he'd said, but he couldn't quite see where it had gone off the rails. 'I didn't say that, did I? I don't know why you should suggest that.' He lifted his huge arms in the air for a moment, as if he proposed to take a swing at his questioner, then let them drop back awkwardly to his sides. He looked like an amateur actor caught wondering what to do with his hands on stage.

Lambert let him sit awkwardly like that for a moment. 'Sent you to frighten Martin Carter at the university last Monday, didn't he?'

Jolly felt his first spurt of apprehension. How could they know that? Had they been watching him, even then? Had they rumbled what the boss was up to, as early as that? 'Don't know what you're talking about. I wasn't anywhere near no fucking university. Don't even know this Carter bugger you're talking about!'

It was his first mistake. He should have merely refused to comment. He had given them a lie, which they could use

206

against him, in due course. Lambert smiled an open satisfaction at that. 'Strange, that. Mr Carter gave us a very accurate description of you. He's in custody, you see, so I suppose he's happy that you can't get at him to beat him up. Surprising how it loosens people's tongues, when they feel they're safe from thugs like you, Mr Jolly.'

He didn't like that use of the title. They used that sort of politeness when they had you in the station, when they were going to charge you with something. A full minute too late, he snarled, 'No comment!'

Lambert laughed openly into his face, a small, mirthless sound. 'You've chosen the wrong man to work for, I'm afraid, Mr Jolly. You could be in for quite a sentence here. Unless you choose to be more frank with us than you've been so far. But I expect you won't be bright enough to see that.'

He turned his head sideways to Hook, who nodded and said, 'In a lot of trouble, you are, Mark. Can't see you getting the benefit of any doubt, either, a man with your record.'

He should have known they'd be aware of his previous, experienced pigs like this. He should have been ready for it. But he hadn't been, and now he was on the defensive, as they weighed in on him from both sides. Like all bullies, he didn't like it when he felt himself to be outnumbered. Physically, he could have smashed either of these men to the ground, and then put the boot in and finished them off, if the situation had called for it. But he knew he was at a disadvantage in any battle of words. And now there were two of them ganging up on him. As he felt himself losing his mental bearings, he fell back into the automatic, meaningless whine of the career criminal. 'I ain't done nothing wrong. I'm trying to go straight, keep out of trouble. And you bastards come trying to fit me up. This is harassment, this is!'

But his voice rang with desperation, not conviction, and the two men on the other side of the desk ignored him completely, contemplating their next move. He was softening up nicely, in Lambert's judgement. 'I'm afraid you've not made a very good job of going straight, Mr Jolly. You've chosen the wrong company, for a start. And the wrong employer. Once we've investigated everything you've been up to over the last twelve months or so, we should be able to lock you away for quite a few years. Wouldn't you think so, DS Hook?'

'Six to eight would be my informed guess, sir. Unless we discover more than we know already, of course.'

Lambert nodded thoughtfully. 'Your best policy now would be to cut your losses and give us all the help you can, while you're still a good citizen helping us with our enquiries, rather than a man under caution. But I don't expect you'll have the sense to see that. And I don't see why we should counsel you to do it. It's our job to lock away villains, and in my view the public would be much better off with you behind bars for eight years.'

Hook leaned forward. 'He's right, you know. I expect even you can see that, by now. I always like to give people, even the worst people like you, the chance to help themselves, but in this case—'

'You need to speak to Mr Hudson, not me. I act under orders. I haven't done anything that—'

'Mistake relying on Mr Hudson, Mark.' Bert Hook shook his head sadly at the mistaken tactic. 'He's in big trouble. You backed the wrong horse there.'

'He runs a legitimate business. Office supplies. It's very successful.' He mouthed the phrases he had heard the boss use in the past, but they fell from his thick lips like phrases in a comedy sketch.

'He's going down for drugs offences. Serious drugs offences. He's been running quite a network, as you know. And those who worked for him are going to go down with him. All of them. Including the muscle he used to put the frighteners on people. I could almost feel sorry for you, being caught up with something like that.'

Mark Jolly licked his lips, searching for the clever rejoinder which would not come. It was better to say nothing, let the pigs make the running, he decided belatedly.

Lambert regarded him with undisguised distaste. 'I'd rather expect a rat like you to desert the sinking ship, save as much as you could of your miserable skin. But perhaps you're not bright enough for that. And we'll be quite happy to put you away. Don't have any illusions about that.'

The man who had been determined to say nothing found

that he had to fill the silence. 'I ain't done nothing. I've just done whatever the boss asked me to do. Odd jobs around the place and—'

'Driving, you said. You do a bit of driving for Hudson, when called upon.'

'I have done, yes.' He glared suspiciously at his tormentors, a great bull of a man waiting for the picador's next dart.

'Different vehicles, I should think. I expect you're quite versatile, when it comes to driving.'

'I do what I'm ordered to do.'

'Without asking many questions about it, I'm sure.'

'Not my job to ask questions. I'm paid to—'

'Driven old white Ford vans in your time, I should think. Bit of a comedown after the boss's Merc, but all in a day's work, I expect.'

He felt the colour draining from his bloated face as he stared at them. He couldn't work out how they'd led him to this. And he knew now that he was going to talk.

Twenty-Eight

They drove for a little way by the Severn, not far above the spot where the body of Clare Mills had been discovered ten days earlier. The river was sluggish here, wide and unruffled between its low banks, still as a lake in the low evening sun, as if even the water was feeling the heat. It was nine o'clock now, but the temperature had scarcely dropped from its afternoon peak and there was not a breath of wind. Nature itself seemed to be waiting for something to happen.

Hook glanced occasionally at the grim profile beside him, but spoke not a word. After a little while, Lambert turned the old Vauxhall away from the road by the river, into the Forest of Dean. There were few other cars about as they moved beneath trees heavy with leaf, through the silent village and up to the house where this had all begun.

It was Roy Hudson who opened the front door of the high stone house with the immaculate gardens. There was no sign of his wife, and he chose not to explain her absence to them. He offered them no clue as to whether he had sent his strange partner out of the way, whether he considered Judith Hudson's affliction an advantage or a danger to him. Right to the end, they were not to see this strangely assorted couple together.

Hudson took them through into the room which looked down the long rear garden. Not a leaf moved on the full-leaved hawthorns at the end of it. The blazing roses and the first bright blooms of the dahlias looked especially vivid on this perfect July evening, their colours enhanced by the special light of the warm dusk. As the sun set in a blaze of red over the Bristol Channel, twenty miles beyond the trees of the ancient Forest, the sky over the hills beyond the end of the garden was shading from a brilliant crimson into purple.

Hook found himself filling with a reluctant admiration for

210

the nerve of the man. Hudson must have known by now that the police were on to his drugs operation, and maybe more, but he had chosen to stay and brazen it out, not to flee. He had no real alternative, of course: his movements had been tracked for the last two days. But he could not know that, and there was courage of a sort in his choosing to face them here, in this refuge he had built from his profits.

He looked scarcely shaken. His hair was still becomingly silvered at the temples, his tan as deep as ever, a defiant statement of his physical health amidst his collapsing world. The brown, deep-set eyes were as watchful as they had been the first time they had interviewed him, but there was no evidence of panic in them, no paling of the slightly florid cheeks.

Hudson said, 'Have you arrested that illegal immigrant for Clare's murder yet? The one who stole her jewellery and pawned it?' There was the first suspicion of anxiety in the way he had opened the conversation, but he cloaked it with the appearance of a challenge to them.

Lambert said, 'The man who called himself Denis Pimbury has been investigated. He didn't kill your stepdaughter.'

'I'm surprised you feel as confident about it as that.'

'Oh, we do, Mr Hudson. How he got into the country is another matter. It seems that he came in through an illegal-immigrants ring, but he is more a victim than a criminal. It's the people who are organizing the entry of such people who are causing misery and making millions. A lot of the crime bosses involved in the sale of illegal drugs are beginning to develop unsavoury sidelines with people desperate to get into Britain at any cost. Drug operators like you, in fact.'

He let his distaste for the man in front of him come out in the last phrase, perfectly content to provoke him into indiscretions if that were possible. And Hudson, visibly rattled for the first time, resorted to bluster. 'You'd better be careful what you say, Chief Superintendent. I've been very patient with you all the way through this business, but I have lawyers who would be interested in what you're saying.'

'I'm sure you have. And the time for lawyers is certainly at hand.'

'You should really be much more confident of your facts before you begin making allegations.'

'And you should really be much more selective in the work-ers you employ and the tactics you use. Fear only silences people up to a certain point.'

'I haven't even an inkling as to what you might be getting at.' It was meaningless and Hudson knew it: weak, where he wanted to be aggressive. He forced a contemptuous smile, but he knew now that this was not going to work, that his lawyer would be at work before the day was out. The only question now was what charges he would be confronting. He did not like the confidence of this grave senior policeman and the stolid, unsmiling acolyte at his side.

Lambert said like a man concluding the preliminaries, 'We know that Hudson Office Supplies is a loss-making business.'

'Bloody Chris Tillcock.' The words were out before he could stop himself, the thought springing to his lips even as it entered his brain.

Lambert smiled at his mistake. 'Mr Tillcock offered us certain accounting facts, as a good citizen should. And even banks begin to release information, once they know that murder charges are in prospect.'

It was the first mention of the word, and with it Hudson's eyes darted past them to the closed door behind them. But they surely couldn't have anything to support the charge. Roy kept his voice calm as he said, 'It's not a crime to have a struggling business, is it? I'll admit we were short of capital for a time, but once Judith had put her money into the firm we soon—'

'Married her to get your hands on that money, did you?' Lambert was gratuitously insulting now, watching his man like a predatory cat, pawing him to provoke him into further indiscretions.

'Of course I didn't!' For the first time, and perhaps when they had least expected it, his voice rose towards a shout. 'I married Judith because I cared for her, because we were in love.' Suddenly, ridiculously, it was important to him that he should convince these two hostile strangers of the truth of that.

'But you didn't pour her money into Hudson Office Supplies. You used it to develop a business which was much more sinister.'

'The office supplies stuff was always a loser.' He offered that in a low voice, almost like an afterthought. He did not seem to realize that he was now tacitly accepting what Lambert said, reinforcing his arguments.

But it was Bert Hook who now said softly, 'But you couldn't frighten Clare Mills, could you?' From the harmless-looking village-bobby face, the words emerged as a fact, not a question. It was so accurate that Roy Hudson wondered for an instant of panic how on earth the man could know such things.

'I don't know what you're talking about. I had a good relationship with my stepdaughter. There were a few problems at first, as you might expect when a mother remarries, but—'

'No wonder Clare gave that brooch and ring to Denis Pimbury to sell. She didn't want them, because they came from you. They were the first things she thought of when she wanted to raise money for him.'

'All right. I suppose the jewellery might have been a mistake. She never wanted gifts of any value from me, but—'

'You wanted her to work for you, I suppose. Wanted her to set up a drugs operation in the university, once she became a student there. That would have tied her to you for life, wouldn't it?'

'She could have had everything I had, eventually. She could have taken over the lot. Her mother wanted us to be close.' It sounded pathetic, but it was the key to everything, Roy thought. Your love made you vulnerable, made you do foolish things. He would never have involved himself with that damned girl, if his wife hadn't said she wanted them to be close, to be a family. And the irony was that Judith herself couldn't seem to conjure up maternal feelings for the girl, couldn't forgive Clare when she rejected her stepfather.

'But Clare resisted. Kept turning you down when you tried to involve her. But that was no reason to kill her.' Hook's voice, with its soft Herefordshire burr, went on as softly and calmly as if he had been discussing their next meal.

Roy Hudson could not understand how this harmless-looking figure seemed to know all this, how he could be so certain about it. He said desperately, 'I didn't kill Clare Mills.

213

You haven't a shred of proof. That bloody husband of hers killed her. Ian Walker killed her. Drove her body to the river in that old van of his. Dumped her in the Severn and drove away.' He worked his brain furiously, wondering what other particulars he could summon; he had a sudden impulse to pile up the detail, as if that alone could convince them of the dead man's guilt.

Hook smiled at him now, looking straight into those deepset eyes for the first time. 'Clare's body was driven there in that van all right. But not by the man who cleaned out the vehicle so thoroughly afterwards. Not by Ian Walker.'

'You've no grounds for saying that. And certainly no grounds for saying that I—'

'Mark Jolly drove the van on that Saturday night. Took away the body that you had strangled and dumped it like a dead kitten in the Severn.' Hook allowed the first surge of passion into his voice, his anger a homage to the dead woman.

'Prove it!' It was no more than desperate, unthinking defiance.

'We have a statement from Mark Jolly to that effect. As we said, you should have chosen your staff more carefully. But then, only a fool would hold back the truth when he's an accessory to murder.'

Hudson said doggedly, hopelessly, 'Ian Walker killed Clare. And then killed himself with his own shotgun, when he knew you were on to him.'

'No, Mr Hudson. It was you who discharged that shotgun last Monday night.'

'I have a perfectly good alibi for both these killings. I was with my wife when Clare was murdered. And as for Monday night, I can prove that my car was parked in Cheltenham throughout the evening. And you've already been told that—'

'Mr Jolly has already told us where you were on the Saturday night. Helping him to load the body of Clare Mills into the van owned by Ian Walker. Directing him to the spot on the river where it would be slid into the water.'

The game was up. There was a kind of relief when you abandoned the resistance that you had always known would be pointless. Roy Hudson, speaking it seemed as much to himself as to his adversaries, said dully, 'Clare was going to the police. She wouldn't join in the work, whatever incentives I offered her. She was going to tell them everything she knew about the enterprise and the people involved in it. I couldn't let her do that.' He spoke almost regretfully, as if once they understood the full situation they would see the logic of his actions.

'And Ian Walker was in no position to prevent you from using his van.'

He nodded, all defiance gone now. 'Walker was working for me. Pushing a few drugs around his dubious friends. He was in Gloucester on that night. I paid him a hundred pounds for the use of his van and he jumped at it. All he had to do was to clean it thoroughly afterwards.' He smiled mirthlessly at the cheapness with which the man had been bought. That Saturday seemed a long time ago now.

'But Walker wasn't the kind of man you could trust.' Lambert sounded almost sympathetic now as he led his man on into the familiar territory of violence breeding more violence.

'He wasn't up to much, Ian Walker.' Hudson sounded regretful, not for the man who was dead, but for his own foolishness in involving him. 'He'd have let me down once you began to press him. He'd have panicked and tried to save his own skin as soon as he felt you were on to him.'

'So he had to be removed.'

He nodded, as if the whole thing was perfectly rational. He was at this moment as devoid of any moral sense as that strange wife of his, without the mental problem which overlaid and explained her deficiencies. 'We had to get rid of him, and quickly, or he'd have told you the truth about Clare's death.'

Lambert sighed softly. 'So on Monday night, the man who you claimed was with you in Cheltenham, Mark Jolly, drove you out to Walker's caravan in his car. He's now admitted to that, by the way.'

But Hudson had no intention of prevaricating now. He merely nodded. 'I thought of using a taxi, but you could have traced that. It seemed safer at the time to use my own man.' He smiled bitterly at the irony of that thought. 'I was intending

215

to garrotte Walker, like Clare, take him from behind when he wasn't expecting it. But he had his own shotgun in the caravan. It occurred to me that I could make it look like suicide, give you a murderer for Clare Mills.' Again he had that slight, acerbic smile, as if he scarcely credited that what had seemed so logical could go so wrong.

Hook stepped forward and pronounced the words of arrest. Roy Hudson nodded slowly, all resistance gone. He said, 'Will someone look after Judith? I sent her out when I knew you were coming.' He was suddenly weary with guilt. 'She had nothing to do with this, you know. She knew nothing about any of it.'

It wouldn't be true of most wives. But with the strange, detached Judith Hudson it probably was. And it seemed that a genuine love for his wife was the one decent quality present in this man who had caused such suffering. Lambert said stiffly, 'Mrs Hudson will be told what has happened in due course. A woman police officer will explain things to her.'

It was over. They took him out to the police car which had eased into the drive behind them. Hudson rode in the back, handcuffed between two grim-faced uniformed officers, as the car followed Lambert's big Vauxhall back through the Forest to Oldford police station and the cells. It was a strange little procession which moved steadily through the warm summer darkness of woods in full leaf.

In Shakespeare, nature would have echoed momentous events in the world of man, with a storm shattering the heavy days of heat. But on this night, the world sweltered on, with no end yet to the heat wave which gripped the country. Perhaps the murderer of poor, innocent Clare Mills and the less worthy Ian Walker did not merit any momentous tribute from the elements.

Perhaps only Lambert and Hook and Rushton would sleep more easily, with the squalid little tale concluded.